A MOME

Frederica was ne -
dent that had lef r
spirits and streng

Why, then, did she not protest when Lord Lucien dared to visit her alone? Why did she not cry out for help when he actually sat on her bed?

Instead, silence reigned in the room as he took her hand in his. Her fingers curled naturally around his in response, and she licked her lips nervously. Slowly he bent down to kiss her, gently at first and then hungrily, and Frederica returned that kiss. He wrapped his arms around her then, lifting her up so that she was pressed against him, her heart echoing the beats of his own.

There was still time for her to stop him . . . and to stop herself . . . but that time was rapidly running out. . . .

The Impulsive Governess

by

Barbara Allister

A SIGNET BOOK

SIGNET
Published by the Penguin Group
Penguin Books USA Inc., 375 Hudson Street,
New York, New York 10014, U.S.A.
Penguin Books Ltd, 27 Wrights Lane,
London W8 5TZ, England
Penguin Books Australia Ltd, Ringwood,
Victoria, Australia
Penguin Books Canada Ltd, 10 Alcorn Avenue,
Toronto, Ontario, Canada M4V 3B2
Penguin Books (N.Z.) Ltd, 182–190 Wairau Road,
Auckland 10, New Zealand

Penguin Books Ltd, Registered Offices:
Harmondsworth, Middlesex, England

First published by Signet, an imprint of New American Library,
a division of Penguin Books USA Inc.

First Printing, January, 1993
10 9 8 7 6 5 4 3 2 1

Printed in the United States of America

1

GAZING UP into the midnight blue eyes of Lucien Devereaux, Lord Forestal, Frederica Montgomery felt her heart pounding. Taking a deep breath, she forced the words from her mouth. "I regret that I must decline your offer." She quickly lowered her eyes, knowing she was making the right choice. Her hands pleated the folds of her gray gown nervously, recognizing the urge to agree to his offer, yet hoping that she could escape before she acted impulsively. "You never think before you act, Frederica," she imagined her brother George saying once again. After more than a year of stubbornly refusing to back down from one impulsive gesture, she was not about to let another interfere with her life—no matter how fast her heart was pounding, no matter how much she wanted to agree.

"You cannot. I mean, it is unheard of. Everything is arranged," he said angrily. He rose and began pacing the room, his long strides quickly quartering the library. Frederica sat quietly, only her hands revealing her nervousness. He towered over her, his over six-foot lean frame handsomely displayed in dark blue coat and buff pantaloons. His dark brown hair was more tousled than when his valet had finished with it.

"I have no choice, my lord," she added quietly. She glanced up quickly and found him standing over her, his usually pleasant face twisted into a scowl. "The situation has changed since we exchanged letters." She took a deep breath. His eyes narrowed as he noticed the improvement in her figure. Noting where his eyes focused, she let her breath out hastily.

"Dash it! You must agree. There is no one else. I sent the rest packing when I received your last letter. I do not have time to find anyone else," he said angrily, gripping the back of the chair where he had been sitting so tightly his knuckles turned white. "If it is money—"

"Money? No, my lord. I would not break my word for something as trivial as money," she said hastily. Her hand flew up to her mouth, but that did not hide the look of mingled dismay and confusion that flickered across her face.

Forestal had been walking away from her, pacing as he normally did when he had any problem to solve. Hearing her words, he slowly turned back to face her, a look of surprise and shock on his countenance. "Trivial?" he drawled in his deep, rich voice that reminded Frederica of her favorite chocolate. "Trivial?" he asked again, walking slowly across the room until he stood looming above her.

"That is not really what I meant at all," she said, stammering. She could feel his eyes staring at her even though he was behind her. "Sometimes situations occur when money is the least of our worries." Silently she cursed her too quick tongue.

"I am not certain the poorest of my tenants would agree with you, Miss Montgomery. Indeed, I am surprised at your attitude. A woman who must make her way alone in the world turning down a position that would give her security." He returned to his seat behind the large desk and stared at her as if daring her to repeat her refusal. The late spring sunlight that spilled through the window behind him created splotches of gold in his otherwise dark brown hair.

Frederica had the grace to blush. Her eyes returned to her clasped hands. "I can only offer my apology, my lord," she said quietly, hoping that the interview would soon be over, yet dreading that time too. The first moment she had seen him that morning she could hardly breathe. In spite of her resolve, she had had to force the words of refusal out. Even now she was biting her lips in order to keep from blurting out her willingness to change her mind.

"Is it because mine is a bachelor household?" he asked. He leaned forward, peering at her, wishing he could see her face better. The gray bonnet and dress she wore were an effective disguise, one she had learned was a necessary part of life as a governess. Never beautiful, she deliberately hid behind clothing that made her pleasant features and medium brown hair seem nondescript. That morning she had deliberately chosen a bonnet with a brim. Shadowed by the brim, her face did not reveal much of what she was thinking, a factor Frederica had considered before she donned it that morning. "My man of business did discuss that issue with you?"

Drawing on training that had been instilled in her before she had ever begun her own schooling, she took a deep breath to settle her nerves. Then she said as calmly as she could, "Yes, my lord, he did." Wishing that she could get up as he had and pace about the room herself, Frederica forced herself to stay seated. "I must be honest and admit that your situation made my original decision difficult, but it was not the reason I must refuse the position. As I told you earlier, my situation has changed. I am no longer free to accept your offer."

"Why?" he demanded. He ran his hand through his dark hair, disturbing its casually wind-tossed style. "Come, Miss Montgomery, you must admit that you owe me more of an explanation than that." He sat back in his chair and waited for her answer. For a few moments he was still, willing her to comply with his demand. He stared at her, hoping he could force her to change her mind.

Across the desk Frederica watched him. Then she took another deep breath as she considered him. If she was fair, and she always tried to be fair, she had to admit that she was leaving him in an awkward position. The previous governess had already departed. Four children—especially active, imaginative ones that he had described in his letter—should not be in the sole care of servants. No wonder Lord Forestal seemed to be wearing a perpetual frown. To be left as guardian to four children who were under their mother's care was one thing, but since the lady's death six months earlier, he alone had been responsible. Frederica wet her lips with the tip of her tongue. "Since I wrote agreeing to take the position . . ." she began. Then she paused, wondering how she could explain without giving everything away. Finally she said quickly, "My former governess needs my help. I cannot abandon her."

"Does she own a school where you will be teaching?" he asked. Two of the governesses he had hired in the past six months had used that excuse when they had given their resignations. The look on his face said that he would not believe her if she too tried to use that ploy.

"Nothing so simple. She helped me when—" Here Frederica broke off, realizing that she had almost said too much. She looked down at her folded hands and then back up at the gentleman in front of her. "You must understand I cannot abandon her."

"Surely the woman understands that you must make your living. She would not want you to jeopardize your chance for employment." Once again he got up and started pacing the room. "You can send her part of your salary. If you need an advance to care for her, I will have my man of business send her a draft immediately." He walked back to the corner of the desk and sat on it, one long leg swinging carelessly.

"Money is the least of the problems, my lord." He raised his eyebrows. She hurried on. "Because she once helped me when I was having difficulties, she has no one else to turn to. She only wants my company until she can find another position." Her voice quavered just a little as she remembered how brave her friend, Violet Witherspoon, had been as she told

Frederica what had happened. "It may take some time. No one seems to want an elderly governess." This time her voice broke as she thought about how discouraged her friend had become. In the past week, Violet had been turned down several times, the last time so harshly that Frederica had found her friend in tears.

As she thought about that time, Frederica could still hear her friend's voice as she had explained through her sobs, "She said I am too old. What am I to do? What am I to do?" Violet's sobs had overcome her at that moment. And Frederica had made herself a promise that she would do anything to make Violet happy—even if it meant renewing her relationship with her own family, a relationship she had broken over a year earlier.

Her reverie made her miss the first few words Lord Forestal said. ". . . perfect solution." He smiled at her, obviously expecting her instant agreement. But all she could think about was that the dark blue coat he was wearing made his midnight blue eyes even darker. He smiled as if willing her to accept. Frederica had to bite her lip again to keep from agreeing with him even though she had no idea what he had said. In contrast to his earlier brooding good looks, the smile made Frederica's heart race faster, although, as she reminded herself firmly, she must remember not to get foolish ideas.

Not really wanting to admit that she had not been paying attention, she asked hesitantly, "Would you please repeat what you just said?"

Delighted with his own proposal, Forestal stood up and smiled. He pulled the cuffs of his coat farther down. "Took you as much by surprise as it did me, I suppose. I really cannot blame you." He smiled at her again, and she caught her breath. He walked back behind the desk and took his seat. "I wonder that I did not think of it before. If one governess cannot handle my four wards, maybe two can." He laughed ruefully. "At least I hope you can. If this does not work, I suppose I must send them off to schools."

"What two governesses?" Frederica asked sharply.

"You and your friend." Once again he smiled at her. "You said you had some doubts about working in a bachelor household. If you and your friend were together, no one could talk." He paused and looked thoughtful. "I suppose I should know her name before I hire her. And I will need references that my man of business can check out. She does have references, does she not?" he asked with a renewed frown. If Miss Montgomery did not agree to this solution, he would have to start the process again, and he had already spent too much time on the project.

"Impeccable ones," Frederica reassured him. She had written one of them herself. "Her name is Violet Witherspoon. She is the former governess of the Viscount Basset and his sisters."

"Yorkshire, hmmm. Never see much of the family in London except maybe during part of the Season. But I seem to remember that one of the girls married very well. Have her send the references to the same place you sent yours. Start packing. I will let you know as soon as I have checked them out. I must have this problem settled as soon as possible."

Frederica sat as still as a mouse held captive by the eyes of a cat ready to pounce, too surprised to respond. She stared at him as though she had never seen him before. Finally, when he was becoming impatient and worried that she would refuse, she asked, "You want to hire both Violet and me?"

"Yes!" he said impatiently.

Slowly she let her breath out, realizing that she had been rescued from crawling home, her hand out. She stood up and took a minute to smooth her gray skirts. "We will await word from you, Lord Forestal," she said, a small smile on her lips. "I am certain Miss Witherspoon will be as delighted as I am to accept the position."

As the front door shut behind her a few minutes

later, Frederica felt like laughing for the first time since she had arrived in London a few days before. Noting a hackney cab discharging a passenger a block away and very conscious that she might meet someone she knew if she was not very careful, she signaled for him. Soon she was jolting over the rough streets toward the small house in an unfashionable section of town where both she and Violet were guests.

Convincing her former governess that she had found a solution to their problem was much more difficult than Frederica had thought possible. The moment she heard the news, a look of consternation crossed Violet's face. Before Frederica could question her about it, the older lady asked, "But how can you know that we can trust him, my dear?" Her brown eyes held a hint of dismay. "Why would any gentleman hire two governesses when one will do? And shouldn't the boy have a tutor instead? Perhaps we should write your brother and ask him," she suggested gently, a hint of panic in her voice. Although her face showed only a small portion of the panic she was feeling, Violet could not imagine a more impossible situation. She reminded herself that it was no more impossible than that of the previous year. But she did not want to explain a disaster of that nature a second time. No matter how fond Viscount Bassett was of her, Violet knew he was depending on her to convince his sister to return home.

"Violet, you know that cannot be," her former charge explained patiently, controlling herself with an effort.

"And who is this Lord Forestal?" Violet asked. "I do not remember seeing his name on any of the lists of those attending parties at the best homes. How can you think about accepting a post with a man whose background we know nothing of?"

"Apparently Lord Forestal is noted as a traveler. Until about two years ago, he was in the colonies exploring. I did make inquiries before I agreed to accept the position. Apparently he prefers his club to *ton* parties, although he attended a few last Season before his cousin died. This year he has been too busy caring for the children."

"Humph!" Violet's face was set in a disapproving line. Small but plump, she was generally easygoing, but when she took a dislike to someone, it was difficult to get her to change her mind.

Frederica plastered a smile on her face and explained once again. "Apparently Lord Forestal's wards have been creating havoc with his bachelor household. He has decided that to ensure that a governess will stay longer than a few days or weeks, he will hire more than one. Four children from sixteen to four can require more attention than any one person has to give, especially since they lost their mother before they came out of mourning for their father." Frederica glanced at her friend from under incredibly long lashes and sighed. "I do hope to be some help to them, but if you really . . ."

In spite of herself, Violet felt a stirring of pity. "I am certain his lordship is doing his best," she said firmly. "But we do not have to get involved in his problems. If we remain in London, I am certain that we can find a better solution to our problem." She sighed: in spite of her dismay over the disaster to her plans, her tender heart reacted to the thought of four orphan children with only a cousin to care for them.

"My conscience will not allow me to desert them. Apparently the housekeeper, worn down by the unexpected turmoil of the last few months, has been ordered to her bed by the doctor. At present the butler has been handling the situation with the help of a few young maids." Frederica imbued her words with the suggestion of gloom.

"You mean those babies have been left all alone with a butler?" Violet demanded, her sense of propriety outraged.

"Yes. Lord Forestal explained that at least the butler was fond of the children. He did try to gain some help from members of his family. After all the few remaining members of the family had refused him aid, Forestal could see no other solution than to leave the children in his butler's care and come to London to interview a governess himself. He told me that if I refused his offer, his only remaining choice would be to send the children away to school. I do not think I can allow the youngest, a four-year-old girl, to be subjected to that." She glanced at Violet and noted with satisfaction a look of horror on the older lady's face.

Violet's loyalty to Frederica's brother kept her silent only a few seconds. Then her protective nature yielded to the inevitable. "Boarding school for a four-year-old!" The light of battle filled the older lady's face with religious zeal. "You find a boy to deliver my letters of reference. I will get them out of my trunk. A boarding school. Humph!" Violet bustled out of the room, her shoulders set as if she were going into battle. Mentally she began composing a letter to her employer. She would have to explain the situation carefully to Viscount Bassett, but knowing how much he loved his own children, she was certain he would understand the problem. Four children in a butler's care. Then she smiled wryly. Even if he did complain, she would be too far away to hear him. At least she would be with Miss Frederica this time and not have to face him herself.

The door snapped closed behind the lavender muslin skirts Violet wore. Frederica relaxed for a moment, a soft smile playing across her lips, transforming her face into that of a beauty. Then she too hurried from the room, filled with satisfaction.

That satisfaction was sorely tried in the next four days. When Lord Forestal notified Frederica that Mrs. Witherspoon's references were acceptable, he also sent a list of errands for her to accomplish. Although their mother had been dead for only six months, he was determined that the children return to colors once more.

"And what kind of respect is he teaching them?

That is what I want to know," Violet said as she read his letter for herself. "It is not right." She straightened her skirts as though she were straightening his mind. She had received a letter from Viscount Bassett that morning, and he was not pleased. Certain that his sister would be returning home soon, he had made certain plans. The governess's dismay at having to disturb his ideas caused her to snap at Frederica.

Her former charge looked at her rather strangely, wondering what had disturbed her. "But, Violet, even after Papa died, we did not wear black for the whole year. You know he told us expressly that we were not to do so. And these children have been in black for a year and a half, poor things," Frederica reminded her. "How they must be longing for a bit of color in their lives."

"You at least wore gray and lavender. Look at what he says here: 'Choose something bright—reds, blues, greens.' A child dressed in red? And who will make up the clothes once we arrive? You do not expect to find a seamstress in that household, do you?"

"Someone in the neighborhood is certain to sew. If not, Lord Forestal can hire someone to stay for a while. Think about choosing bolts of fabric in bright colors." Frederica smiled. "If we must, we can sew." Violet frowned. "And we can teach the young ladies to make their own clothing," Frederica said with a smile. "Remember my first lessons."

"If the oldest does not know how to sew by now, we will never be able to teach her. Miss Frederica, are you certain we are doing the right thing?" Violet asked nervously.

"You must not call me Miss Frederica, Violet. You will make everyone suspicious. Come, let us put our bonnets on and search for those fabrics. We will need to buy some material for ourselves too. I do not intend to be outmoded much longer. Your cousin has told me of a fabric warehouse that has excellent merchandise but where few of the fashionable go." She smiled at her friend, mischief twinkling in her eyes. "Even if we did meet someone we knew, I do not think they would recognize me in this outfit." Violet took one disapproving look at the drab brown dress Frederica wore and had to agree.

After a final interview with Lord Forestal before he left the city, an interview in which Violet said little but observed her friend and their employer most carefully, Violet quickly reversed her position and threw herself wholeheartedly into the completion of their shopping. Finally the two ladies boarded the stagecoach. Sitting opposite each other in the more expensive corner seats, the ladies watched the bright spring countryside outside their windows. Because the road was one of the most heavily traveled in England, their progress was slower than they liked. However, they were pleasantly surprised to discover at each rest stop that Lord Forestal's secretary had insured them some privacy, hiring private rooms where a meal better than that served the ordinary passengers was waiting. Already drawn to their employer's handsome appearance and rich voice, Frederica was charmed once again. Violet, her opinion already changing to a more favorable one, positively gushed. "So thoughtful. You were right again, my dear. A gentleman of his caliber deserves our support," she assured her companion.

After a remarkably short journey, less than two days when only a few years before it would have taken them four, they stepped from the coach into a prosperous inn yard. Once again an innkeeper welcomed them, providing a maid to show them to the rooms reserved. "You go inside and freshen up. I will identify our luggage so that this gentleman can take charge of it," Frederica said, smiling at her friend, who, although trying to be cheerful and pleasant, appeared exhausted. Violet nodded weakly. Although much more comfortable than she had expected, this journey had reminded her of how lucky she had been the past few years. She had forgotten how much more comfortable a journey in a private carriage was than in a coach.

No sooner than Violet had walked into the inn, a groom appeared, wiping the last of his ale from his mustache with the back of his hand. "Would you be Miss Montgomery?" he asked, coming up behind Frederica. She jumped and then nodded. "Show me what is yours, and I will load it. His lordship said to remind you we still have some way to go, so you had better have a bit of a rest and something to eat before we start off. Are you the only one? Thought there were to be two." Before she could answer him, the groom had picked up the luggage the innkeeper pointed out and headed toward the stables.

Frederica stared after him for a moment and then hurried into the inn after her host. "That would be Masters," the innkeeper explained. "His lordship's head groom. His lordship must be impressed with you. He never sent Masters for any of the others. No fine parlor for them neither. First room up the stairs on the right," he said in a kind manner. As she walked slowly up the stairs, the innkeeper shook his head. "Fancy arrangements for governesses, I say," he said to his wife as she walked back from waving the coach on its way.

"You've no call to be questioning anything his lordship does. After his problems this year, he deserves some peace. Remember if it hadn't been for him, we would never have had this place," she reminded him. "Besides, what he does is his business. Now, see that those men gambling over there in the corner pay up before they lose their last ha'penny." She frowned at him until he bustled away. Then she hurried toward the kitchen.

Upstairs, Frederica was washing the dust of the last few hours from her face. Feeling much better, she turned and looked toward the small bed where her companion lay. "May I get anything for you?" she asked. Violet shook her head. "Lord Forestal sent his head groom to take us to his home. I think the innkeeper was impressed." She walked toward the small window and looked out into the busy inn yard, rolling her head in a circle in hopes of relieving some of the pressure she felt in the back of her neck. "Masters—that is the groom's name—said we had some way to go before we arrive and that we would need to eat. But if you are too tired, perhaps I can ask the innkeeper's wife to make up a basket that we can take with us."

"A basket for two governesses? Miss Frederica, you forget yourself." Violet swung her feet over the edge of the bed. "And do not tell me not to call you Miss Frederica again. What am I to say when you forget your station? I will be fine once I have eaten," she reassured the younger lady. A few minutes after she had washed her face and hands and brushed wrinkles from her skirts, she watched a maid arrange the food on the table. Violet said with enthusiasm, "I believe this repast is even better than the one this morning."

By the time the groom scratched on the door to their parlor, both ladies felt more refreshed. Gathering the small valises that had traveled inside the coach with them and putting on their bonnets, they walked down the stairs to their waiting transportation, a coach instead of the gig they had expected. Violet paused for a moment, sending Frederica on ahead and spoke furtively to the innkeeper's wife, handing her a small piece of folded paper. Then she hurried after Frederica.

"He must be in desperate need. He sent his own coach," Violet said in surprise as she entered the carriage. "Oh, this is more the thing." She settled into a corner and smiled. Then she yawned delicately, covering her mouth with her gloved hand. "I am sorry."

"Do not apologize to me. I am just as tired as you are. Perhaps both of us can sleep for a little while. We do not want to be completely exhausted when we arrive at our new post."

"If we are very late, I do not suppose we will meet the children until tomorrow," her friend said calmly. "After the care Lord Forestal has provided on this journey, he will want us to see them at their best."

"I wonder what they did that caused four governesses in the last six months to leave?" Frederica wondered as if to herself.

Hours later, Frederica crawled into the fresh, well-aired bed assigned to her. Sighing deeply, she relaxed and snuggled down into the bed, enjoying the feel of crisp linen and the scent of lavender. Though this might be a bachelor household, someone competent was in charge of the housekeeping. She stretched one last time and slid even farther down in the bed. Then she felt it. Something cold, damp, and alive.

Opening her mouth to scream, Frederica quickly closed it without uttering a sound. Slipping from the bed, she threw back the covers. There near the foot of the bed she discovered the culprit, a fat frog who was more frightened of her and its new situation than she was of it. Drawing on lessons learned in childhood, she captured it and crossed to the bell pull. When the maid appeared, she handed the frog to her and gave her orders to release it in the garden. She was ready to climb back in bed when a terrible thought struck her. "Violet!" Throwing her dressing gown about her, she hurried down the hall to her friend's room.

"Violet?" she called as she opened the door cautiously. When no one answered, she opened it farther and walked in. Realizing that Violet was not there, she hurried to her bed and threw back her covers to reveal another frog.

"Frederica? Is there something wrong?" her friend asked as she entered the room.

"Nothing. I just wanted to see if the children had left you a friend too," Frederica explained, holding out her prize. "Where were you?"

"I simply had to see the little girl. She was in the nursery, sleeping peacefully with a nursery maid close at hand." Violet took one look at the frog and shivered. "I am glad you rescued that poor creature. I would have frightened the poor thing to death. Which of the children do you suppose is responsible?"

"I suppose we will have to wait until tomorrow to

discover that. Thankfully, all of us played with frogs when we were growing up."

"Except your sister," Violet reminded.

"Yes, except my sister," Frederica said in a lifeless voice. "Good night."

Cursing herself for reminding Frederica of her sister, a subject that still had the power to wound, Violet watched Frederica walk from the room, the frog still held gently in her hand. Then Violet glanced at the bed and shivered again. If Frederica had not come to her rescue, she would have put her foot against that creature. She inspected the rest of the bed carefully, making certain no other surprises were waiting for her. Then she crawled into it, shut her eyes tightly, and went to sleep.

2

THE NEXT MORNING the sun was shining through the lace curtains when Frederica awoke. She glanced at the light, and her eyes flew open wider. She gasped in dismay. After tossing and turning for hours, she had finally fallen asleep as the clock at the top of the stairs struck two and as a result had overslept. Jumping from bed, she dashed to the basin to wash her face, amazed to find the water still warm. Dismayed at her tardiness, she dressed, noting with surprise that someone had ironed the wrinkles from her dresses. Finally attired in one of her plainest and primmest dresses, a gray muslin that did little to make the best of her brown hair and blue eyes, she coiled her long hair into a sober knot at the back of her neck and hurried from the room.

Apparently someone had been on the watch for her. No sooner than she stepped from her room than a maid appeared. "His lordship asked me to show you to the breakfast room," she explained.

"But I must see the children," Frederica protested. "I should have been with them hours ago. Someone should have awakened me earlier."

"That would have been more than my position is worth, miss. His lordship gave us strict orders that you and Miss Witherspoon were to sleep as late as you wished this morning," the maid explained. And the servants who had had to watch those four children for the past few weeks would do anything in their power to insure that the governesses stayed this time.

"Then I will have breakfast," Frederica said. "I am Frederica Montgomery. What is your name?"

"Sally—Sally Wright," the maid said, obviously flustered yet flattered that a governess would be interested in her. The last four had ignored the household staff except to give them orders.

"Sally, has Miss Witherspoon come down for breakfast yet?"

"Daisy just took her a cup of tea about half an hour ago, but she is still in her room," the girl said in soft country tones.

Once more Frederica stopped at her friend's door. Before she could announce herself, it opened. "Shockingly spoiled, that is what I am," the older lady said with a smile. "His lordship is much too easy an employer. Imagine our sleeping so late. We must hurry through breakfast so that we can meet the children, Frederica," she said with a smile.

"His lordship wants to see you in the library when you finish with your meal," Sally said as she showed them a room where a variety of foods were still spread along a sideboard. "Someone will show you the way."

After a hasty breakfast, the ladies walked to the library, where their employer waited. As they entered the room, he stood and motioned them to be seated. "I understand that you have already fallen victim to one of the children's latest tactics—frogs," he said in his deep, rich voice. Frederica could not take her eyes from him. Dressed in a dark brown jacket over buff pantaloons, he made an imposing figure. "I congratulate you on disappointing them with your reaction."

"You have Miss Montgomery to thank for that, my lord," Violet said quietly. She smiled. "I am afraid I would have reacted exactly as they would have wished. She removed the frog before I found it." She glanced at her companion. Catching a glimpse of the emotion Frederica was trying so hard to hide, Violet felt both pleasure and a hint of dismay. She looked at her employer once again, this time paying more attention to him physically. He was lean, the kind of lean that seemed to promise power. His shoulders, though not as broad as some, filled out his jacket nicely. Trying not to be too obvious with her inspection, she studied his face. Too rugged to be considered handsome in the classical sense, it was still attractive. His mouth . . . Violet looked carefully away, not wanting to admit the sensuality she noted there.

Surprised by the rush of enjoyment she had felt when she first saw Lord Forestal, Frederica quickly hid her emotions under the calm mask that, early in her career as a governess, she had learned was necessary. She was a governess in Lord Forestal's employ, she reminded herself. But when he turned to look at her, approval on his face, her heart raced.

"Well done, Miss Montgomery. We will teach those four rascals that they cannot have their own way any longer." He smiled at her as he took a seat near theirs. She could not resist smiling back. Not for the first time since the two ladies had entered the room, Forestal experienced increased interest in Frederica. When she smiled, her face took on a warmth, a beauty that was hidden when she was impassive. She lowered her eyelashes as if to escape his scrutiny, and he noticed the way they swept her cheek.

Just before the silence became uncomfortable, Violet asked, "When shall we meet the children?"

"Very shortly. I sent them out to ride with Masters and the other grooms. As soon as they return and put on fresh clothing, they will join us. I thought you could meet and spend some time with them before we dine. Unless I have guests, I expect the children to join me. I will expect you to accompany them." He intercepted the worried glances between the two. "What is the problem?"

"You expect the four-year-old to sit down to dine with you every day?" Violet asked, not very successful at masking her disapproval.

"How will she ever learn to behave if she eats only in the nursery? Besides, she would be lonely without her brother and sisters." To himself he acknowledged that he would miss the little one if she had to eat in the nursery.

"If that is what you wish, my lord. And what about the times when you are not at home?" Frederica asked. In their correspondence he had mentioned that he was often from home, maintaining a watch over both his own and his wards' properties.

"That is for you to decide," he explained. "Do you have any further questions?"

"You said you wished your oldest ward trained so that she can be presented soon. Have you found a suitable lady to present her?" Frederica asked, remembering the hours of planning that had gone into her own Season.

"Not yet." He glanced from one to the other. "Diana is just sixteen. She wants to be presented next Season, but I would like her to wait. Although none of her relatives will stir a finger to help her, I have some hopes of enlisting the wife of one of my friends. But she will be presenting her niece next Season, and I could not ask her to present Diana too. She will simply have to wait." When he finished, his chin was set in a firm line. "Is there anything else?"

"As questions arise, may we approach you for answers?" Violet asked hesitantly. In her experience governesses were expected to handle all the problems themselves.

"Of course. I plan to stay at the Priory at least for another week." Before he could explain further, the door opened.

"Cousin Luc, cousin Luc, we saw a deer with her babies. They ran away from us. You should have been there," said a tiny golden-haired girl who rushed into the room. She had obviously just escaped from her nursery maid, for the bow on her dress was still untied, its ribbons dragging on the ground. Luc raised his eyebrows at the sight of her. Then he smiled.

"What color were they, imp?" he asked.

"Red." Then the little girl cocked her head to one

side as if considering her answer. "And the color you wore yesterday."

"Blue?"

"No, silly. On the bottom."

"Oh, fawn."

"Fawn. That is what Masters called the little deer. Fawns." She put her hands on her hips and glared up at him, her brown eyes dark with disapproval. "That was not a real . . . ?"

"No, Belinda, the color is called fawn after the color of the baby deer," he explained, his smile carefully hidden. Violet and Frederica had been watching the episode with controlled amusement. The little girl was single-minded in her determination to share her experience with her guardian. She had not noticed they were there. "Now that you are here, you must make your curtsy to Miss Witherspoon and Miss Montgomery. You do not wish them to think you rude."

A look of dismay on her face, the little girl turned around to stare at the two ladies. A frown from her guardian reminded her to curtsy. "Hello," she said shyly and retreated until she was as close to Forestal as she could get without climbing onto his lap.

Before either of the ladies could answer, the door to the library opened again. "See, Diana, I told you she would find cousin Luc. She always does," said a boy who was tall but whose voice still had not changed. Catching sight of the other occupants of the room, the three young people halted.

"Come in," their cousin urged them, restraint evident both in his voice and on his face. As Frederica and Violet watched with amusement they were careful not to show, dismay, embarrassment, and hint of defiance crossed the faces of the children. "Miss Witherspoon and Miss Montgomery, here are your other three charges. Children, these are your governesses."

At the word *children,* the oldest girl's face flushed angrily. She bit her lip but said nothing. The next oldest girl put her hand on her brother's arm to stifle the protest she saw there. Violet and Frederica exchanged rueful glances.

"Miss Witherspoon, Miss Montgomery, may I present to you my wards. The oldest is Diana." The girl made her curtsy, a very credible one both Frederica and Violet noted. They had little to correct there. The girl, like her little sister, had golden curls and deep brown eyes. Already pretty, she held promise to become a beauty, but the sullen look on her face marred her appearance.

"The next oldest is Hester." Her hair, more brown than gold, had been ruthlessly kept out of her face by a ribbon, but a few curls spilled over untidily. Her eyes, a lighter shade than either of her sisters, dropped shyly. She grimaced and made a sketchy curtsy. "The next is Thomas, and you have already met Belinda," he said as the boy made his bow. Thomas was a study in browns and golds. His skin, already tanned from the hours he spent outside, glowed with good health. Although only twelve, he was almost as tall as his older sister. His hair, bleached by the sun, was lighter than either Diana's or Belinda's. As handsome as his sisters were pretty, he carefully made his face a mask of indifference even though he was angry. At least he seemed intelligent, Frederica thought.

The children stood there quietly, their faces impassive. Belinda deserted her cousin to stand next to her brother, her hand creeping into his. "Perhaps the children could show us the nursery and the schoolroom while we are waiting to dine," Violet suggested. Diana's and Thomas's shoulders stiffened as though they wished to refuse, but they remained silent.

Violet got up and went to stand beside Belinda. Turning the child around, she tied her ribbons into a bow as she said, "I am Miss Witherspoon, and this is Miss Montgomery. We would appreciate your showing us where we will be working."

The children looked at their cousin, and he smiled at them. "We will all go," he said, his deep voice leaving no doubt in anyone's mind that he expected to be obeyed. "Diana, you lead the way. Ladies."

By the time the tour was completed, both Frederica and Violet were pleased with what they had seen. The schoolroom and nursery were bright rooms that showed signs of recent renovation. The supplies and furnishings were of the highest quality. Obviously, Lord Forestal was willing to spend both time and money to make his wards happy.

Although Violet said nothing when she first saw the suite, she made up her mind to approach her employer at the first opportunity to ask that she be allowed to move into the vacant bedroom that adjoined the nursery. While no governess had been in residence, it had been perfectly acceptable to have a nursery maid sleep near by, but now that she had arrived, Violet was determined that Belinda would not spend another night without her governess close at hand. Shy around strangers but warm and loving with her family, the little girl had quickly captured Violet's heart.

The midday meal was a silent affair. The children answered in monotones when they were addressed. After a few false starts, the adults allowed them to relapse into silence. When the uncomfortable meal was over, Violet took Belinda to the nursery for a nap while Frederica directed the other three to the schoolroom, where she planned to discover the extent of their education. Forestal watched them go, his face impassive but his mind easier than it had been in some time. He hurried to his study and pulled out the letter he had received a short time earlier. It was brief. "Return to London as soon as possible. Situation unstable." He stared at it for a moment. Then he pulled out a piece of paper and picked up his pen. If hiring the two governesses worked as well as he hoped, he could return to London and his courier duties for the government with a clear conscience.

Both his hopes and those of Frederica, that the children would quickly grow resigned to the fact that their new governesses were of stronger stuff than their old ones, were soon blasted. When she handed each of them a book and asked them to read a selected passage, all three—Diana, Hester, and Thomas—looked at her as though she were a bedlamite. Turning to a new subject, she wrote some simple sums on slates. The problems too were ignored. Finally she approached the pianoforte that occupied a prominent place in the room and played a few notes. The discordant notes that came from the instrument produced a few giggles that were instantly silenced.

Hester was the weak link, Frederica decided, allowing herself the faintest hint of a smile. She got up and lifted the lid. "Just as I suspected," she said calmly, as though she had planned the incident. "When you are asked to play during a musical evening, Diana, always remember to have someone check the instrument. Some young ladies who are proud of their own talents will do anything to spoil your performance." As soon as she had lifted the doll and toy soldiers out, she turned around, a look of horror on her face. "You do play, Diana?"

"Of course she does!" a young voice said indignantly.

"Hush, Hester," the older girl whispered angrily.

"Well, you do. You play even better than Mama could. And she was very good indeed!" The younger girl regarded her brother and sister impatiently. "I do not see why we have to be quiet. If your putting a frog in her bed did not frighten her away as it did the others, I do not know why you think Coventry will work, Thomas."

"Hester!" Her sister pinched Hester angrily.

"I told you we should not tell her," Thomas said to Diana. "Now see what has happened."

"Well, I do not see how we could keep her from knowing," his sister said indignantly. "If we had tried to stay quiet without telling her, she would have asked us endless questions about what we were trying to do."

"Do not expect me to tell you anything else, Hester," her brother said. "Even Belinda can keep a secret better than you."

"If you had listened to me, you would not have tried the frogs the first night," Hester retorted. "And who do you think you are talking to me like that, Thomas? You are my younger brother—two years younger. I do not see why we always have to do what you and Diana want."

Frederica sat quietly as the three children bickered among themselves. Diana was the first to realize how much they were revealing to the newcomer. She sat back, her lips firmly shut, and pulled at Thomas's sleeve. He too sat back, stifling his words. For a few moments only Hester continued to talk. Then she too fell silent. The three young people glanced at one another and at Frederica nervously.

Before she had decided exactly how to handle the situation, the door opened and Violet walked in, holding Belinda by the hand. "Come and show your brother and sisters what you have learned today, my dear," the older woman urged. She released the child and smiled down at her.

Shyly the little girl looked up at her governess and then at the other people in the room. "Belinda, B-e-l-i-n-d-a," she said hesitantly and looked to see their reactions.

"That's wonderful, my dear," Frederica said warmly, smiling at the tiny girl.

Although both ladies could tell that she was upset, Diana reached down and hugged her sister. "I am proud of you, little one." Both Hester and Thomas forgot their differences to shower her with praise.

Frederica noticed how close the four of them were. Diana looked up to see her watching them and wiped the emotion from her face. She stood up and glanced defiantly at her new governess.

Violet and Frederica exchanged a glance and sighed.

3

THE NEXT FEW days were anything but pleasant ones for Frederica. Determined to show their displeasure, the older children tried her patience daily.

Although their Coventry treatment did not work, Diana and Thomas found something else that did. The next morning before their governesses were up, they left the house, returning tired, sun-browned, and smug hours later. As soon as Frederica realized that the two were missing, she began searching for them cautiously, determined not to allow the servants or the children if they were hiding where they could observe her actions to know how worried she was. Her soft red mouth was set in a tight line that both Violet and anyone who had known her for long would have recognized as a danger sign. It was the same look that she wore whenever one of her brother's letters arrived, the ones filled with demands that she return home and stop being foolish.

For Hester the morning was a success rescued from disaster. When she had realized that Diana and Thomas had deserted her, her eyes stung and her lips trembled as she fought to keep her tears from falling. It was the first time her brother and sister had deserted her, and Hester felt betrayed. She wanted to cry like a little baby. Only the presence of the two governesses and her baby sister kept that tragedy at bay.

Frederica, walking into the sitting room attached to the schoolroom, knew at once that something had happened to upset her charge. She remembered all too well how often she had smiled and blinked rapidly to disperse her tears. But she had been more successful than Hester. But then she had been much older—twenty-one, a veteran of three Seasons. No one had suspected her heart was broken—not until she had run away. Her heart went out to Hester. She smiled at her as she asked, "I suppose it would be too much to hope for that your sister and brother told you where they were going?"

"Yes," Hester whispered, not at all certain how her new governess would react. She glanced up and was happy to see the tight line around Frederica's mouth soften into a smile.

"Do you mean that the other children have run away?" Violet asked indignantly. She glanced down at the sleeping child who sat in her lap to make certain their remarks had not awakened her.

"Oh, they haven't run away," Hester assured them. "They will be back when it begins to get dark. Or if they run out of food." She paused for a moment. "Or if they are bored. But they probably won't be. There are lots of things to do this time of year. Maybe they will catch a trout for cousin Luc's supper. Thomas is a good fisherman. But lately Diana does not want to get her hands dirty. Dirty! How can a fish that has just come from the water be dirty? I asked her to explain it to me, but all she would say was that when I was her age I would understand." She turned her big brown eyes on Frederica. "Do you understand what she meant?"

The two ladies exchanged knowing glances. "Diana is growing up," Frederica explained. "She knows that the *ton* may not approve of young ladies who go fishing."

"That is the most ridiculous thing I have ever heard," Hester said indignantly. "Just a few months ago, Diana could hardly wait for the sun to come up to escape to the stream. She was almost as good a fisherman as cousin Luc."

Recognizing that nothing she said would make sense

to her charge, Frederica suggested, "Perhaps you could show me the house. Last night I did not have much time to look around." And it will give me a chance to search for those two at the same time, she added to herself. A look at Violet revealed that her friend had recognized her strategy and was nodding.

Eagerly, Hester agreed. Neither the baby, the oldest, or the only boy, Hester often longed for more attention than she received. Escorting her governess throughout the house, showing her rooms still unfamiliar enough to hold an air of mystery, the girl tried to forget the shabby treatment she had received at the hands of her brother and sister. Even though they did not find Diana and Thomas, Frederica was pleased to see the excitement on the little girl's face as she showed her favorite places in her home. "Cousin Luc told us we could play anywhere but his study and the estate office. But Thomas goes there sometimes anyway. Cousin Luc's manager lets him, but I do not understand why Thomas likes it there. There is nothing interesting in the office. I prefer the library or the picture gallery. They are just as nice as ours at home. Oh, Miss Montgomery, I wish you could see my home." Hester paused, her face sad. "Cousin Luc brought us here after Mama died. He thought we would be happier. But sometimes I miss my home."

"Perhaps Lord Forestal could take you there for a visit someday," Frederica said gently, determined to mention the idea to her employer.

"He cannot. It is rented," Hester said sadly. Then she brightened up again. "Let me show you the books cousin Luc has ordered for me." She paused and then added, "For all of us."

When the midday meal was announced, Frederica shepherded Hester into the dining room and braced for the questions she knew were coming. To her surprise and, truthfully, her dismay, Lord Forestal was not present for the meal. "I told you he would not be here, Miss Montgomery," Hester said smugly. "This is Thursday. He visits Mr. Smithers on Thursday."

Turning to Violet, she added, "Mr. Smithers was his tutor before cousin Luc went off to school. When Luc inherited, he gave Mr. Smithers the living. You will see him when we go to church this Sunday." Belinda tugged at her sister's arm, but Hester only ignored her and continued. "They play chess and discuss writers who are dead. At least that is what cousin Luc says. He will not allow any of us to accompany him—not even Thomas, and Thomas knows how to play chess."

Violet and Frederica exchanged knowing glances. After a few hours of Hester's chatter, they both would have enjoyed a moment to themselves. Frederica reminded herself that Hester was a pleasant girl in spite of her constant talking. She sighed, wondering when she would learn to think before she made impulsive decisions. Instead of having a meal with a fourteen- and a four-year-old, she could be at home with her family. And next door to her sister. The last thought brought her out of her slight melancholy. She shook herself mentally, reminding herself that it was early days yet, and at her first job it had taken her several weeks before the colonel's children had been willing to model their behavior after hers.

Not wanting to waste the day completely, Frederica used the afternoon to review the extent of Hester's education. Although the girl had a dreadful Italian accent, she could write a passable hand. And she loved to read and talk about new ideas she had read.

By the time they joined the others for the evening meal, Frederica and Hester were friends. Pleading a need to establish a more definite evening routine, Violet had asked to share Belinda's supper. But her main reason was unspoken. She knew Frederica's temper and was not certain how her former charge would react when she saw Diana and Thomas again. The past year, however, had taught Frederica much about controlling her emotions. Not by word or glance did she reveal that her head was pounding and her stomach in knots from the worry she had suffered that day. Although she knew when the children returned, she ignored them, concentrating instead on helping Hester into her prettiest gown and selecting one of her own most becoming dresses, a muslin sprigged in soft blue with blue ribbons.

Complimenting Diana on her choice of frocks, the governess waited until her employer arrived before she began the first sally. "How delightfully healthy you look, Diana," she said brightly. "That slight hint of bronze on your skin makes you seem so alive."

To Frederica's delight, Luc said, "I am so glad that you still enjoy being outside. Some of the younger ladies I met last Season were so pale, I wondered if they ever saw the sun."

Diana blanched. Both Frederica and Luc could tell that she wanted to ask a question, but her stubbornness kept her silent. Fortunately, Hester rarely was silent. "Why were they so pale, cousin Luc? Were they ill?"

"No, Hester. Pale skin—milky white skin, as I believe some of the gentlemen referred to it—was all the rage. Was it fashionable when the young ladies you chaperoned were presented, Miss Montgomery?"

"Definitely. And when I came out, I was the despair of my family." Everyone stared at her in surprise, but she did not notice. "I refused to wear my bonnets with the wide brims to protect my face. Not even strawberries or Denmark Lotion could whiten my skin to the proscribed paleness." Her voice, light and amusing, held an undercurrent of dismay. "My sister, however, was the belle of her Season. I believe several of her beaux claimed that her skin was so clear and white they could see right through it."

"Disgusting," Thomas said. "Who wants to see through a person's skin?" He glanced at his older sister, a hint of worry on his face. Her face was gloomy.

Luc laughed and put his hand on his younger cousin's shoulder. "One day you will understand."

"That's what you always say," Hester complained. She and Thomas exchanged disgusted looks. The boy nodded. Diana bit her lip nervously and glanced down at her brown arms. She looked up and caught Frederica observing her. Tossing her head defiantly, Diana ignored her governess. Instead she smiled at her cousin. "But you did not admire those pale young ladies, did you, cousin Luc?" she asked with just the hint of a couquette in her voice.

"I was much too busy to dance after anyone as young as them," he said with a smile, remembering a singer who had captured his attention. The contrast between her black hair and alabaster skin had held his attention long after his interest in her other charms had faded. That memory and a quick mental review of the young ladies he had met during the last Season made him turn to Frederica and ask, "Diana is not too brown, is she?"

The question set his oldest cousin's teeth on edge. Diana shivered slightly. Frederica, discreetly observant, managed to hold back a grin of satisfaction.

"Dash it, Diana, you are not going to fall for that kind of trick, are you?" Thomas demanded, glancing from Frederica to his older sister. His usually pleasant face was set in a frown. "Miss Montgomery probably talked to cousin Luc before coming to supper, and they planned what they were going to say just to scare you so that you would not spend tomorrow outside as we did today."

"Would you repeat that statement, Thomas?" The dark, rich voice of their cousin made both pranksters sit up straight in their chairs. Luc looked first at Thomas and then at Diana. His blue eyes darkened with anger. "Well?"

"You might as well tell him, Thomas. You already gave most of it away," Hester said smugly, a satisfied smile on her face. "And you say I talk too much."

"Hester!" Three voices rang out at the same time, differing only in tone and loudness. Frederica exchanged a rueful glance with her employer and then said calmly, "Yes, Thomas. You might as well tell us."

"Well, I will! At least he will hear our side of the

story and not just yours," the boy said, glaring at Frederica. Remembering a similar look that her brother had once worn, the governess was certain that she would be made to pay for the boy's humiliation.

"I am waiting," his cousin reminded him, giving no hint of the dismay he felt. "And it will be the first time I have heard this tale. Miss Montgomery and Hester entered the room only moments before you did this evening."

"I could have told you that," Hester added. "Miss Montgomery and I were reading a story. She brought the latest books from London. And the latest pattern books." She smiled triumphantly at her sister, whose usually wide brown eyes were narrowed to slits. "You should see what everyone is wearing."

"Hush, Hester. Let your brother explain," her cousin said firmly. "Thomas, begin."

Slowly, hesitantly, the story came out. As Luc listened, his face did not reveal the uneasiness he felt. As calm as a marble bust, he listened to Thomas's report and skillfully questioned Diana. "Tomorrow I will be visiting you in the schoolroom," he said firmly. "Then I will see each of you in my study."

To Frederica's surprise, Thomas and Diana exchanged pleased looks. Over the uncomfortable evening meal and as she drifted off to sleep, she wondered about it.

Over the next few days there were no more incidents. Neither Thomas nor Diana willingly participated in the lessons, not unless their cousin was present. Then they were all cooperation. Diana, after resisting as long as she was able, did suggest that perhaps Miss Montgomery might want to show her the fashion plates she had brought from London. But Thomas's scornful laughter changed her mind quickly.

Violet, on the other hand, was widely successful. A happy, loving child, Belinda enjoyed her new governess. The servants, relieved of their responsibilities of watching the children while they maintained their usual jobs, were only too willing to run errands for her. Even the temporary housekeeper found time to visit with Miss Witherspoon once a day, declaring to the other servants that it was wonderful to have someone who knew how to run a house to give a suggestion now and then.

After the governesses had been at the estate for almost two weeks, the day both Frederica and the children had been dreading arrived. First, Luc called the younger lady into his study. As she entered the room, he turned from the window, where he had been staring into his garden. The riding clothes he wore were not new, but they fit him as though they were a part of his skin. He held a piece of paper in his hand.

"You wanted to see me, Lord Forestal?" Frederica asked, wondering what had created those shadows in his dark blue eyes.

He frowned. "It is not what I had planned," he said as though talking to himself. He looked at her carefully, inspecting her as he would one of his horses. Dressed in a dull gray gown, her hair pulled back in a bun, she seemed too young for the responsibility he planned to put on her shoulders. And he had no doubt that it would be Frederica who had to shoulder the burden of his absence. As kind and loving as Violet Witherspoon was, she was not one who would be strong enough to enforce her will on the three older children. But Frederica might. She was, after all, his only choice.

"I have to go away," he said bluntly, thinking of the urgent message he had just received. When he had been asked to help his government, he had agreed immediately, never giving the danger a thought. Now, with the children his sole responsibility, he wondered. But he had no choice; he was already committed.

Frederica waited for him to say more, her face carefully schooled to hide the dismay that made her stomach tighten. His dark hair shone in the sunlight streaming through the window, making the strong planes of his face sharp. When the silence grew uncomfortable, she asked, "And?"

"The children. Are they behaving well? Will you promise to stay with them until I return? No matter what they do?" he asked, the words tumbling over one another as though they were acrobats in the middle of a precision routine.

Drawing herself up, Frederica stiffened her shoulders as though she were under inspection. "Miss Witherspoon and I agreed to stay, Lord Forestal. We do not break our word." Each word was cold and crisp.

Luc, realizing that he had offended her, hurried on. "It is just that every time I leave, the governess leaves before I return. I know it must be something the children are doing. And I cannot be interrupted this time. Do not be offended, Miss Montgomery. I am simply concerned for the children's safety," he said.

Instead of mollifying her, his words enraged Frederica. "I can assure you, my lord, that neither Violet nor I will disturb you. You can be certain of that."

"Blast it!" Frederica raised her eyebrows in protest at his language. "Excuse me, but I am making a mess of this, Miss Montgomery. Let me assure you that if it was not an emergency, I would not be leaving." Luc ran his hand through his hair, disarranging the curls his valet had so carefully combed. One piece stood up, and Frederica had to fight back the impulse to reach up and smooth it into place.

"Do the children know?" she asked.

"I will send for them as soon as we have finished talking. They will not be pleased," he said with a sigh. "I had promised to stay home for a time."

And they will take their anger out on me, Frederica thought. Something clicked in her mind. She remembered the look that Diana and Thomas had shared the evening after they had disappeared. "Perhaps they can write to you and tell you what they are doing. Although it will not be the same as your being here, it will make them feel as though you are not forgetting them."

"I could never do that," he assured her. Then he looked rather uncomfortable. "It is just, well . . ." He stumbled over the words. "I do not think it would be a good idea. I do not know where I will be, and the letters might miss me."

Frederica's face, which had softened as she made the suggestion, froze into a look of disapproval. "Then I will not encourage the children to write," she said.

Luc did not have any trouble reading the disapproval in her voice. Although the attitude of his cousins' governesses had never bothered him before, now he was uncomfortable, unwilling to have her think badly of him. He looked at Frederica, wishing he could make her smile, wishing he could stay close to her. "You do realize that I will be writing to them. I simply do not think it would be a good idea for their letters to be chasing me around England." He looked at her, trying to force her silently to return his gaze. She kept her eyes fixed on a spot just over his shoulder. He frowned. "I will be leaving tomorrow morning."

"And when do you expect to return?" she asked, wishing her heart would stop pounding, wishing she did not feel so desolate.

"I do not know." He fell silent. Just when she had decided that it was time for her to leave, he said quietly, "Take this." He held out a small sheet of paper. She looked at him, puzzled. "If an emergency arises, something life-threatening, you may write me at this address." She nodded and turned to leave. "Please do not show this to anyone else, Miss Montgomery."

Startled by the seriousness of his voice, she turned back to look at him. He appeared taller than usual, the sun throwing his shadow across the floor. Her breath caught in her throat, and it took three tries before she could get out the words "Yes, my lord." Then she was gone.

Luc's interview with the children was even more disastrous. Both Diana and Hester began to cry. Thomas puffed up with anger, his face growing red. "You do not care for us," he cried. "I told you how it would be," he said to his sisters. Then he turned to face his cousin. "As soon as I saw those two, I knew it would not be long until you left us again."

No matter how much Luc tried to explain that he had no choice, the children refused to listen. Their faces wore frowns, and, secretly, each was certain that he or she had done something to cause this to happen. "I do not want you to go," Hester said with a sob, grabbing the tail of Luc's coat and refusing to let go.

"I thought you liked Miss Montgomery and Miss Witherspoon," he said as he stroked her hair.

"I do." Her face was covered with tears. "But they are not family. If they do not like us, they could go away."

"Hush, Hester," Diana said angrily, trying to pull her away from Luc. "You are acting like Belinda. Do not be such a baby." Thomas watched them from the corner of the room where he had retreated. He muttered something under his breath. Diana glared at him and shook her head.

Luc managed to pry Hester's hands loose and took them in his larger ones. "Look at me, my dear," he said softly, wishing there was some way he could stay at home. When he had become involved in this dangerous plan, he had had only himself to consider. Now every time he left, he worried about the children. "If I could stay with you, I would," he said, looking deeply within her eyes. Then he looked across the room at the other two. They refused to meet his gaze. He sighed. "Miss Montgomery has assured me that no matter what happens, she and Miss Witherspoon will remain here with you."

Thomas said something, but it was too low for his cousin to understand. Diana moved close to her brother and grabbed him by the arm. She whispered something in his ear. Glaring at her, he clamped his lips together.

"Do you understand?" Luc asked, knowing once he had said the question how foolish it was. Of course they did not understand. After their losses in the past two years, all they understood was that he was once again leaving them with someone he had hired to look after them. If the message had not been marked *Urgent,* he might have chosen to ignore it.

Diana looked at her brother and sister. Slowly each nodded. "You will come back, cousin Luc?" Hester asked, her recent tears making her voice quaver.

"Certainly. And the sooner I leave, the sooner I can return," he assured her. But her question had shaken him. As soon as the children had returned to the schoolroom, he pulled out a sheet of paper. Then he crumpled it up. He would be in London before the letter arrived. While he was there, he could make his arrangements for the children's future if something should happen to him.

As soon as their cousin's coach drove away, the older children disappeared—even Hester. Having a suspicion why they were acting as they did, this time Frederica did not worry. Instead she spent her day visiting with Violet and Belinda, becoming better acquainted with the servants, and reading a book she had set aside for a quiet moment. When the three of them returned that evening, tired and sun-washed, she smiled. "Did you enjoy your holiday?" she asked calmly. Violet smiled at them too.

As usual, Diana and Thomas ignored her. But Hester rushed to her side. "We found a bird's nest with three little birds. They were so funny. They would peep and open their mouths as soon as they saw their mother. And she would drop food into their mouths. They were greedy."

"How wonderful." Frederica smiled at her and smoothed Hester's hair. "But it was not just the mother feeding the birds. The father does too."

"He does? Well, I suppose he would have to in order to keep those greedy chicks filled," Hester said with a smile. "Would you like to see the baby birds?"

"Hester!" Both her brother and sister practically shouted her name. Startled, she turned to look at them. Then she hung her head, remembering the promise she had made. "I'm sorry," she whispered.

Her happy mood destroyed, she sat down on a sofa near Miss Witherspoon and Belinda.

"This is the time of year to enjoy the gifts of nature and to learn from them," Miss Witherspoon said gently. "Belinda and I visited the gardens today. She helped me cut the flowers for the bouquet on that table, didn't you, love?"

Belinda nodded shyly. Then she walked over to Hester and tugged on her skirt. "You can come with us tomorrow," she said with a shy smile. Hester shifted uncomfortably and did not answer. Belinda's happy smile disappeared. "You don't want to go with me?" she asked, her lip wobbling.

Diana rushed to her side and swept her into her arms before Violet could do the same. She kissed her younger sister's cheek and whispered something in her ear. Belinda's eyes grew large. "For me?" she asked excitedly.

"For you," her older sister said assuringly. "But you must remember that it is our secret." The little girl nodded and slipped out of her arms. She smiled up at Diana and then at Hester, and hurried back to Violet, leaning against the lady who in just a few days had come to mean security. Both Frederica and Violet looked on without making a comment, although later that evening they both revealed their uneasiness.

"I know they are plotting something, Violet," Frederica said in a worried tone.

"Well, they had better leave Belinda out of their schemes," her friend said firmly. "She is only a baby." She got up and glanced into the room where her charge lay asleep. "I simply do not understand the older ones. They do not seem to be naturally mischievous." She settled herself in her chair and took up her handiwork.

"They are not. At least no more than any other children. I think they have lost too many important people in their lives already." Frederica sat on the sofa and closed her eyes for a moment. "I wish I knew what I could do."

"Give them a little more time, my dear. They are bound to respond to you before long." Violet's voice was as calm and soothing as it had ever been when Frederica had come to her when she was a troubled child. This time, however, Frederica was not calmed.

4

THE NEXT FEW days were trying ones for Frederica. The older children disappeared as soon as they awoke and remained gone all day. One morning, thinking to follow them to their hiding place, Frederica arose early, lying in wait in one of the bedrooms across from Thomas's. She had watched him leave and hurry toward his cousin's suite. Diana and Hester had followed a short time later. Although she watched carefully, they did not reappear.

Feeling as though she were intruding where her employer would not have wanted her to go, Frederica crept down the hall and silently entered the sitting room. It was empty. She hurried into the empty bedroom and searched the dressing room next door. She was just about to open the door that led into the adjoining rooms when she heard a noise behind her. "Miss Montgomery?" the maid asked, a puzzled look on her face. "Is there something you want?"

Knowing she had no reason to be in her employer's rooms, Frederica blushed and began to stammer and stumble. "Ah, well, not . . ." Then she caught herself. "How did you get in here? I did not hear you open the door?"

"No need to do that, miss. There is a staircase that leads from this room to the lower floors. Makes it ever so easy to take care of his lordship. It even has a rope and pulley so his lordship can have a hot bath or a neat supper without too much bother. His lordship's grandfather had it installed." The maid lowered her voice carefully. "According to those who knew him, he liked to entertain his lovelies up here. My, the stories they tell. Glad I was not living here then. My mum wouldn't let me work here if he were still around." She smiled at Frederica and set to her tasks.

"Where is this staircase device?" Frederica asked, her voice curious.

"Behind that door. That's the stairs. Right steep they are too. Have to be careful if I'm carrying anything. Suppose that's why they installed the pulley." The maid finished sweeping an already clean grate and moved around the room, flicking her feather duster over the furniture.

"And where is that?"

"In the dressing room."

Frederica quickly located the additional exits, noting the lock on the stairway exits. "Do you use this stairway every morning?"

"Not when his lordship is home," the maid assured her. "Mr. Smythe, his man, takes care of him then. When he is ready for us to clean, he rings for us, and we go in through the hallway door."

Frederica nodded and hurried off to find the housekeeper. Having taken the post only temporarily to allow her aunt to recuperate, she was aware of the situation. Although she liked the children, her sympathies were with the governess. Therefore, she listened to Frederica politely. "Since Lord Forestal entrusted them to my care—mine and Miss Witherspoon's, that is—you must see how worried I have been. Why, anything could happen to those girls. Thomas, I believe, can take care of himself, but with all the men roving about the countryside, I worry about the girls. You, I am sure, have warned the maids to be careful when they travel," Frederica said with a frown.

"There is danger everywhere. And a good girl must be very careful," the housekeeper said slowly. Although she had never thought that there were dangers lurking outside the house, Miss Montgomery made sense. "And if something were to happen to one of the young ladies?"

"Well, I would not want to have to write Lord Forestal. Would you?" Frederica asked. The housekeeper shook her head. "So we are agreed? You will lock the doors to the stairs and call in a carpenter to seal the other opening until Lord Forestal returns."

The housekeeper nodded. "But that will not keep them inside. They have been allowed to run free. They will find another route to escape."

"Then I will block that too," Frederica said confidently.

"Just as stubborn as Miss Diana, she is. I wonder, who will win this contest?" the housekeeper asked the butler when she told him of the conversation later that afternoon.

"Do not speculate about your betters, Mrs. Greene, if you hope to rise permanently to the rank of housekeeper," Dudley said crushingly. Then he lowered his guard just a little. "I favor Miss Montgomery," he said in almost a whisper. Mrs. Greene looked up, startled. "She has a way about her as if she were used to being in charge. Don't you agree?" The housekeeper nodded and then lowered her eyes. Over the next few days they watched carefully to see who would win the battle.

At first everything seemed to go Frederica's way. She was waiting when the children crept out of their cousin's rooms after finding the staircase and pulley blocked. "Good morning," she said brightly. "It is so nice to see all of you up so early. We can eat breakfast together."

She watched while Hester took a step toward her. Her mouth thinned to a line when she saw Diana grab her sister's arm and pinch it hard. Hester fell back a pace or two. "We will have breakfast in our rooms, Miss Montgomery," Diana said with a sneer.

"No."

"What do you mean, no?" Diana demanded. Thomas, who had begun walking toward his room, turned back to glare at them.

"Just that. We will have all our meals together. Or you will not have anything to eat," Frederica said quietly, reasonably. She smiled at the children, hoping she was not letting a hint of superiority show through.

"You can't do that!" Thomas said.

"Oh, but I can," Frederica assured him. "Your cousin left me in charge."

"You and Miss Witherspoon," Diana reminded her. "We will see what she says about this."

"She agrees. I believe she and Belinda are waiting for us in the schoolroom. We do not want to keep them from their breakfast any longer."

"The schoolroom," Diana said with a sneer. "You expect me to eat there? We eat in the dining room." She glared at her governess.

Had Frederica been a mere governess, she would probably have wilted under the look. But she knew that as soon as she wanted, she could return to the *ton* and that she did not have to depend on this position to support herself. Of course, she did not want to return to her brother yet, but nothing this chit could say had any power to harm her. "I believe it is the proper place for you. Were Lord Forestal not so lenient, you would have been expected to eat there every day. Until he is once again at home, we will do so."

"Then I will not eat!" Diana turned and stalked toward her room. She reached her door, flung it open, and walked through. Before she slammed it behind her, she could not resist throwing a triumphant glance over her shoulder at the little group that still stood in the hall.

"Will the two of you follow her lead?" Frederica asked. "I believe Cook has sent up some fresh strawberries to tempt your appetite."

"No, Miss Montgomery. I will eat with you and Belinda," Hester said with a smile, relieved that she could return to her books.

Thomas held a hand over his stomach. He could feel it growling. "I suppose it will be all right."

"Good. Hurry to the schoolroom. You will find Miss Witherspoon waiting for you there. She has been very concerned because Belinda has been feeling neglected. I must speak to Mrs. Greene, and then I will be along too."

"Mrs. Greene?" Thomas said as he and Hester climbed the stairs to the schoolroom. "What does Miss Montgomery want with our housekeeper?"

"If she wants us to know, I am certain she will tell us," Hester told him. He glared at her, but she refused to rise to the bait.

About two hours later, they found out. They were in the schoolroom doing their mathematics. In spite of himself, Thomas had not been able to resist the problem which Frederica had set him, involving as it did cannons, horses, and shot. Hester was converting a recipe for plum pudding for six to one for twenty-four. Belinda sat on Miss Witherspoon's lap, reciting the letters of her name. Everything was quiet until the door flew open and crashed into the wall.

"How could you?" Diana screamed. She flew at her governess, her hands shaped into claws.

Frederica caught her easily, taking both of her wrists in her hands and sat her down on the settee. "Once you are calmer, I expect an explanation for your behavior," she said calmly.

"As do I," said Violet Witherspoon in a haughty tone.

"You had no right!" Diana twisted and turned, trying to get free, but Frederica had no intention of letting her loose.

Belinda began to cry and tried to run to her older sister. Violet held her back. "Perhaps you should take her into the nursery, Violet," Frederica said.

"Do you want me to take the other two?" her older friend asked, shaken by the behavior of the girl so near her presentation.

Frederica looked from Hester's face to Thomas's. "No, they can stay." Unconsciously the two let out the breath they had been holding. Diana twisted and struggled more. She opened her mouth to scream. "No, Diana, you are not to say another word until they are gone. I know you do not want to upset your little sister," Frederica said firmly. The oldest girl gulped and then fell silent.

"What did Miss Montgomery do to you, Diana?" Thomas demanded as soon as the door behind Violet and Belinda had closed. He glared at his governess.

Diana was obviously making an effort to control herself. "She—she told Cook not to give me anything to eat!"

"That is all?" Hester asked indignantly. "She told you that you had to eat with us if you wanted anything."

"This is my home. She has no right to deny me food."

"And I did not," Frederica said. "If you share our meals here in the schoolroom, you may have whatever you wish. You, however, said you did not want anything to eat." Wishing she was not enjoying Diana's discomfort so much, Frederica watched the emotions playing across the children's faces.

Thomas was the first to burst into speech. "Cook baked macaroons today. They are Diana's favorite. You are doing this just to punish her." He glared at the governess.

"No, Thomas. I simply thought it was time to let you know that I will not be manipulated by you any longer," Frederica said.

"Manipulated? What do you mean?" he asked, his face contorted into a frown.

"I know what you are doing. What you did to the others. And it will not work with me."

Diana, though still angry, had managed to regain some control. "We do not know what you mean," she said in a hateful voice. "If you do not like your treatment, you can leave."

"Yes, children, that is a choice I have," Frederica said with a smile. Hester sat down beside her, looking worried. "But it is not one that I will make. I promised your cousin I would remain here until he returns. And I will." Her voice grew quieter and more icy. "Make no mistake about that." She glanced from one child to another, making certain they recognized her resolve. Hester hung her head, but the other two stared back at her in anger.

"I do not know why cousin Luc hired you. I am too old for a governess. I should have a tutor," Thomas said angrily. "What do you know of Latin and Greek?"

"And I need a companion, someone who can help me prepare for my presentation. Not someone who did not take," Diana said spitefully.

Having watched her charge slip into slumber and leaving her in the care of her nursemaid, Violet reentered the room just in time to hear Diana's remark. "Not take? My dear girl, Miss Frederica had her choice of suitors."

"And she chose to become a governess instead of accepting one of them, I suppose?" Diana said, her tone implying that Violet was lying.

"It surprised me too. I tried to talk her out of it, really I did. It is most unsuitable for a lady of her birth," Violet said in a perplexed tone.

"Violet, you have said enough already," Frederica said through clenched teeth.

"Her birth? Miss Montgomery, what is she talking about? What does she mean?" Puzzled, Hester leaned close to Frederica.

"Yes, do explain," Diana said mockingly. Thomas, not at all certain of what was happening, was silent.

"No." The single word stunned them.

"No?" Diana echoed.

"But you must. I want to know," Hester pleaded.

"No. However, if you feel this strongly about not wanting to let me teach you, I will tell your cousin he will have to find someone else." She watched smug pleasure sweep across Diana's and Thomas's faces. "After he returns home, of course. I have no intention of disturbing him now." Their faces fell again.

"No, I do not want you to go," Hester said, tears beginning to well up in her eyes. "Promise you will stay with us. I will be good. I will not run away again.

I will do all my lessons, even my mathematics. Please, Miss Montgomery, do not go away." She turned toward her brother and sister. "See what you have done? Now I suppose we will have some horrible, stern woman who will make me wear my backboard all day and keep you practicing your curtsys, Diana, and make Thomas write essays over and over again."

Violet glanced at Frederica and then back at the children. Her face showed her confusion. "Can it be that you do not know?" she asked.

"Know? Know what?" Thomas asked in a belligerent voice. "No one ever tells us anything. We did not know we were coming to live with cousin Luc until he came to get us. The servants knew, but no one had told us."

"Oh, my dears." Violet closed her eyes in despair. "Frederica, you must tell them what Lord Forestal told you when he hired you."

Her friend frowned. "If he wanted them to know . . ." she began, her face thoughtful.

"Know what?" Thomas demanded.

"Does it concern us?" Diana asked, her voice trembling. She remembered hearing some of their servants talking about what was to become of them before everyone knew that cousin Luc had been appointed their guardian.

"Yes," Frederica whispered.

"Tell them," Violet urged.

Frederica took a deep breath. "When Lord Forestal hired us in London, he told us that we were his last hope. For some reason." Here she paused for a moment and looked around the room at the children. "He could not keep a governess. If we did not take the job, he could see no other choice but to send you away to school."

"School? Hooray!" Thomas shouted.

"Away from here?" Hester asked.

"Together?" Diana asked, her face paler than a sheet of foolscap. She glanced toward the door into the nursery.

Frederica shook her head. "He did not want to do it," she explained. "He simply did not know what else to do."

"But you came," Hester said with a smile. "So we do not have to leave here."

"I want to go to school," Thomas said defiantly.

"And leave us?" Diana demanded, her face as cloudy as a June sky before a thunderstorm.

"I do not know why you are complaining. Next year you plan to leave us and go to London to be presented," he said scornfully. Every time Diana had mentioned London, something had hurt within him.

"But you would have come along. We would not have to be separated. How will Belinda know who we are if we are not here to talk to her?" Diana asked mournfully. "I want us to be together. Mama and Papa would not have wanted us to be separated." Big tears began to roll down her cheeks, making her look more Hester's age than that of young lady getting ready for her presentation. She sat down beside her sister and wrapped her arms around her. Hester turned away from Frederica and put her arms around her sister's waist.

Frederica got up and walked across the room to where her friend was seated. She put her hands on Violet's shoulders, wishing there had been some other way to win the children over. She did not want them always worrying whether Lord Forestal would change his mind and send them away.

Thomas took Frederica's empty seat and sat close to his sisters, too much a growing boy to embrace as they were doing. "I would not want to leave Belinda alone," he said gruffly.

"What are we to do? Have you already written to cousin Luc?" Diana asked, her eyes brimming with tears.

"No."

"No? Oh, Miss Montgomery, you will not write and tell him about us, will you? Please, do not say a word," Diana begged.

"Miss Montgomery would not do something like that," Hester said confidently. Then she added, "Would you?" Her voice revealed her doubts.

Frederica looked at her friend Violet and raised her eyebrows. Violet shrugged. "And what would she have to tell him?" Violet asked. "She was hired to teach lessons and manners, not to maintain a correspondence with her employer." She looked at Hester and Thomas and wished they were smaller so that they could sit in her lap and hug her. Diana already seemed too grown up to even imagine her accepting that fate.

Worrying about the fears they had embedded in the children's minds, Frederica asked, "You do know that your cousin, Lord Forestal, has gone to great lengths to keep you with him?" She looked from Diana to Thomas to Hester. At first they just looked back at her with doubt in their eyes.

"If he wanted us to stay with him, why did he say that you were his last hope?" Thomas demanded.

"My dear, think of what has happened to the gentleman in the last few months!" Violet said quickly.

"What?" Diana asked, her eyes wide. Frederica looked at her and had to struggle over the pretty picture the girl made; if she forgot to be angry, Diana was a beauty.

"How many governesses have you frightened away?" the older lady asked. She kept her voice interested but not condemning. The three of them hung their heads. "And you have not considered what you have done to his daily routine. Unlike many gentlemen of my acquaintance, he does not demand that you stay in the schoolroom but insists on your presence—even Belinda's presence—when he dines. That, my dears, tells me a great deal about how much he cares."

"And before we even met you, he had us buying you things in London. Mostly for the girls, I admit, Thomas. But you did receive several new books lately, did you not?" Frederica said. She was pleased to see the children's faces begin to light up once more. She and Violet glanced at each other. "What would happen if we pretended that we had never met before today?" Frederica asked, looking from one face to another. "Would that make a difference?"

"You mean start over?" Thomas asked skeptically.

"As though you just walked in the door," Hester said, a wide smile on her face.

"Yes."

"I am so happy to make your acquaintance, Miss Montgomery and Miss Witherspoon," Diana said politely. "May I introduce my brother and sister?"

5

Over the next few days everyone began making an attempt to get along, one that did not always work. Among four children, upsets were the order of the day.

Once Diana accepted her governess, she was insatiable for details about Miss Montgomery's presentation. Her mother had told her about hers, but to Diana that was eons past. Miss Montgomery was old but not as old as her mother had been. As a result, she constantly asked Frederica questions, much to the chagrin of her sister Hester. "But you don't even like her," Hester told Diana after the older girl had asked questions for almost an hour. "She's my friend."

"Well, she may be your friend, but she is my governess too," Diana said, tossing the curls she longed to wear up over her shoulder. "It is her job to get me ready for my presentation. You have plenty of time."

"I liked it better when you and Thomas were not here," Hester said in a low, grumbling voice. "Then Miss Montgomery would let me read what I wanted and then discuss it with me."

"You had better watch out, little sister," Diana said in a condescending voice. "Soon you will have the reputation of a bluestocking. And you know what that will do to your chances of a good marriage." She laughed at the look on her younger sister's face.

Frederica walked in just in time to hear the last of the conversation, although the girls were too busy sniping at each other to pay attention to her. The governess noticed, however, that Thomas had used the few minutes she had left the room to escape. Frederica sighed. She too would like to leave the bickering girls alone, but she could not. She narrowed her eyes for a moment, wondering what she could do to improve Diana's attitude. "But gentlemen do not want someone who has an empty cockloft either, my dear," she said when Diana had finished.

The girls whirled around, their faces flushed. "I, ah, did not mean . . ." Diana began.

"Yes, you did," Hester said angrily. "That is all you do—tell me what I am doing wrong. You think you are so smart simply because you are the oldest. Well, you do not know everything. Does she, Miss Montgomery?"

For a moment Frederica felt once again like a sixteen-year-old with a sister three years younger who resented her. Hester was giving her a different perspective on what her own sister must have felt. "Hester," she said gently. "Diana does not think she knows everything. Do you, my dear?" She smiled at the older girl, willing her to answer properly.

"No. I am sorry, Hester." Diana hugged her sister and then took her seat at the table again. "Sometimes I do not see the purpose in studying all this math or geography. And Mama never had us read the newspapers. In fact, I never saw her do so."

"Oh, she read the notices and the accounts of the balls," Hester told her. "When she was ill, she let me read them to her."

"Well, I do not understand why we need to study any of these things," her older sister complained.

"Perhaps this next lesson will help. You will need your best handwriting, a knowledge of mathematics, and many social skills," Frederica said encouragingly. She had spent two hours that morning persuading the housekeeper that the lesson was necessary. Now all she had to do was get the girls involved. Then she would turn her attention to Thomas. At that moment, the boy looked into the room. "Thomas, do not go away. I have a role for you in this exercise."

"Do I have to?" he asked, his face set in unhappy lines.

"Yes," his governess assured him. She really had to find some way to interest him in education.

"When will we begin?" asked Hester, taking her chair beside Frederica.

"Now. You will be planning a formal dinner and a ball." Thomas groaned and lowered his head. "Not you, young man," she assured him. "Your job will be to see that the young ladies do not overspend their budget."

He raised his head from his crossed arms, looking interested. "Does that mean I can tell them what to do?"

"Not exactly." He dropped his head to his arms again. "It will be your job to make certain that the ladies' expenditures match what they were given to spend."

"Who will tell us what we can spend?" Diana asked, her eyebrows going up.

"That will be part of your assignment," Frederica assured them. "Here are the details." Carefully she went over the requirements. "And each expenditure must be written up and given to Thomas, who will approve or reject it."

"Reject it?" Both Hester and Diana frowned at this remark. Thomas smiled.

"What does that mean?" Diana asked, her lovely face marred by a frown.

"If he does not believe you have enough money to pay for the item, he will not approve it."

"What will happen then?" Hester asked, piqued by the idea of planning a party, but not certain her younger brother should have any say in it.

"You will have to make changes somewhere in something else if you think it is an item that is essential. If it is not, you can eliminate it. Remember, the more you use products that come from the estate, the more money you will have to use elsewhere." Frederica smiled at them.

"But we have never planned a party before. How are we to know what to do?" Hester asked.

"I will help you and so will Miss Witherspoon and Mrs. Greene. Perhaps the first thing we should do is make a list." Thomas groaned again. "How will you know whether an item is essential if you do not know what is involved?" Frederica reminded him. Then another thought struck her. "And you will need to make some plans too."

"I will?"

"The gentleman of the house always makes the arrangements for the stabling of the horses. You will need to find out how many extra servants and how much hay will be needed," she told him, thankful she had thought of something. She knew, of course, that the estate manager could have taken care of this, but she wanted Thomas involved.

"How will I find that out?" he asked, intrigued despite himself. The girls looked at each other and rolled their eyes.

"The same way the girls will. You will need to consult with the servants. Shall we make the list now? Hester, you write." The next few minutes were busy ones. A few disagreements broke out among the siblings, but they did not disrupt the spirit of excitement that pervaded the schoolroom for the first time since Frederica and Violet's arrival.

The older lady looked in and smiled. "What I can I do to help?" she asked.

"Take over here for a moment," Frederica said. "You know more about this than I do." She got up and crossed to her friend. "There are a few more people I need to see," she explained, glad she had discussed her plan with Violet ahead of time. With the change in Thomas's duties, she needed to see the estate manager and the head groom.

"Certainly. Now what have you done so far?"

Gratefully, Frederica slipped from the room. After seeing the two men and winning their support, she took a few minutes to sit in the library, absorbing the quiet and picturing her employer's reaction to her newest plan. She closed her eyes and could see him standing in front of her as he had done that day he had told her he was leaving. As usual when she thought of him, much more often than she wanted to, her heart began to beat more rapidly and her cheeks flushed.

After a few minutes, she got up. Then she remembered something Hester had said about her employer and the vicar. Quickly she sat down again and penned a letter.

The next day brought not one but three pieces of mail for Miss Montgomery. As usual, she was in the schoolroom with her friend and the four children when the butler entered. "I thought these might be important," he said as he handed them to her on a silver tray. He had worked for a nobleman all his life and recognized the name of one of the leading solicitors in the country. He had taken careful note of the franked letter that rested directly under it. His master had never written one of the governesses before. Even before Miss Witherspoon had mentioned Miss Montgomery's family, he had recognized her for quality. And it was not his place to wonder at anything they might do, he reminded himself. He bowed and left the room reluctantly, wondering just what was in those letters.

The children clustered around her. "Who are they from, Miss Montgomery?" Hester asked, her eyes wide.

"Do not be silly, Hester. She will not know until she opens them," Diana said in a condescending voice.

Frederica could have disagreed with her but chose not to. Putting the letter from her man of business to one side, she opened the one that made her heart beat faster. Although she had received only two letters from him before, she would recognize Lord Forestal's handwriting anywhere.

"Well?" Thomas asked impatiently.

"Children," Miss Witherspoon scolded. "Do you not know it is rude to comment on someone else's letters?" She too tried to put her impatience aside. Had she been Frederica, she would have opened the letter from the lawyer first, certain it contained word from the viscount. She was certain Frederica's brother would have some comment about this latest venture of his sister's. "Come. Let us finish this discussion." She smiled at the little girl beside her. Belinda nodded and then yawned.

"Well, I do not think they need new gowns for the party," Thomas said firmly. "They have enough clothes as it is. And the budget will not allow it," he added as though that were the last word.

"There has to be some money for this. It is important," Diana said angrily. "You just enjoy saying no."

"Well, maybe we can cut back on something else. Do we really need ostrich plumes for an evening at our own home?" Hester asked.

"This is a ball," Diana explained.

Her mind more on the letter that lay on the tray than on what she was saying, Violet said, "Her presentation to the queen was the only time I remember Lady, er, Miss Montgomery wearing ostrich plumes."

"Miss Montgomery was presented to the queen!" Diana's eyes grew wide.

Violet blanched when she realized what she had said. "Yes," she said quietly, wishing she could recall her last comment. Frederica would never forgive her if she had given her secret away. She glanced over to her former charge, happy to see that she was still involved with her letter. Just then Frederica looked up, and Violet's heart sank.

"Children, good news. Your cousin will be home shortly," she said, her voice and the smile on her face revealing her excitement. She would see him again soon.

"When?" Thomas demanded.

"He does not give a specific date. But soon."

"I hope he stays home this time," Diana said wistfully. Then realizing that her words might be considered an insult, she added, "Not that we do not like you now, Miss Montgomery. And you too, Miss Witherspoon."

"That is quite all right, Diana," the older lady assured her. "Of course you will be happy to see your guardian."

"Then maybe he will agree that I will be old enough to be presented next Season. Do you think he will, Miss Montgomery? Will you help me so that I can be presented to the queen too?" Diana said in a most beguiling voice.

"What?" Frederica looked up from the letter she had been rereading. For a moment she could have sworn she heard the deep, rich tones of her employer's voice.

"Will you persuade cousin Luc that I should be presented to the queen? Was it very exciting? Did she speak to you?" Diana asked, her questions falling over one another in her haste to get them out.

Frederica looked at her friend Violet, puzzled. Then she looked back at Diana. The girl was leaning forward, her eyes open wide. Hester too had moved closer. Only Thomas looked bored. "If you are going to talk about your presentation again, Diana, I am going to the estate office," he said in disgust. "At least there I will not have to listen to any more discussions about ostrich plumes or gowns." The boy paused. "Will cousin Luc's arrival change our assignment, Miss Montgomery?" he asked hopefully. Although he enjoyed telling his sisters they had to economize on their plans, he got to do it too little to suit him.

"No."

His face fell. "I will be in the estate office if you need me," he said with a sigh.

"I will call you when we are ready for geography," Frederica told him, knowing that the subject was his favorite. The girls grimaced. Belinda began to whimper. Frederica looked at the small girl, who was yawning and rubbing her eyes. "Take your sister and put her to bed while I talk to Miss Witherspoon," she told the girls.

Violet felt her stomach knot. She knew she should have held her tongue. But to her surprise, Frederica did not address her slip of the tongue. "I hope this is what I think it is," she said as she slit open the letter with no identifying marks. She read it quickly, and her face fell. "He will not agree unless Lord Forestal approves," she said finally.

"Approve of what?"

"To tutor Thomas. I told you I wrote the vicar asking his assistance, didn't I?"

"No. But it was a good idea. How wonderful that Lord Forestal will soon be here to approve of your plan. What will the vicar be teaching him?"

"The usual. Latin and Greek. I wish I had a better classical education so that I could help him," Frederica said resentfully. Violet looked at her and sighed. More than once she had heard that complaint. As a girl Frederica had tried to convince her father that she should study the same subjects as her brother.

"Well, you do not. This is the best solution to the problem. Unless he sends him off to school. Sometimes I think Thomas would be happier at school, where he would have some friends his own age," Violet said thoughtfully.

"I suppose you are right. But he is such a little boy."

"Nonsense. Your brother was much younger when he was sent to Winchester."

"And look how he turned out. Dictatorial and—and . . ." The door to the schoolroom opened again. The girls walked in. "Has she gone to sleep?" The girls nodded. "Since you have changes to make in your plans for the gowns for the party, you should sit down with the pattern cards again. You do not want Thomas to say you do not have enough money another time." Although the girls wanted to argue, she would allow no discussion. "Make those changes. Remember, you must be finished by the end of the week." She put the three letters into her pocket, resolving to use her free time that afternoon to read what her man of business had to say—another complaint from her brother, she supposed.

When she remembered the letter later in the day, she opened it, thinking once again how fortunate she was. When her inheritance from her aunt had been disclosed, her father had retained her aunt's solicitor to manage her property instead of turning the whole affair to his own overworked agents. Although Mr. Bridges did not approve of what Frederica had done, and was unwilling to advance her money to set up an establishment on her own, at least he did not owe his allegiance to her brother. He simply received the letters and sent them on to her, usually with a request that she reveal her whereabouts to her brother.

As usual, her brother pleaded with her to come home. He despaired of her reputation and worried about what the world would think. Frederica sighed. Every letter had said the same thing. Then her eyes narrowed; she read the line again. "And how did he know Violet was with me?" she muttered as she reread how grateful he was that Violet, dear Violet, was with her this time. How did he find out that Violet was with her? And wasn't he supposed to be angry with their governess? Her frown furrowed her brow. What was going on?

Before she had given the problem much thought, another message captured her attention. Her sister was expecting her first child. Frederica paused, waiting for the burst of pain that messages about her sister and her husband had brought before. Surprised, she read the line again. Nothing but a faint regret and that mostly because she was so far away. Surprised, she smiled and stretched. Finishing the letter, she left the room to find Violet and tell her the exciting news.

Violet's reaction was one Frederica was not ready for. "I must go to her at once," she said, standing up.

"You cannot. What would Lord Forestal think? Besides, you said my brother told you never to return," Frederica reminded her.

Looking perplexed, Violet frowned. Then she smiled. "Miss Ernestine had nothing to do with that. Had she been back from her honeymoon when I left, I am certain she would have invited me to live with her," she said confidently.

Frederica was not as certain. Her younger sister was very like young Diana, thinking only of her own pleasure. But she did not say that. "Tina. Remember how Ernestine decided that her name was too long and told us to call her Tina as her beaux in London had done? Besides, it will be years before she will need a governess. And Nanny Swift, Henry's nurse, is right at hand. Remember how protective she used to be when Henry would come to play with George?" Her sister had married a gentleman who had grown up on the next estate. From the time they were small children, Frederica and her brother, George, had been friends with Henry, who was a year older than Frederica and a year younger than George. Frederica thought about her friend, the man she had always thought she would marry, but to her surprise she could not picture the man clearly. A little boy kept chasing him out of the way.

"If she needs me, I will go no matter what Nanny Swift says or does," Violet assured her. Remembering what had caused Frederica to run away, she asked, "How are you feeling?" She looked at the younger lady carefully, trying to read more than the surface expression.

Frederica smiled. "You know, Violet, when you told me I would forget him, I thought you were lying. But I have. Now I feel nothing but happiness for them."

"Good! You can write your brother, and we can go home."

"No. I promised Lord Forestal I would not leave these children, and I keep my promises," Frederica said fiercely, feeling weak at the thought of leaving the one place where she was certain to see him.

"But there is no need—"

"I will not listen to another word. I promised."

Nothing Violet could say would make her listen to reason. Over the next few days, the older lady tried every tactic she knew. None worked. All simply made Frederica grow stronger in her resolve.

"There is a coach coming up the drive!" Thomas said three days later. The children tumbled through the doorway and down the stairs before Frederica and Violet had a chance to straighten their hair or their clothes.

"Be careful of the little one," Violet scolded as Diana pulled the baby after her.

"Did you order anything special for tea?" Frederica asked. Since their assignment to plan the party, Violet had taken Diana and Hester under her wing, keeping them with her as she met with the housekeeper each day to plan the meals.

"The young ladies made some suggestions. I added others. There is nothing a man likes more after a long journey than a nice, hot bath and a hearty tea," she explained. "Lord Forestal has the right to be comfortable in his own home."

"I agree with you. But what does that have anything to do with tea?" Frederica asked.

"He may not appreciate being surrounded by children when he has just finished a long journey."

Frederica said nothing, hoping that her friend was wrong. When they arrived in the front hallway, both ladies made a few adjustments in the children's clothing. Then they retreated to the salon. In a few minutes, the children's happy voices echoed down the corridor. The door opened and they entered, a tall man surrounded by handsome children.

He smiled at the two ladies, enjoying especially the sight of Frederica in a blue muslin. Not only had the children been on his mind often during his time away, but so had Frederica Montgomery. He had found himself thinking of her whenever he was alone, wondering if she were happy. "So you are still here," he said with a laugh, pleased to see her once again.

She bristled. "I said I would stay until you returned," she said coolly.

"You won't go away, will you?" Hester asked, her eyes brimming with tears.

"She is going nowhere," her cousin promised. "I was simply teasing her. Reassure her, Miss Montgomery," he said ruefully. His rich voice made shivers run up and down her spine. Not really wanting to, she smiled at him. "See, Hester? You have nothing to worry about." He sat down and pulled Belinda onto his knee. "Tell me what you have been doing."

For the next several minutes, the children surrounded him with noise, spilling out their joys and disappointments. They carefully avoided the pranks they had pulled on their governess, however. Frederica simply smiled at the sight of her employer surrounded by his family, dreaming forbidden dreams. Then a question of Diana's pulled her out of her own thoughts. "When I am presented next year, will I be presented to the queen as Miss Montgomery was?"

Frederica sat up straight. She held her breath and waited for his reaction. But in the past eighteen months Luc had been involved in many scenes that required a quick reaction. Without letting his surprise show, he asked, "And who said you were to be presented next Season?"

"Cousin Luc?" Diana's big brown eyes filled with tears. "You said it was a possibility."

"And that is what it remains. You are very young. Next Season you will only be seventeen," he reminded her.

"How old were you, Miss Montgomery?" Diana asked, turning to someone who she hoped would be her ally.

"A few months before my nineteenth birthday," Frederica said, wishing she could tell the girl to hush. "Most of my friends were my age or a little older."

"Oh." Diana looked at her cousin. He was watching her with a hint of amusement.

Frederica seized the moment to change the conversation. "Whenever you have time, Lord Forestal, I have a problem I would like to discuss with you." The children's faces grew somber. "It is nothing serious, just a minor change in the way I am teaching."

"Tomorrow at ten in the library?" he asked. Frederica nodded, trying to decide why the smile he gave her made her feel so strange. He thought she was a governess, she reminded herself. Then she laughed to herself. She was a governess. And being one was her own decision. She had better keep her mind on her supposed station and stop getting ideas she knew would never come true.

The next morning, she arrived a few minutes early for their meeting. Instead of choosing one of her more stylish dresses, she had chosen one of the gray ones she had had made when she had accepted her first position. The color, never a good one for her, made her remember the role she was playing. Luc looked up when she entered, noting with displeasure the tired look around her eyes. Frederica could have explained; she had spent the night trying unsuccessfully to get him out of her thoughts. He watched her sit down, returned to his own seat, and finished signing the document before him. Then he leaned back.

"What is the change you wish to discuss? You know you have my full support with whatever you wish to do," he said, smiling at her. "You have managed to survive the first few weeks. You and Miss Witherspoon must be doing something right."

"Thank you, Lord Forestal," Frederica said carefully. She had planned what she was going to say, but now that she was sitting in front of him everything she wanted to say disappeared. She cleared her throat.

"Is it Diana's demands to be presented?" he asked, wondering what had happened to the calm, collected governess he had hired.

"No. The girls are no problem. And neither is Thomas," she added hastily. "But—"

"But what?"

"Thomas needs more than I can give him."

"What do you mean?"

"I am not proficient in Latin and Greek, Lord Forestal. If Thomas is to go to school eventually, he will need to be well grounded in both subjects. You could tutor him yourself," Frederica suggested tentatively.

"No, I cannot. My visit here is a brief respite only." He thought of the meetings he was missing while he was in the country and frowned. Everything seemed to be moving smoothly, but with the country at war, he was cautious. "I wanted to see how the children were progressing, but I must return by the end of the week," he explained, noting that the little light in Frederica's face seemed to disappear with his words. "However, I would not want the children to think I had abandoned them. As soon as I can return, I will. Now explain what you would like to do about Thomas."

"Your estate manager has already taken him in hand. I hope you do not object, Lord Forestal, but I thought he needed to learn how to manage an estate. Apparently his father was too ill to teach him much."

"A sound plan. I should have thought of it before I left. But that will not take care of the Latin and Greek. Perhaps I could visit my old tutor, the vicar, and ask him to help," he suggested and smiled at her. Suddenly the dull spring morning light seemed radiant.

"I had thought of that. But the vicar would not agree to help without your approval," Frederica said, returning the smile. Luc stared at her, transfixed by the way her face glowed with happiness and satisfaction. The silence in the room grew. He had to fight the urge to get up and find out what it would be like to hold her in his arms.

Finally, uncomfortable with his thoughts and feelings, Luc cleared his throat. He looked out the window near him. His forehead wrinkled as he worked out a problem. Then he smiled again. "Is there anything else you need to ask me, Miss Montgomery?"

She shook her head, wondering at his strange behavior.

"Good. Then I declare the next few days a holiday."

"A holiday?"

"I want you, the children," he said hastily, "to spend some time with me. Do you think they would enjoy a picnic?"

"Of course."

"Then meet me back here in . . ." He looked at the clock on the mantel. "About an hour with the children."

"All of them?"

"Even Belinda," he assured her. "And Miss Witherspoon too if she wants to come."

"Shall I order the picnic?" Frederica asked, feeling rather overwhelmed by the thought of spending hours with him.

"No, I shall speak to Mrs. Greene myself. I need to talk to her anyway. My former housekeeper has decided that she does not want to return. Something about too many misbehaving children, I believe she said. I hope Mrs. Greene will take the position permanently."

"I am certain she will," Frederica said in encouragement.

When the housekeeper was shown in a few minutes later, Mrs. Greene was certain she knew what he was going to say. But when she heard his question, she beamed. "It will be my pleasure, my lord," she said, sparkling with pride.

"Oh, I sent the butler to tell Cook that I wanted a picnic lunch for the children, governesses, and me. Would you see her personally and apologize for the short notice?" he asked. "I get home too seldom, and when I am, I wish to spend as much time with my wards as possible." He smiled at her, and she would have agreed to anything. "Oh, one more thing, Mrs. Greene. I must leave someone in charge. I hope you do not mind taking orders from Miss Montgomery even though she is only a governess."

The housekeeper laughed. "Not a bit, my lord. Anyone can see from her behavior and her manners that Miss Montgomery is quality. And Miss Witherspoon has obviously been used to ordering a large household. Life has been much simpler since the ladies began taking charge. Even Miss Diana and Miss Hester are no problem. Cook says Miss Diana has a way with a menu. She will make someone a fine wife."

"Miss Diana and Miss Hester?" he asked, wondering how his wards had become part of this conversation.

"The practical part of their lessons, my lord. Miss Montgomery insists that they learn to manage a household. And that means planning menus and checking the linen. Your linen closets have not had such a good cleaning since your mother—" She changed her mind and said, "For years." She rose, shaking out her skirts and causing her keys to jingle. "Is there anything else?"

"No." He watched her walk away. He thought about Frederica Montgomery, wondering if he would ever know what had caused her to become a governess. In the next few days maybe he could find out more about this mysterious woman.

6

THAT PICNIC by the stream was the first in a series of adventures that Lord Forestal, the children, and their governesses shared. Even though he had planned carefully to safeguard the children, had even shared his meals with them so that they could become comfortable with him, he had had little knowledge of them as individual persons. The next few days changed that.

On the picnic that afternoon, he watched in amazement as Thomas refused to sit still, roaming about the area, discovering rocks with interesting shapes that went into his pockets. The boy skipped rocks on the small brook and lay down to try to tickle a fish. His hands wet, he chased his sisters, sprinkling them with water. When they scolded him or appealed to their guardian or governesses, Thomas merely laughed and shrugged his shoulders. When Belinda pulled on his leg, begging to be lifted to his shoulder, he reached down and put her up there.

"Be careful, Thomas," Violet Witherspoon called, her heart pounding as she watched her charge lifted into the air as casually as if she were a sack of grain. She twisted her hands, certain there would soon be an accident of terrible proportions.

"He will do nothing to hurt her, Violet," Frederica said, patting her friend on the hand. She could remember how anxious the older lady had been when George had swung Ernestine about. "Look. He is holding her quite firmly, and she is holding on tightly."

"What is wrong?" Luc asked. Frederica jumped because she had not heard him walking up behind her.

"Nothing," she said.

As if unwilling to challenge her and ruin the spirit of the afternoon, Luc merely lifted an eyebrow and smiled. A few minutes later, he rescued Thomas when he lifted Belinda from the boy's shoulders and set her on his own. Violet gave a sigh of relief. Frederica simply smiled.

Although both ladies expected him to forget about the children as his own affairs grew more pressing, much as Frederica's brother did, they were pleasantly surprised. The next morning and every morning of his stay, Luc took Thomas with him as he inspected farms or went hunting. When he discovered that Thomas did not know how to use a gun, he began the instruction himself. The boy was so puffed up with pride that the girls were indignant.

Even that did not last. Wanting to get to know Hester and Diana more fully, Luc invited them to accompany him for a drive and on visits to his tenants. Hester, he discovered, was more comfortable with books than people, but she tried. She really cared how they felt and asked intelligent questions. Diana, on the other hand, seemed to be interested only in herself.

Not certain how he should proceed with his oldest cousin, Luc called Frederica to the library. "What are we to do, Miss Montgomery?" he asked, running his hands through his dark hair, already rumpled by the breeze that was blowing that day. "All she can talk about is clothes and how she looks. And if I hear one more word about a presentation, she will never have one. How do you stand it? Do I pay you enough?" He had been pacing the room and returned to his chair. Stretching his long legs out and staring at his boots, he sighed. "What is wrong with the chit?"

"Nothing." Her employer raised his eyebrows. Frederica tried another approach. "What was her life like with her mother and father?"

"From what I can gather, my cousin was in poor

health for some time. Oh, he had his good and bad times, but the bad outweighed the good. His wife was constantly at his side."

"Leaving the children to their own devices," Frederica said, trying to keep her disapproval out of her voice.

"Not completely. They had governesses and nursery maids. And Caroline saw them at least part of each day. At least she did until her own health began to fail." He paused and stared at the lady in the chair in front of him. "What point are you trying to make?"

"Only this. Diana is a lovely young lady." She waited until he nodded before she continued. "The attention she should have received from her family was directed in other channels. When I was her age, my family allowed me to attend dinner parties and even country dances among our closest friends. I had young men who asked me to stand up with them, who paid me compliments. Diana is different. She has had little social experience. And she knows she is not prepared for the life a young lady must lead; she is afraid she will disgrace you in public, that when she is finally presented she will not know how to behave. And I can understand those fears," Frederica said quietly. "She does not want to appear foolish." Her own words echoed in her mind. Only by a stiff effort was she able to keep her emotions from showing on her face. She realized she had run away from home because she too had been afraid of looking foolish, not because she was in love with Henry as she had thought. She could not face the gossip when her younger sister married before she did.

Her thoughts kept her from hearing her employer's question. "Miss Montgomery, are you all right?" he finally asked after she had ignored his first two questions.

"What?"

"I asked you what I needed to do to help Diana," he explained patiently, puzzled about her behavior.

"Will you be at home any this summer?"

"Some. Why?"

"Do you entertain?"

"Only a few of my friends. Usually bachelors like myself," he explained. He frowned. "You are speaking of something different, families in the neighborhood, are you not?" She nodded. "I am invited to some of the country events, but I am rarely home. And I am not certain Diana would enjoy those events without me."

"Without you she could not attend," Frederica said. "And I did not mean that you should take her with you when you choose to accept an invitation. Instead I think you should have some sort of fete sometime during the summer. You could invite everyone from the neighboring estates, introduce Diana, and repay your social debts very easily."

"You make it seem so simple, yet I remember my mother agonizing for weeks over a simple dinner party," he said, a worried frown creasing his forehead.

"The children will be delighted to help. Diana and Hester worked diligently on the party I asked them to plan," Frederica reminded him. "This time their plans would be carried out."

"But I do not even know when I will be returning. You cannot give a party if I am not here to host it."

"Check your calendar, Lord Forestal. We will plan around your schedule."

Luc wondered how he was going to explain this situation to his superior. When he had agreed to be a special courier for the war effort, he was unencumbered. Now with the children depending on him, he had tried to withdraw from the network. But he had been told he was too involved, vital to the group's plans. Only when he insisted had they agreed that he could return home for a visit. Then Luc's head lifted; his eyes grew more serious. The children were his first responsibility. "Tell me the date, and I will be here," he said firmly.

Frederica nodded. Before she could continue, the door to the library flew open. "Luc, you must return to London!" Seeing Frederica, the gentleman stopped. He made his bow and then stared at her, his brow wrinkled with an effort to identify her. "Sorry. Did not mean to interrupt."

"I told him you were busy, my lord," the butler said, frowning.

Luc gave his friend John Wentworth a look that told him to watch what he said. Then he turned back to the governess. She had her eyes fixed on her lap and her head lowered. All he could see was the top of her glossy brown hair. "Is there anything else, Miss Montgomery?" he asked. She shook her head. "Then we will talk again later."

Still without looking up, Frederica hurried from the room, afraid to look up into the face of one of her sister's former suitors. John Wentworth stared after her. "Montgomery? Montgomery?" he whispered to himself.

"Now, what brings you bursting in here on such a beautiful day, John?" his friend asked, noting the travel-stained clothing his friend wore. He braced himself.

"They sent me to get you. Too dangerous to trust anything to paper at this time," Wentworth explained. He glanced at the door, frowning. "Who was that woman?"

"One of the children's governesses."

"You have more than one?" his friend asked, his face a study in confusion.

"Trust me, John. You do not want to know the details. Even I am not sure what happened," Luc assured him, smiling. "Now, what has happened since I left London?"

"Philpot has disappeared," Wentworth said.

"But the man is legend. No one can stop him. That is why he has been so valuable in getting messages to the Peninsula." Luc stood up and unconsciously squared his shoulders. He walked to the door and opened it slightly, checking to make sure no one was listening. "Are you certain?" he asked when he returned to his seat.

"The Old Man is," his friend said. "And you know how often he is wrong." They looked at each other, remembering the man who had persuaded them to join this enterprise.

"What does he want me to do?"

"Get back to London immediately. He expected you last week," his friend reminded him.

"Something came up," Luc said, frowning. He wondered if he would have to break his promise to Frederica. If things were so bad that he had been recalled, he might not be able to return.

"Not in your usual style, Luc," his friend said with a smile. "But she seems familiar."

"You have a loose screw if you think I would do anything to damage my wards' reputation. And an affair with their governess certainly would," Luc said angrily. He thought about the lady who had left just a short time before, acknowledging there was more truth than lie to his friend's assumption. She was no beauty, but something about her intrigued him.

"Sorry." Wentworth pointedly brushed some dust from his riding outfit. "I would think you would offer a thirsty man something to drink," he said.

Luc nodded and walked over to a decanter and glasses that rested on a small table in an alcove between tall cabinets filled with books. "How soon should I be ready to leave?" he asked as he handed his friend a glass of wine.

"Today. As soon as you can be ready. I will need a horse and someone to take mine back to London. I rode him hard." Luc got up and went to the bell pull.

When Luc visited the schoolroom a short time later, he said good-bye to the children, assuring them that he would return shortly, a statement he hoped he could keep. Frederica listened to his instructions carefully but without animation, keeping her eyes fixed on the floor. When she raised them to meet his once, he was surprised at the disapproval he read there. He had no way of knowing that she had heard his valet discussing their departure with the butler. "Probably has to do with that bark of frailty he's been keeping this year," the valet had said. "Big brown eyes, flame red hair, white skin, and a bosom a man could get lost in. Lord Forestal don't like to share. If she's gone wandering, he'll have something to say." The valet laughed. The butler nodded his head, and Frederica felt her heart breaking. She was no innocent; she knew her brother had had mistresses since the first year he was in the *ton,* but she had not thought of them in connection with her employer.

Carefully she listened to his instructions, nodding when appropriate. Then she and Violet escorted the children outside so that they could wave good-bye and send him off with hopes for a speedy return. As Luc disappeared from view, Frederica shivered.

Had she realized what he would be facing in London, she would have tried to keep him at home. The problems facing the couriers had never been greater. The messages were not getting through. And Philpot was not the only man who had disappeared. "Gentlemen, we must change our strategy," said their leader, an older man with white hair. Although his name was known to most of them, no one said it aloud.

"What is your plan, sir?" asked Luc, as usual the spokesman for the group.

"It is too soon to say, Forestal. Too soon. I will see all of you tomorrow night. By then I should have more information," Lord Moulton said, his voice thoughtful, his eyes searching the group. Those eyes boring into each person there made a few men shift nervously. Luc met them openly. He nodded.

While Luc struggled with intrigue, Frederica, Violet, and the children began to plan the fete. Her heart bruised, Frederica did not approach planning this party with as much enthusiasm as before, but everyone else did. Diana was in alt, and Hester was not far behind. Even Thomas entered into the spirit of the planning.

Since he had begun his lessons with the vicar, he no longer felt so dominated by his sisters.

Finally the invitations were sent, replies began arriving, new clothes were ordered, entertainment planned, and the most appetizing food and drinks put on the menu. All that remained was the return of the host and the arrival of their new clothing.

"What if it does not arrive?" Diana worried. "We should have told the dressmaker that the fete was a week earlier than it is."

"And how would it look when everyone else who wanted a new dress went in and told her something different?" her sister asked, her voice revealing her disgust at Diana's preoccupation with clothing. "Anyone knows that the food is the important part of any party."

"Then why is Almack's so popular? According to Miss Witherspoon, all that is served there is stale cakes and watered wine," Diana replied haughtily. "And everyone wants to be invited there." Hester had no answer and could only glare at her. Diana turned her worries to another front. "Cousin Luc will be here, Miss Montgomery. You said he would be here. We will be thought most improper if he does not arrive."

"His last letter assured us that we could count on him. In fact, he is bringing his friend Mr. Wentworth as well," Frederica said soothingly. "You are very fortunate to have a guardian who cares so much about you."

"What's she done now, Miss Montgomery?" Thomas asked as he walked through the door. He frowned at this older sister. In the past few weeks he had changed from her ally to her tormentor. "I know." He made his voice a high treble, not difficult because it had not yet begun to change. "Oh, Miss Montgomery, is he going to come? My dress is not ready. What shall I do?" He put his hands on each side of his face and let his eyes grow wide with wonder. Hester laughed. Diana frowned.

"I do not sound like that," Diana said, trembling with anger.

"Yes, you do," her sister assured her.

"All you care about is yourself," Thomas said fiercely. "You have not been outside for days."

"I cut flowers for the house just yesterday," Diana said indignantly. "You remember, Miss Montgomery."

"That's not the same thing, and you know it, Diana," her brother said angrily. "When have you gone for a walk or taken Belinda out to play?"

"Miss Witherspoon takes her outside now. Besides, I have been too busy," his older sister explained.

"Too busy worrying Miss Montgomery whether Cousin Luc will return on time or when our dresses will arrive," Hester said. She glared at her sister.

Finally, Frederica had had enough. "Children—yes, you too, Diana—find a book to read for the next few minutes. If you cannot talk without arguing, you do not need to talk at all." The two younger children glared at their older sister as if blaming her for their punishment. But soon all three were reading. Frederica breathed a sigh of relief. It was growing more difficult to maintain her temper. If Diana was not so like her younger sister, Ernestine, there would have been no problem. As it was, she was reliving Ernestine's presentation over again, wondering if she could have changed the outcome. But she knew that even if she rather than Ernestine had married Henry, she would not have been happy. How could she have wasted three years of her life—no, almost five, counting the years she had been a governess—thinking she was in love with a gentleman like Henry? She picked up her own book, a collection of poems she had bought in London, and sighed. Soon she would have to tell Lord Forestal that she was leaving. There was no reason to stay away from home. But the thought of leaving Lord Forestal made her feel more desolate than she had ever felt when she thought she was in love with Henry.

In London, Frederica's employer struggled with his own worries. The problems with the couriers had not vanished. In fact, they were growing worse. Philpot had been discovered, beaten, drugged, and unable to give them any information. And two other messengers had disappeared, two men who could travel unnoticed in the stews and slums of London.

"How many of us knew of the work these men did?" he asked his superior one afternoon after the others had left. Luc was standing by the door, one hand on the frame. His shoulders, very straight, were encased in an afternoon coat of deep blue. His eyes seemed unfocused, as though he were looking at something no one else could see.

"All of you," his mentor said. He searched the face of the gentleman in front of him carefully before he said his next words. "You think someone in the organization is betraying us."

"Don't you?" Luc asked, staring into the older gentleman's sharp brown eyes. His eyes seemed to dare his mentor to break his silence. When a few moments had gone by, he added, "You must! There is no other conclusion." Still there was silence. "Have you made a list of who knew where Philpot and the others were going?"

"Yes. There are seven of you on it."

"Of us? Do you suspect me?"

"At first I suspected everyone. With the type of information with which we are entrusted, you must realize that I could trust no one," his mentor said. He shut his eyes for a moment and drew a deep breath.

"But now? Do you still suspect me?" Luc asked, trying to keep the resentment out of his voice.

"No. You must admit, though, you were the ideal suspect. You wanted out."

"Only because of my family responsibilities, blast it! If something happens to me, the children will be left alone. I cannot do that to them." He stood up, anger still evident on his face.

"Would you rather I had lied to you?" His mentor got up slowly, limping across the room to a table where wine and glasses waited. He glanced at his protégé, his shoulders even more squared than before.

"No." Luc took the glass he was offered and stared at the wine. He raised his head. "Where does this leave us now?" he asked carefully, swirling the wine in the glass.

Lord Moulton sat back down in his chair with a sigh. He smiled ironically, but his eyes were still cold. "Now, with your permission, you become our bait."

Luc smiled sardonically. Then his face became serious. "I must return home for the fete. Nothing will keep me from honoring my promise." He thought of Frederica sadly, regretting the fact that he would not have more time to become better acquainted with her.

"Just so. The fete is a wonderful idea. All you have to do is invite a few more people to be your house guests."

"But I do not have a hostess."

"My wife will be happy to act for you," his mentor said, silently asking him if he had any objections.

"Please extend her my thanks," Luc said quietly, taking a deep breath. He could hardly wait to write to Frederica. If he could interest his mentor's wife in Diana, perhaps the child could have her presentation after all. "How many people would you like me to invite?"

When Frederica received Forestal's letter, her heart sank. She immediately went looking for Violet. "We will be discovered," she said frantically.

Her friend said a silent prayer of thanksgiving. "What do you mean?" she asked calmly.

"Look at the people he has invited. And not just to the fete. To stay," Frederica cried. "What are we to do?" She waved the list in front of Violet's face. "Half of these people know me or my brother!"

"We will think of something," her friend said soothingly, wondering if she could get a message to Frederica's brother to have him close at hand. "You have always known there was a possibility of discovery," she reminded Frederica.

"Discovery, yes. But how am I to explain? And what will they think? I am a governess in a bachelor household. What will George say when he finds out?"

"Maybe we can keep him from learning about it."

"How? It will be the *on-dit* of the *ton*. Miss Montgomery, who turned down at least five suitors for her hand and her wealth, has become a governess. How shocking! And what will Ernestine say?"

Exactly what you think she will say, Violet thought. If there had ever been a more selfish individual than Ernestine Montgomery, Violet had never met her. But Ernestine was lovely and could be sweet when she wanted to be. That sweetness had never been part of her relationship with her sister, however. Instead of worrying her friend, Violet said soothingly, "I cannot believe the danger is so great. Let me see the list." She took it from Frederica's clenched hand. Her eyes widened. "Oh, my!"

"Now you understand," Frederica said in a low moan. "What are we to do?" Given her own choice, she would have left the county that instant, but she had given her word. "What are we to do?" she asked more insistently.

"One thing we must not do is worry ourselves over something that may change tomorrow. Lord Forestal simply states he has invited them. They may already be engaged elsewhere," Violet reminded her. Frederica moaned again. "If they accept, we shall think of something."

7

As ARRANGEMENTS for the fete continued, Frederica worried and fretted, finding fault with arrangements that only days before she had declared were perfect. The children began avoiding her. One afternoon when she had gone to search out Mrs. Greene to give more instructions, Violet entered the schoolroom in time to hear Hester say, "You talk to her. If you do not, everything will be destroyed."

Diana agreed. "Thomas, you are the perfect one. She cannot accuse you of self-interest. You do not care whether the party is successful or not. All you think about are the horses. You talk to her."

Thomas glared at the two of them. Then he caught sight of the older lady. "If anyone talks to her, it should be Miss Witherspoon." He got up and pulled her over to the table. "You have known her longer than we have. You have to do something." He scowled as he thought of the time he had been forced to spend with his sisters, time he could have spent in the stables or outside.

"What are you talking about?" Violet asked, knowing in her heart what they were going to say. She sat down and carefully arranged the skirts of the rather ordinary lavender dress she wore. "I assume it is something about the party." She looked from one to the other girl questioningly.

Diana finally broke the uneasy silence. "Miss Witherspoon, can you talk to Miss Montgomery? She is destroying everything." The girl had tears that threatened to fall from her big brown eyes, creating a perfect picture of distress, but she was not thinking about the picture she made. "Everything was going so well. Miss Montgomery was excited as we were. Now it seems she is trying to change all our plans. It is not fair. You have to talk to her."

"She does not even let me discuss what I am reading with her. It's almost as though she were in a different world," Hester added, the neglect she felt adding a sharp edge to her voice. "And our lessons are not even fun. All she wants us to do is calculate the yield on the corn crop. Can you do something? Please?"

Violet looked at the pitiful faces on the three and nodded. "I will speak to her this afternoon." The children brightened. "But I do not promise that anything will change." They nodded, their faces serious, but Violet could tell that they expected her to be successful.

Later that afternoon when she and Frederica were alone, Violet wished she felt as confident as the children. She cleared her throat several times until Frederica turned to stare at her. "You are not coming down with something, Violet, are you? I do not know how I would manage without you," Frederica asked sharply. Then her face brightened. "Of course, if you do have something, something contagious, no one would expect us to continue with this party."

"I am fine," her friend assured her. Frederica's face fell. Violet cleared her throat again and then, before she lost what little courage she had, began to speak again. "Miss Frederica—"

"Frederica. How many times have I told you not to call me Miss Frederica?" her former charge snapped. Feeling badly for her hasty words almost as soon as they left her mouth, Frederica put her arm around her friend. "I am sorry, Violet." She took a deep breath, reminding herself that even if the *ton* discovered that she was a governess, the most that would happen would be a flurry of gossip for a time. But she did not think she could bear to see Lord Forestal's face when he discovered how she had deceived him.

"That is all right." The older lady smiled at her

friend. Then she grew serious. "But what you are doing to those children is not all right," she said sternly.

"What do you mean? What am I doing to those children?"

"They are not unaware. They know that something is distressing you, something that is causing you to interfere with their plans for the party."

"Interfere? I am simply trying to solve a few problems," Frederica complained. "They have never had the responsibility for such a large party before. They should appreciate what I am doing."

"They do, but they would appreciate your allowing them to continue making the decisions you assigned them. Frederica, you cannot tell them they have responsibilities and then take over the planning. The children do not understand."

"But I am not taking over."

"Yes, my dear, you are. Diana and Hester arranged the menu, and you approved it days ago. Now you are changing it. And that is only one instance," Violet said firmly. "What kind of example are you setting?"

Frederica sat down and put her head in her hands, wishing she could get rid of the headache that had plagued her since early that morning. She thought about what Violet had said and had to admit that her friend was speaking the truth. "But I want everything to go well. The girls have never planned a house party before," she said defensively.

"Neither had you the first time your father invited guests home after your mother died," Violet reminded her.

"I had no choice."

"But I did. I could have made the arrangements or left them to the housekeeper," Violet reminded her. She watched her friend sit up straight again, a thoughtful look on her face.

"What if everyone that Lord Forestal has invited comes?" Frederica asked, revealing the question that was haunting her every waking moment of her day.

By night, her nightmares caused her to toss and turn as she pictured Lord Forestal, his dark blue eyes blazing fire, as he tossed her out of his house as soon as Lord and Lady Moulton told him what an impostor she was.

"We will think of something," Violet reassured her, her voice as calm and peaceful as she could make it. "Besides, no one expects to see the governess at a party."

"But if they stay several days?"

"Then *you* can develop some contagious disease," Violet promised. "And I will dedicate myself to your care," she said grandly, a pious expression on her face.

Frederica smiled wryly. "I suppose it would work," she said thoughtfully. "But how will we explain it to the children?"

"Leave the children to me. Now, stop moping about here. Pull yourself together. Life is not going to stop because Lord Forestal has chosen to invite a few guests to stay. Besides, think what a good opportunity it will be for Diana to practice her manners. This is just what she needs," Violet said bracingly.

"I suppose you are right." Frederica sighed.

"Now, you need to straighten up and apologize to the children." Violet paused. "And Mrs. Greene as well." Frederica grimaced like a child. "The sooner you get this over with, the better it will be," Violet reminded her much as she had done when Frederica was a girl and had to admit her errors. Her friend nodded and straightened her shoulders.

The interview with the children was not an easy task for Frederica. But once it was over and the children's hurt feelings had been soothed, everything began to proceed much more smoothly. As Diana and Hester drew table settings and assigned their houseguests rooms, Frederica tried to hide the uncertainty that still plagued her.

In London, Luc was experiencing uncertainty of his own. Slowly, carefully, the plan was leaked to the members of their small group. The story they had decided on used the cover of the house party; Luc would be carrying very sensitive plans to turn over to someone who was to get them to the Peninsula. The exchange would happen the day everyone left so that no one would suspect. Only Luc and their mentor, Lord Moulton, knew the name of the second courier.

While his circle buzzed with rumors, Luc went about his usual activities. Never one to attend the balls of the fashionable, he refused most of the invitations that came his way as the Season wound to a close, preferring to spend his time at Tattersall's, sparring with Jackson, or playing a few hands at his club. After visiting her the first evening he returned, he said goodbye to his current mistress, finding her flame red locks and gaudy figure oddly unsatisfying. Instead he found that in quiet moments his thoughts lingered on Frederica, wondering what it would be like to hold her. Although not as dramatic as the women he usually pursued, there was something about her pleasant appearance that would not let him forget her. And when she smiled, the world seemed brighter. The thought made his heart race. More than once he pulled out paper to begin a letter to her but crumpled it minutes later when he could not think of anything to write.

Had Frederica known how often he was thinking of her, she would have been much happier. Although she finally learned not to allow her emotions to control her actions, her moods swung from joy at the thought of seeing Lord Forestal, of being in the same room as him, to despair because her secret would be revealed and she would be forced to leave him. But she was happiest when she was thinking of him. The letter he finally sent made her heart pound as she looked at his handwriting. Slowly she broke the seal. Running her hand across the letter, she imagined it was his skin and shivered deliciously.

He was returning home within the week. But the good news was merely the prelude to the bad. His guests would be arriving the day before the fete and would remain some days afterward. The rest of the letter was a blur. It dropped from her limp hand. Violet, catching a glimpse of her despair, hurried to her side. "What is wrong?"

"They are all coming. They will arrive a day before the fete and remain afterward," Frederica said lifelessly. "I suppose I might as well write George and tell him where I am. The word will be out soon."

"Nonsense! I've never known you to give up so easily. You are not the same lady who decided to run away rather than face the wedded bliss of your sister and the man you had decided to marry. For shame. I expected more of you," Violet said. Then she added, "Of course, if you did want to write your brother, I would agree. Maybe we can convince everyone that you became a governess for a lark."

"And chose to spend more than a year of my life caring for someone else's children? Violet, even you could not persuade the *ton* of that," Frederica said, her eyes haunted. "And how would we explain your presence?"

"I came along to be your chaperon," her friend said heartily, hoping that Frederica never had to find out how true that statement really was. "And if you do not like that idea, we can tell Lord Forestal that we prefer to remain in our rooms."

"And who will look after the children? I cannot see Belinda wanting to stay in her room too. And Diana and Hester would be horrified if I even suggested it."

"Do not borrow trouble. We will think of something," her friend said positively.

Miles away, Luc was reminding himself of the same thing. As soon as the word had gotten out that he was to be the courier for the latest plans, strange things had been happening to him. One night as he and John Wentworth left their club, a stone crashed to the pavement behind him, missing him by inches. "Dash it, Luc," John complained. "Look at the dust. I am simply covered with it. Would have thought they would take better care of the place than this."

Luc stared up at the corner where the stone had been, his eyes narrowed dangerously. "Yes, so would I," he said thoughtfully. The two men continued on their way, one more cautiously than he had been previously.

That caution served Luc in good stead a few nights later. Leaving a group of his friends still sitting over their brandy, he walked out into the street, letting the cool, damp air brush the fumes from his brain. He stretched and then set his hat jauntily on his head. As he had begun doing, he took a quick look down the street before he stepped off the step. The slightest movement disturbed the darkness of a recessed doorway a few doors away. Before the stone had fallen, Luc would have paid no attention to something as insignificant as a furtive movement at night. But now he was more cautious. He swung his cane nonchalantly, testing at the same time the ease with which he could pull his sword free from his stick. Then he stepped into the street as if unaware anyone else was around. Walking briskly, he turned the corner. Footsteps echoed behind him, ones that moved rapidly. He walked faster. So did they, growing closer. He turned another corner, looking for a doorway that would hide him until he could get a look at the person following him and almost ran into a man with a lantern. "Evening, sir," the watch said, holding his lantern high.

Luç cursed under his breath. By the time he turned back around the corner, he could hear only faint whispers of running steps. "If the watch had been only a few minutes later, I would have had him," he told Lord Moulton, his voice letting the older man know his disgust at having lost his chance to unmask the traitor.

"Or he could have had you," the older man reminded him. "No more of those heroics, Forestal. Remember your promise. Take someone with you from now on."

"But whom can I trust?" The question was one that had haunted him lately.

The older man nodded thoughtfully. "Then surround yourself with several of your friends, stay with a party. Or better yet, invite them to your lodgings. Someone must be very nervous by now. And we do not want to lose him or you."

"Maybe it would be better if I returned home," Luc suggested, his face brightening.

"Not just yet. But you can leave soon, very soon."

Every day Luc waited for the letter releasing him, spending his days as his mentor had suggested, surrounded by friends. Careful to add a few Corinthians not part of the courier network to any activity he favored, he spent his days and evenings gaming or visiting the greenrooms of the various theaters still open for the members of the *ton* still in town. Where once he would have flirted with every pretty wench he saw, now no one appealed to him. "They are too showy," he complained to John Wentworth when his friend twitted him about his disinterest.

In spite of his diligence, he was not completely safe. One evening he picked up his brandy glass and raised it to his lips. A smell of bitter almonds hit his nostrils before the first sip touched his lips. Quickly he set the glass on the edge of the table and then carefully brushed his arm against it, knocking it to the floor.

"No fair," one of his friends complained. "Broke my concentration. Insist on a redeal."

"Ha! If you had been concentrating, you would never have gotten into a game with Forestal. His luck's unbeatable the last few days," Wentworth said, a rueful look on his face. "Can't say much for his steadiness now, though." He laughed and poured his friend another drink. "Any time now it will be my turn to win."

Luc took the glass from his outstretched hand, twirling the brandy up the sides of the glass, sniffing the aroma. Nothing unusual. He took a tiny sip and then sat back in his chair, a thoughtful look on his face.

By the time he made his report the next day, his mentor had learned about the incident. "Young Wentworth has become suspicious. Seems to think you have been involved in too many accidents," the older gentleman said, his eyes boring into Luc. "He may be right. What happened last night?"

Quickly Luc told him what he knew. "We have no proof that someone was trying to kill me," he reminded his mentor. "There was no way I could slip the drink from the room."

"No. That would only have increased the suspicion of the traitor. I wish I knew what game he was playing. Why does he want to get rid of you? There is something we are missing." He tapped his fingers together slowly, trying to solve the puzzle. "Why would he want to kill you? What would your death gain him?" He stared thoughtfully into the distance. He raised his head and stared at Luc sightlessly for a moment. Then he smiled, not a pleasant smile but one that warned the watcher to beware. "I think a scare might be in order," he said firmly. "You need to disappear for a short time. Take young Wentworth and return home. Leave as soon as it is light tomorrow."

"Wentworth?" Luc's face showed his relief. John Wentworth had been his friend since they were at school together. If the slight man with the keen gray eyes and sharp tongue was the traitor, Luc did not know how he would react.

"He did not need to tell me what had happened. Been in his best interests to forget it if he had been the traitor." The older man laughed. "Besides, you need someone to guard your back. Can you be ready? We want them to think the plans are on their way." He laughed mirthlessly. "Wish I could see their faces when they discover you are gone."

"I thought you were traveling with me," Luc said.

"You will travel faster without my coach and my wife's luggage. We will arrive the day before the fete. Take care of yourself, Forestal. I would not like to have to explain to your wards if something happens to you," he said gruffly, standing up and holding out his hand. Luc shook it and quickly left. Lord Moulton stared after him, hoping he had made the right decision.

While Luc was playing hare and hounds in London, Frederica gradually regained her composure as she checked the final details about the party. Everyone who was at home had accepted their invitation, especially after word leaked out that Lord Forestal was bringing some of his London friends to stay. Ladies with daughters to settle found suddenly that their plans had changed so that they could attend. Frederica and Violet exchanged a quiet chuckle over those notes, and even Hester and Diana exchanged knowing glances.

Although the fear of discovery was never far from Frederica's consciousness, it was pushed to one side by a catastrophe of major proportions. The dressmaker in the nearby town entrusted with the girls' dresses sent a frantic note that she had failed to take a vital measurement and could not complete the gowns until she did.

Diana went into hysterics. "I will be ruined. No one will pay any attention to me. I have nothing to wear. All of my gowns are above the ankle. Everyone will think me a little girl," she wailed.

"Well, you do not sound much older than Belinda now," Hester told her in acid tones that hid her own disappointment. "What do you expect Miss Montgomery to do? Make you a dress herself?"

"Hester," Frederica said, scolding.

"I do not mean to be such a crybaby, Miss Montgomery, but the dress was going to be so pretty. It made me feel grown up," Diana said, wiping her face on her handkerchief. A sob broke through occasionally.

"It will be a beautiful dress, Diana," Frederica assured her. "Fortunately, we have everything else in hand and can spare the time tomorrow to go into town."

"But the fete is this week. She cannot get them finished in time," Diana explained, letting the smallest amount of hope creep into her voice. "And we must stay here to check the final arrangements. We do not have time to go into town."

"Nonsense. I am certain Mrs. Greene is quite capable of making any decisions while we are gone," Frederica said in a soothing manner.

"Good heavens, Diana. We are not leaving forever. The trip takes only a few hours," Hester reminded her.

"We will leave very early tomorrow morning and be in town almost as soon as the shop opens. After she has taken whatever measurement she missed, we can shop. Mrs. Greene and Cook told me today that they needed to send someone into town for supplies. We can serve as their messengers," Frederica said firmly. "By the time we have luncheon and finish our errands, the dressmaker should have finished your gowns. We will make a day of it."

Only Thomas, who had planned to spend the morning out hunting, protested the plan. Finally, even he gave in. Sending the children to bed early so that they would be ready at first light, Violet and Frederica sat back and breathed a sigh of relief. "Are you certain the dressmaker will be able to finish the dresses?" Violet asked, shutting the door to the nursery, where Belinda was sleeping.

"She had better be," Frederica said firmly. "I sent her a message today, reminding her of Lord Forestal's position in the county." She closed her eyes and sighed. "How glad I will be when this is over," she said wearily. "I almost wish I would be discovered. It would be so much easier."

"Maybe you should write your brother before the party. Tell him where you are and what you are doing. Then he can pretend he knows everything, and you can confess your secret to Lord Forestal," Violet suggested tentatively.

Her friend laughed. "I wish I could see George's face when he read that letter. No, Violet, I have no wish for my brother to die of apoplexy. I will trust to my luck." She stretched and yawned. "I'm for bed. I will see you in the morning."

With three girls bubbling with excitement and one twelve-year-old boy seething with resentment, their coach pulled away only a half hour later than Frederica had planned. Determined that no country dressmaker would intimidate her or her charges, Frederica had dressed in one of her London frocks, a blue and white sprigged muslin with a blue pelisse and ribbons, with a matching bonnet, gloves, and slippers. Although no longer the first stare for London, Frederica felt the dress would send the dressmaker a message. And she was right.

From the moment Frederica and Violet escorted the girls into the dressmaker's small shop, the woman was all apologies and promises. Thomas, growing uncomfortable with all the material and groveling, soon got permission to visit the shops. The girls, however, enjoyed every moment. Even Belinda stood patiently for the hem to be pinned into the dresses. When Frederica was satisfied that the woman would have everything done to her satisfaction, she swept her group from the room like a mother shepherding her daughter from a ballroom.

By the time they had finished their other errands, found Thomas, and had luncheon, the dresses had been delivered to the inn where the carriage waited. Wearily, Belinda tried to climb in but stumbled and began to cry. "She is tired, poor dear," Violet explained as she picked up the little girl. "You can put your head in my lap and go to sleep." Soon everyone in the coach was nodding, everyone except Thomas.

Traveling to town, he had been occupied by playing a game with a string, but he had grown tired of that. Frederica had allowed him to purchase a new book. He turned the pages slowly but did not care to read. He pulled up the window sash to peer outside; Diana complained about the draft. Disgusted, he began to count the number of squabs in the upholstery of the coach, punching his finger into each recess. Even that grew tiring in a few minutes. Then in an effort to discover secret panels that he had heard of in some coaches, he began tapping the side of the coach beside him. When his hand hit something solid, he stopped. He glanced at the others to see if they had noticed anything, recognizing with a pleased smile that all had their eyes closed. Slowly he slid his hand into the pocket he had found. His hand curled around something hard. He glanced around again. Then he slowly drew the object out. It was a pistol. He checked it carefully. It was loaded. Not wanting anyone to know what he had found, he slipped it back into the pocket, keeping his hand resting lightly on it. Gradually he too drifted off into a half-dream–half-waking state in which he was a hero fighting off highwaymen.

They were about halfway home, and everyone was beginning to stir, when a shot rang out. Violet and Diana woke with small screams. Frederica sat up straight and put her hand over Hester's mouth to keep her from crying out. She leaned closer to the window. While Violet held Belinda close, Thomas took Diana's hand in his and picked up the gun with his other one.

Another shot rang out. The coach pulled to a stop. "We've nothing but ladies and children," the coachman said, staring into the barrel of a gun. The groom stayed still. "Nothing for you here."

"Let us decide that," a man snarled in a cultured voice. Then to her horror, Frederica heard him tell his confederate, "Look at the crest. This is his coach. Remember: take only one of the children. We don't want to be slowed down too much."

Her heart pounding, Frederica whispered, "Children, you must pretend I am your mother. Violet, you are my companion. Do you understand?" All of them nodded, their eyes wide with fear. Belinda began crying loudly.

"Hush, sweet," Violet said, frightened, pulling the child tightly against her.

Thomas began to pull the gun from the pocket. The door to the coach opened. He stopped.

"Get out," a rough voice demanded.

"How dare you frighten my children! I demand that

you leave us alone," Frederica said, her anger overcoming her fear.

A tall man with a mask laughed and leaned into the carriage to pull her out. "Just what I like. A lady with fire." He laughed evilly. He had just gotten his hand around her arm when Thomas fired. The man clutched his shoulder and fell backward.

"Check the pocket on your side," Thomas told his sister. She fumbled inside, pulling the other gun out. Her hand was shaking so badly, she dropped the gun. Thomas bent down to grab it. Before he could pick it up, the coach started up with a lurch.

"Quick! Lie down on the floor," Frederica commanded, practically throwing them from their seats. She hovered over Thomas, Hester, and Diana while Violet held Belinda close. Suddenly another shot rang out. The coach picked up speed, bouncing along.

The coachman glanced back over his shoulder and then down at his tired horses. Seeing a side road up ahead that led to a small village, he made the turn, tossing his passengers about wildly. In spite of the ruts, he continued as fast as he could. Only when the village was in sight did he begin to slow down. Finally he pulled up to an inn, a place more frequented by farmers and shepherds than the gentry.

When the coach stopped, the children sat up, taking stock of themselves. Thomas reached down to help Violet to her feet while Hester turned to Frederica. Suddenly she screamed.

The coachman, still shaking, scrambled from his seat while the groom pulled the door open. Hester continued screaming as she stared at her hand, covered in blood. Violet took a deep breath and slapped her, not hard enough to hurt but enough to get her attention. Then she took charge. "Thomas, take your sisters into the inn. And remember what *your mother* told you." He nodded solemnly, beginning to shake himself. He could still see the man falling backward, his hand to his shoulder. Diana picked up Belinda, and Hester followed them, her hand held out stiffly as though it had been injured.

Once Violet had room, she felt for Frederica's pulse, fearing the worst. She breathed a sigh of relief when she found it, weak though it was. The amount of blood that stained the back of Frederica's dress worried her, though. Outside the coach she could hear people questioning their servants. "Enough of that talking," she said in a ringing voice. "I need someone to carry my mistress into the inn and another person to fetch the doctor." Quickly the two servants moved forward. The groom lifted Frederica carefully in his arms. She moaned, and his face whitened. "Hurry now. Get her inside," Violet demanded, allowing the coachman to hand her from the carriage.

8

FOR A FEW minutes all was confusion. The common room was filled with people, and the harried innkeeper, unused to quality, bustled around but accomplished little. In only a few moments Violet assessed the situation. "Your best room immediately," she demanded. She saw the two girls huddled in the corner. "Diana, you and Hester take Belinda into the kitchen. Have the cook start a restoring broth. Order some tea too." Without checking to see that they were following her orders, she turned back to the groom. "Up the stairs. Follow the landlord." She hurried up the narrow flight after them. Just before she reached the bend in the stairs, she turned around. "Thomas, you watch for the doctor."

As soon as she was out of sight, the men in the common room surrounded Thomas. Still shaken from his ordeal, he backed away until his back hit a table. An old man, bent from years of working in the sun, handed him a tankard. "This will make you feel the thing," he promised.

Thomas took a drink. He began to cough and sputter. "Told ya shouldn't give a young 'un good gin," one of the other men muttered. "Only waste it." The boy set the drink on the table and used the back of his hand to wipe his lips clean. His throat still burned.

When he could speak again, he asked, "How soon will the doctor arrive?" He glanced at the door as if wishing would make the man arrive sooner.

"Depends," the old man said, scratching his head.

"On what?"

"Where he is. If he's at home, be here shortly." The old man, obviously the spokesman for the group, paused. "What happened?"

Just then the coachman, who had just finished settling the horses in the small stable, came in. "Leave the boy alone. He was in the coach and didn't have a good view of the robbery," he said firmly, noting the way they had surrounded his young master as though they were vultures waiting to pick the flesh from his bones.

Thomas flushed angrily. "I saw enough to shoot one of them," he said. Then his words hit him. He blanched, and his knees began to wobble. He sat down abruptly on a nearby bench, his head drooping forward.

"So it was you," the coachman said thoughtfully. "Thought it might be—"

The boy sat up and cut him off before he could give them away. "Mama. He had hold of her," Thomas explained. The coachman's eyes narrowed as he realized what Thomas was suggesting. Then he nodded.

"Wot they want? Heard you say there were two," the gray-haired man asked.

"They planned to take one of us," Thomas said quickly. "Mama and I heard them say something about only wanting one of us." The door to the kitchen swung open, and the girls reentered, Diana carrying a wooden tray with a teapot and cups. One by one the men melted away, leaving the room to the children and the coachman.

"Has the doctor arrived?" Hester asked anxiously. Diana sat down and pulled Belinda up onto her lap.

"I want Miss Witherspoon," Belinda said, her lip beginning to quiver. "I want to go home." Tears began to stream down her face.

The older children looked at one another and agreed with their little sister. "When will he come?" Diana fretted. "Has Miss Witherspoon come back downstairs?" she asked nervously. "What do you think is happening?"

"I wish cousin Luc were here," Hester said, her voice louder than she had intended. She hung her head and looked at her dirty shoes.

Footsteps sounded on the stairs. They turned, but it was only the groom. "Is she awake? Is she all right?" they asked almost in unison.

"Bleeding's stopped." The groom shook his head. "Once Miss Witherspoon realized that, she would not be satisfied until the landlord shook out the mattress and fetched fresh sheets. She had me hold the lady until she had them to her satisfaction."

"Then Miss Montgomery is all right?" Hester asked. Both her older sister and brother glared at her. "Well, he knows who she is," she said defensively.

"And we do not know who might be listening," Diana reminded her angrily. "Until this is over, she is our mother. Watch what you say." She looked down at her smaller sister, but Belinda had drifted off to sleep once more.

Hester nodded. Then she asked again, "Well, is she going to be all right?"

The groom shrugged his shoulders. "Too soon to tell, Miss Hester. Now, what is it you want us to be doing?" He looked toward Thomas, obviously expecting him to make a decision.

For a moment Thomas was frozen. Diana glared at him as though she resented the servants' actions. "I suppose you could take the girls home," he said tentatively.

The coachman, an elderly man called Richards, cleared his throat. Thomas turned to look at him. "Horses be tired, sir. And if they were out there waiting?" He let his voice trail off suggestively. Thomas nodded, wishing he had thought of that.

"But if we do not come home, Mrs. Greene and Dudley will have everyone out looking for us," Diana said practically. "Someone has to go to tell them what has happened." She looked from one face to another, wishing she had the courage to volunteer.

"I will go," Thomas said firmly.

"You cannot," Diana reminded him. "You need to talk to a magistrate." Her brother paled alarmingly. "You need to tell him what happened," she added quickly. "You are the one who fired the pistol." Thomas's cheeks grew even whiter. "Maybe you ought to go, Johnson," she said to the groom. She pulled a coin from her pocket. "Will this be enough to hire a horse?"

"No need of that here," the coachman said firmly. "I'm known in the town. They know I work for Lord Forestal." He turned to his mate. "If you leave soon you will be home before dark. You can take the back roads or cut across fields." The groom nodded and turned to walk out of the room. The coachman followed him. They had just reached the door when it flew open. A round little man hurried in.

"Where's the patient?" he demanded. Thomas quickly escorted him up the stairs.

The girls settled down to wait, more comfortable now that medical help had arrived. Had they heard the conversation between their coachman and groom, they would not have felt so safe. "Tell Mr. Masters and Mr. Dudley what happened. Have them send some outriders with you when you return for the children, and make sure they are armed." The coachman's face was grim. "If they tried once, they will try again."

The groom nodded and hurried toward the stable to begin his journey. The coachman watched him leave and then reentered the inn, calling to the innkeeper to pour him a tankard of home brew.

Upstairs, Violet had forgotten about the girls in her worry over Frederica. Although the bleeding had stopped, her friend was deathly pale. With the innkeeper's wife's help, she removed Frederica's shoes, stockings, and skirt. When they tried to remove the pelisse and bodice, they discovered they were stuck to Frederica's skin. Only by soaking the garments could they remove them. Then the wound began to ooze blood again. Violet closed her eyes for a moment and then eased a pad into place. Only an occasional word broke the silence until the doctor bustled into the room.

"Someone said something about someone being shot," he said without looking at the bed. He put his bag down and rinsed his hands. "Let me see him." The women stepped back from the bed.

"Good God, it's a woman! How did this happen?" he demanded.

"Highwaymen," Violet said briefly. "Doctor, she bled heavily before we knew she was hit. And she has not regained consciousness."

"Smart woman. Best if she stays out. She would not enjoy having me dig for that bullet if she was conscious," he said briskly. He motioned for Violet and the innkeeper's wife to turn Frederica onto her stomach. "Went in, did not come out," he muttered as if to himself "Closer to her back than I would like, too." He glanced up and saw the stricken look on Violet's face. "Do not be burying her yet. Let me see what I can do." Carefully he began to probe the wound. Then he smiled. "This is a lucky lady. The ball seems intact. Now let me see . . ." Working quickly but carefully, he dug the ball out, finally holding it up for Violet to see. "Must have been almost spent when it hit her. Lucky lady."

Frederica moaned. Violet, whose knees had begun to go weak with relief, bent over hastily. "There, there, sweet, you will be fine soon," she crooned much in the same way she soothed Belinda.

"Keep her quiet. She should be fine if infection does not set in," the doctor said, straightening up slowly after he finished dusting the wound with basilicum and bandaging it.

"Infection?" The word sent a shiver of fear through Violet. Frederica's mother had died as a result of a minor injury that had turned putrid.

"Some will have it, some won't," he said. "Keep her warm. I will return tomorrow. If you need me again tonight, send someone for me." Now that his patient had been cared for, his face settled into lines of tiredness. He got ready to leave.

"Doctor, is there any way I can send word to her family?" Violet asked, her face still very pale. "Is there a post road near by?"

"Post road? Why not just send one of your servants?" the innkeeper's wife asked, never hesitant to extract what information she could.

Ignoring her in the same way most people in town did, the doctor nodded. "North or south?" he asked.

"North."

"Give me your letter. I'll see it on its way," he promised. Hurriedly, Violet demanded paper and dashed off a note to the Viscount Bassett, Frederica's brother.

"If she is angry with me, then I will deal with that when she is better," Violet said as she gave him the sealed note. The innkeeper's wife wanted to ask why the wounded lady would be angry but held her tongue. She walked out of the room ahead of the doctor.

No sooner had he left than the children crept up the stairs and stood outside Frederica's room. Violet heard whispering in the hall and angrily opened the door, ready to send the gossipers on their way. When she saw the children, her face softened. "How is she?" Diana asked. "We asked the doctor, but he only muttered something we could not understand."

"Still unconscious." The children's faces paled. "The doctor has assured us that this is good for her. He said sleep is one of nature's ways of healing."

"Then she'll be fine?" Hester asked, crossing her fingers behind her back.

"We hope so," Violet assured her. "Where is Belinda?"

"We left her asleep in the common room. Mrs. Sneed, the innkeeper's wife, promised to watch her for us," Diana explained. "Did the doctor say we could take Miss Montgomery home?" Hester glared at her sister.

"No. We will have to stay here at least for tonight," Violet told them. She looked at Thomas, worried by the white line around his mouth. "Let us go talk to Mrs. Sneed and see if she has supper and some rooms for us." She looked back inside the room, trying to discover some way she did not have to leave Frederica alone.

"You and the girls talk to Mrs. Sneed. I will stay with Miss Montgomery," Thomas said firmly, seeming more of a man than only hours earlier. He refused to listen to any of her objections or Diana's or Hester's claims that they would do much better than he. He needed some time to himself. After listening to a few instructions, he closed the door behind him and took the chair Violet had placed by the bed. He looked at his governess's pale face and wanted to cry. Wearily he leaned back, alone for the first time since the attempted kidnapping that afternoon. Once again the sight of his victim overcame him. He began to tremble.

"Water." A faint whisper from the bed caught his attention. "Water."

"Oh, Miss Montgomery, you are awake. You are awake," he almost shouted, forgetting Violet's careful instructions for just a moment. Then he rushed to pour her some water from the pitcher nearby. Trying to get the cup to her lips was almost impossible. Although a few drops landed on her lips, most of the water soaked the bed. Thomas tried to lift her, but Frederica moaned loudly. Finally he took a spoon and carefully ladled water into her mouth until she refused to drink any more.

"Hurt," she whispered. He looked at the door frantically, wishing that Violet would return. "Hot." Frederica sighed. He moistened a towel and ran it over her face. "Good," she mumbled. He repeated the action until she seemed to slip into sleep again. He sat back down, exhausted.

A few minutes later, the door opened and Violet walked in. "She asked me for water," he said quickly.

"And I spilled some," he explained. "Do you want me to help you lift her off the wet sheets?" He looked at Violet, hoping that he would not see the disapproval he had feared.

"No. You did a good job, Thomas," she said, wondering if the damp sheets would be bad for Frederica. But moving her again would be worse. "Now, you hurry downstairs to your supper. And then to bed. You will have to share a bedroom with your sisters, but I know you will make the best of a bad situation," she said calmly. He nodded and hurried out of the room, only too happy to know that he would not have to sleep in a room alone.

At the Priory, the groom arrived only an hour before his master. Taking advantage of the late hours of sunlight, Luc and Wentworth had traveled the last few miles on horseback, arriving shortly before eleven. When he discovered his house still fully lit and his servants milling about, Luc was worried. The explanation was as bad as he had feared. His mind echoed with the words *Frederica* and *shot* over and over again. Although he had been in the saddle for hours, he immediately began giving orders to leave immediately.

"And what good will you do arriving in the middle of the night?" Wentworth asked him. "Leave at first light." Then his brow furrowed. "When are the other guests expected?"

Luc stopped, every muscle in his back locked. "Others?"

"The house party guests," his friend explained.

"I cannot have that now," Luc said impatiently.

"And how will you cancel at this late date? It is not as though you had a death in the immediate family. Besides, the Old Man would not approve."

"I do not care if he approves!" Luc paced up and down the hallway. "The first thing tomorrow, send out notices the party has been canceled," he told his butler. Dudley nodded.

"And what if she has merely suffered a slight graze?" Wentworth asked. "You know how even the smallest cut can bleed," his friend reminded him. "How would she feel then? Did you not say she had planned the party?" Slowly but surely, his friend convinced him that it was better to wait until morning and that the house party must continue. Although Luc went to his room, he did not sleep that night, instead pacing the floor and worrying about Frederica. The groom had not been very reassuring. Having made up his mind in London to tell her how he felt, Luc felt betrayed.

Finally, morning arrived. Leaving instructions for Wentworth to follow him, Luc left on horseback as soon as it was light enough to ride across the fields. Masters himself was to bring the outriders and other servants to accompany the children to the Priory. And Mrs. Greene, who had offered to come herself, was sending a maid to help Violet care for Frederica. Riding with no care for himself or his horse, Luc was at the inn soon after the children came down for breakfast.

He strode into the room, brushing the dust from his riding clothes. Belinda was the first to see him. She climbed down from her chair and dashed across the room, hugging him about the knees and almost tripping him. He picked her up and carried her across the room to the other children. "How is she this morning?" he asked Diana, his arm tightening around Belinda unconsciously until she complained.

Diana had no doubt whom he meant. "Restless. Miss Witherspoon sat with her all night. I offered, but she would not let me help," Diana explained. Like Thomas, she too seemed to have matured in a matter of hours. "Hester, Thomas, Belinda, and I shared a room. We decided we would take turns sitting with Miss Montgomery today no matter what Miss Witherspoon said."

"Thank you." He smiled at his wards. Putting Belinda back on her chair, he said, "You finish breakfast. I will go upstairs to give Violet a few minutes of rest."

Straightening his shoulders as if preparing for bad news, he walked up the stairs. Just before he reached the door, Thomas stopped him. Annoyed, he turned around. "Cousin Luc, yesterday Miss Montgomery told us to call her our mother. And the innkeeper thinks she is married to you," he said hurriedly. Before Luc could say a word, the boy had turned and run back down the stairs.

"Married to me," Luc said pensively, the idea a pleasant one. He opened the door and walked in. Violet, her face drained by the long night's watch, was wiping Frederica's face with a damp towel, hoping to break the fever that had risen just before dawn. Frederica, lying on her stomach so that she would not rest directly on her wounded shoulder, turned her head from side to side, moaning. She tried to turn over on her back and whimpered in pain. Violet brushed back her hair from her forehead.

Luc stood there, his heart aching, wishing that it was he and not Frederica lying there. The groom had reported what the children had said about the kidnappers' plan, and Luc was certain it had been meant to force him to turn over the secret dispatches. But why had they hurt her? She looked so small, so defenseless.

He walked over to Violet and took the towel from her hand. "You go and rest," he said firmly. "This is not the first time I have tended someone who has been shot." The older lady began to protest. "No! You will need your strength later. Get a few hours' sleep. And later you can arrange a schedule with the maid Mrs. Greene is sending. Off to bed with you," he said, walking her to the door, refusing to listen to her complaints about the impropriety of his behavior.

The minutes of the morning crept by. As they did, Frederica grew more restless, until Luc was forced to give her a few drops of laudanum to keep her from tearing her bandages loose. Like Violet, he wiped her face with water and held her hand, less to give her comfort than to gain comfort himself.

Shortly before midday, the doctor hurried in, followed only minutes later by Violet. He inspected the wound and packed it again with basilicum powder, nodding in a satisfied way. When Violet explained how restless Frederica had been, he frowned. "Find some black willow bark, boil it. Cool it before you give it to her."

"I asked Mrs. Sneed last night if she had any, but she said she used the last for her granddad's aches," Violet said in a worried voice.

"Have her ask around the village. Someone will have some by. I should have her send immediately."

"Mrs. Greene will have some, I am certain," Luc said impatiently. "As soon as Masters arrives, I will send him posthaste. Is there nothing to be done in the meantime?"

"Not that you are not already doing. Lucky for your lady that her companion is so devoted," the doctor said, smiling at Violet. He fancied himself a ladies' man and was not above using his abilities as a doctor to work his way into a lady's confidence.

Violet, however, had no time for him. Leaving her charge to her employer, she quickly found Mrs. Sneed and began making inquiries about the willow bark tea. Alone with the doctor, Luc walked toward the window and then turned. "Now that we are alone, doctor, you can tell me the truth. What are Frederica's chances of recovery?"

"Are you deaf, my lord?" the doctor said with a snort. "As I told her companion, she seems to be improving. It all depends on whether an infection sets in."

"And how long before we know?" Luc asked impatiently. He was standing by the bed, stroking Frederica's hair, which streamed down her back like a brown curtain, covering the bandage.

"A day or two at the most," the older man said. "Now I must be off." He turned to walk out of the room but stopped. "Don't let those children grow too familiar here. They need the security of their own home. They're too quiet. Shouldn't worry if they have nightmares for a while. Do all of you good to talk about what happened, especially with the little one."

Thanking him, Luc closed the door once more and leaned back against it, sighing. Then he heard the bustle of several horses arriving at the inn. Crossing to the window, he watched Masters hand the maid down and saw her hurry inside. Only a few minutes later, he left the patient in her capable hands, pausing a few minutes at the door to stare at Frederica as though he wished to imprint her features on his mind forever.

In the common room downstairs, his friend waited for him. "You could not wait until I was up, could you?" Wentworth said angrily. "Are you ready to destroy all of our plans for a governess?"

"Yes," Luc shouted. The entire room grew silent, and everyone stared at him, Wentworth included. "No—I do not know. But she was injured because of me," he said in a quiet voice. Gradually the other people in the room began to talk again, their eyes still fixed on Lord Forestal.

Wentworth was silent for a moment, not certain what to say. Then he asked, "What can I do to help?"

His friend sighed and closed his eyes for a moment. He looked around the room, finding the small group around Diana. The children were all looking at him, confusion and fear evident on their faces. "See that the children get back to the Priory safely," he said, his voice deep with repressed emotion. "Watch over them for me."

"It is done," Wentworth assured him.

"Let me talk to them first. You organize Masters and the others. We will join you shortly," his friend said.

"What are you going to do?"

"Stay here for a while. I cannot abandon her."

"Watch your back. Or keep a groom with you. He could run errands as well as keep a watchful eye," Wentworth said as he turned to go. Luc nodded, feeling more exhausted than he had ever felt in his life.

He walked over to the corner where the children were sitting quietly, talking among themselves.

As soon as he reached them, Belinda held up her arms, demanding to be picked up. Diana reached for her, but Luc had her in his arms before the older girl could complete the action. The soft, warm body of the child nestled against him reminded Luc that at least the children were safe. He smiled at them and took a seat on the bench. Unconsciously the girls moved closer to him. For a few moments everything was quiet. Then he said, "I am proud of you. You have been very brave during this whole terrible adventure."

The reaction he was expecting was not the one he got. Suddenly everyone was crying. Diana, who had taken charge, clung to him. "It is all my fault," she cried. "If I had not been so preoccupied by my—my clothes, this would never have happened." She shuddered, sobbing, trying to gain control. "I am so ashamed."

"I was so scared," Hester was saying on his other side. She wiped her eyes on her sleeve. Luc handed her his handkerchief, wishing that he had more than one. Thomas scrubbed his eyes with his sleeve and shivered. Belinda wailed loudly. Mrs. Sneed, recognizing his difficulty, took the smallest child from him, promising her a treat.

Luc put his arms around the two girls next to him and smiled at Thomas. When their tears had slowed down, he asked, "Now, what is the nonsense, Diana?"

She took a deep, quivering breath, trying to stop sobbing. "We went to town to get our dresses for the party. If I had not been such a baby about worrying that they would arrive in time, we would not have been on the road then. We waited for them to be finished, you see." She sniffed. Hester handed her the crumpled handkerchief. Without complaining about its dampness, Diana wiped her nose.

"That's not true, Diana," Thomas said. "You heard what that man said." He looked across the table and wished there were room for him closer to his cousin. His dreams the previous night had been particularly gruesome.

"So you heard him too?" his cousin asked thoughtfully. The groom had not been able to swear that the man had planned to take the children. He had been too far away.

"Not clearly," Thomas said. "But Miss Montgomery did."

"Now you did it," Hester complained, wiping her eyes again.

"Did what?" Luc asked, puzzled.

"He called Mama Miss Montgomery," Hester said angrily. "That's not what we are supposed to do."

"Oh." Luc wanted to laugh, but he knew that would hurt Hester's feelings. "Miss Witherspoon thought it best to explain that Miss Montgomery"—he lowered his voice to almost a whisper when he said the name—"was my new bride and that you are my wards and have just recently joined us," he explained. "Of course you may still have difficulty in knowing what to call her."

"She said you were married to her?" Hester asked, her eyes growing large at the prospect. Even though she knew it was not true, her face filled with joy at the thought.

"It is only until we can take her home," Luc reminded them. "Apparently Mrs. Sneed had some difficulty accepting a wounded lady and a coach full of children."

"Well, she certainly did not put herself out to make things comfortable for us," Diana exclaimed. Then she put her hand over her mouth and looked around to see who was near enough to hear.

"She is good with Belinda," Hester reminded her.

"And she did stay with Miss—Mama, last evening so that Violet could be with us until we went to sleep," Thomas added. Luc looked at the boy closely. His voice was almost a monotone, and a white line circled his mouth.

"That's good." He hugged the two girls again. Then he leaned forward over the table and motioned Thomas to come closer. Hester and Diana leaned forward too. "Here is what you are to do. In just a short while Mr. Wentworth, Masters, and some of the other servants are going to take you home. Hush," he said firmly as they began to protest. "I refuse to take chances with you. Besides, Miss Witherspoon needs to be able to concentrate on Miss, ah . . ."

"Frederica, that's what Miss Witherspoon calls her when she thinks we are not listening," Hester said helpfully.

Luc smiled at her. "Frederica if you are still here. At the Priory there are servants who can keep a watch on Belinda. You children have done a fine job in a difficult situation," he added hastily, seeing their faces darken with despair, "but I want to know you are safe."

"We cannot just leave her here," Diana said. "Cousin Luc, she held us on the floor and threw herself on top of us." Her memories caused her voice to begin to shake. "That is—that is why she was shot." Tears began to flow down the faces of both the girls again.

"And that is why you must leave. Do you think she would want you in danger?" he asked, his face stern. Slowly Diana shook her head, her eyes anguished. "Then gather up your things and get ready to return home. I promise that before you leave, I will send Miss Witherspoon down to talk to you."

"You are not going with us?" Thomas asked, his eyes as serious as his voice.

"No. Not just yet. Now, go and get ready to leave." The children got up slowly. "Thomas, stay a moment." The boy stopped, his shoulders set. "Let us walk outside." Expecting the worst, the boy followed him.

Both blinked as they walked out into the bright sunshine of the fresh, clean day. Luc put his arm over the boy's shoulders. "Tell me your version of what happened yesterday," he said gently.

Thomas shivered again. He tried to speak, but at first no words would come out. "I—I shot a man. Oh, cousin Luc, it was nothing like shooting birds! He had his hand around Miss Montgomery's arm, trying to pull her out of the coach. I knew I couldn't let him take her. So I pulled the trigger. It was horrible. He fell backward, clutching his chest." He turned his back on his cousin for a moment, trying manfully to control himself. "Will I be sent to jail for killing him? Diana said I would have to face the magistrate."

Cursing the overhasty mouth of his oldest ward, Luc quickly turned the boy around to face him. "Thomas, you did the right thing. And you did not kill the man." The boy's face brightened. "At least no one found his body." Just by a fragment, Thomas's shoulders lost a bit of their stiffness. "And if anyone speaks to a magistrate, it will not be you." He put both hands on the boy's shoulders and looked him the eye. "Thank you for your swift action."

The boy wanted to cry but swallowed his tears. "It was nothing like I thought it would be," he said. "It was horrible. I do not want to have anything to do with guns again." He shuddered.

Wisely, Luc did not try to disagree. He merely said, "Sometimes life can be ugly. Thomas, on the way home today, you can ride on horseback with Mr. Wentworth if you prefer."

His cousin shook his head. "I will ride with the girls. I can amuse Belinda sometimes when she grows fretful, and since Miss Witherspoon is staying here," he paused. Then he rushed on. "You were not lying to us, were you? Trying to make the girls feel less afraid? She is going to recover?"

"That is what the doctor said," Luc assured him. "I will stay tonight to make certain. Will that make you feel better?" They turned back toward the inn, the tall boy and the even taller man.

As they approached, Wentworth stepped out of the

shadows. "We are ready to go as soon as the children enter the coach," he told his friend. The sight of the bullet hole in the coach had set his teeth on edge. Had the bullet been just slightly lower, Forestal might be laying his governess out for burial instead of hiring a doctor. Wentworth's face darkened in anger as he watched his friend.

"Let's go find Miss Witherspoon so that she can tell you how well your governess is doing," Luc said.

A short time later, he waved them on their way. For a moment he watched the coach move down the road. Then, his face serious, he reentered the inn.

9

WITH THE CHILDREN gone, the inn was quickly returning to normal. The common room began to fill gradually with local residents, who had taken their custom outside while the children were present. Still rather confused by the events of the previous day and wondering just how they had been so lucky to gain the custom of quality, the innkeeper and his wife bustled about, filling tankards and answering questions.

Luc took one look at the assembled group, most of them eyeing him curiously, and headed up the stairs. He knocked on the chamber door and entered. The older maid that Mrs. Greene had sent was seated beside the bed, mending in her lap. As soon as she saw him, she quickly stood up. "Keep your seat, Rose," he said quietly. Rather flustered, she sat back down. "How is she doing?"

"Rather restless. The willow bark tea seems to help, though," she said carefully, watching her pronunciation. "Mrs. Greene sent some restorative jelly. She ate some of that." Having said all she knew of the matter, she fell silent again, wondering what her master was doing here in the sickroom. She had heard what Miss Montgomery had done—everyone at the Priory had heard—but it wasn't right, his being here. But it wasn't her place to tell him so, she reminded herself. Never could tell what quality would do.

Luc stood by the bed, his face not revealing the torment that he was feeling. She looked so small, no larger really than Hester. Someone had smoothed her hair and braided it so that one long braid hung down her back. Through the thin lawn of her nightrail, he could see the thick bandage the doctor had applied. She shifted restlessly, moved her right arm, and moaned slightly. Luc bent over her, his hand barely touching her forehead. Rose frowned, but he was too occupied to notice. "Moisten a towel so I may wipe her forehead. She seems rather warm," he said. The maid quickly handed him a towel moistened with lavender water and watched in disapproval as he personally performed the service.

As he finished, he became aware that Frederica had her eyes open and was staring at him in bewilderment. "What are you doing?" she asked, her voice thick.

"Helping Rose take care of you," he said with a smile, his heart racing. She smiled back and closed her eyes. "Ask Mrs. Sneed for the broth she has ready, Rose," Luc said. "Our patient needs something to keep up her strength." Nodding, the maid hurried out, her face still set in disapproving lines.

While she was gone, Luc sat on the bed and stroked Frederica's hair. She had almost dropped back off to sleep when she remembered what had happened. "The children!" She tried to roll over and sit up but fell back in agony, hurting her shoulder even more. Tears of pain began to roll down her face.

Luc was no more proof against her tears than he had been against Belinda's. He picked her up gently, taking care not to put his hands over the bandage, and held her close to him on his lap. "Shh. They are fine. By now they are almost safe at the Priory," he whispered to her, patting her gently. His arms tightened convulsively as he thought what could have happened, what still might happen. Slowly her tears dried. She put her head on his shoulder, too comfortable to wonder if she were dreaming or awake. Feeling her softness, the warmth of her body, his body responded.

"Lord Forestal!" Rose said, her eyes narrowed in disapproval. No matter what Mrs. Greene or that innkeeper's wife said, it was not right. And if she had not needed her position so much, she would have told his lordship so.

"Give me the cup," he said, ignoring his servant's disapproval and his own reactions. He would worry about what others thought when Frederica was herself again. "Try to drink some of this," he said softly in her ear.

"Don't want any," she said in a grumbling voice.

"Just a little?" he asked, coaxing her much as she would have coaxed a sick child. She opened her mouth and took a sip and then snuggled her head back into his shoulder. "Some more," he whispered, feeling the warmth of her breath against his neck. She shook her head, but he persisted. Over the next few minutes he managed to get her to drink about half the cup. Finally he handed it back to the maid. "I'll hold her until she goes back to sleep," he said, more to himself than to anyone else, not wanting to deny himself that small pleasure. The maid sniffed. He ignored her, surprised at how little he cared about what others thought.

"It hurts," Frederica said, tears beginning to spill down her cheeks again.

"Mrs. Greene sent some black willow bark for tea. Shall I see if Mrs. Sneed has made some up fresh? She drank the last of what we had some time ago," Rose asked, glad to have something to do so that she would not have to watch her master make a fool of himself. He nodded.

As soon as she returned, he suggested. "I'll sit in the chair with her while you put on fresh sheets." Slowly he stood up, wincing as Frederica moaned when he moved too rapidly. "Put some of those extra pillows on the bed so that we can give her extra support for her shoulder," he said, remembering how a doctor had propped up a friend of his after a hunting accident.

Before long, Frederica was back in bed, lying once again on her stomach. She breathed in the sweet scent of the sheets Mrs. Greene had sent and sighed. With pillows under her right side, she was able to move a little without causing herself pain. She shifted slightly and sighed again, drifting off into a drugged sleep.

When Violet reentered the sickroom, she found Luc still there. The innkeeper had brought up a stool so that he could sit; he refused to let Rose give up the chair. Quickly, Violet sent the servant to have her dinner and take a rest, reminding her that she would be needed again soon. "Lord Forestal, you should not be here," she told him sternly as soon as the door had closed behind the maid.

"Everyone thinks she is my wife," he reminded her.

"But she is not. This is not proper. Your servants, at least, know the difference. This will destroy her reputation," she protested, her voice low so that she did not disturb her sleeping charge. "And you need to be with the children," she added persuasively.

"Wentworth is looking after them."

"They do not trust him as they do you. Go home, my lord, and look after them. They will need you close at hand." She stared at him until he nodded.

"I will go. But I will be back," he promised. He frowned. "She seems warmer to me than she did earlier. If you need me, let me know."

"I will watch over her," Violet assured him. "I have prepared a list of things I would like Mrs. Greene to send me. Will you take it to her?"

"Of course. I will see that a groom brings them immediately," he promised, standing up. He glanced once more at the figure in the bed, wishing he were holding her once more. Slowly he walked out of the room, keeping his eyes on Frederica.

"Good day, my lord," Sneed said as he walked down the stairs. "And how is your wife this afternoon?"

"She seems to be better. But she is worried about the children. I must return home to check on them. See to it that Miss Witherspoon and my wife have whatever they need, Sneed," Luc said firmly, his voice promising retribution if his wishes were not met. He handed the man a small purse. "I will return later."

Bowing almost to the ground, the innkeeper put the bag behind him, reveling in its weight.

At the Priory, quiet confusion reigned. Mrs. Greene, uncertain of her master's plans, had continued with plans for the fete although Dudley and some of the other servants were certain that it would be postponed. The children drifted from one activity to the next, never out of sight of one another or some adult. Although he tried to act naturally, Thomas, white and strained, took one look at the stewed rabbit and dashed from the table, returning later looking slightly green.

Wentworth, in charge of children for the first time in his life, was hopelessly out of his element. All he could do was shepherd them from one room to the next. When Luc finally appeared later that afternoon, everyone was happy to see him.

"Is she all right?" Thomas demanded, some color coming back into his face.

"Did you bring her home?" Hester asked.

"Of course he did not," Diana said despressingly. "But when does the doctor say she may return?"

Choosing Diana's question because it was the easiest, Luc said, "He did not tell me that. But she did take some broth and some of Mrs. Greene's restorative jelly."

"Where is my Miss Witherspoon?" Belinda demanded, her bottom lip quivering pitifully.

"She has been asking that all day," Wentworth said with a sigh. "She has looked in every room to see if she can find her." He ran his hand through his hair. "I wish you had brought her back with you."

Luc crouched down in front of his youngest ward. "Miss Witherspoon has to take care of Miss Montgomery, Belinda," he said soothingly. "Remember she was hurt yesterday."

"But she is mine," the little girl said, big tears running down her face.

"You have your sisters and brother," he reminded her, but she kept crying.

"And Nancy, your nursery maid," Diana said encouragingly. "You like Nancy."

"But she does not tell me stories like Miss Witherspoon," Belinda said with a sniff.

"What if I told you a story?" her cousin asked, picking her up in his arms. The action reminded him of how he had held Frederica that afternoon and how he wanted to hold her for the rest of his life.

"And hold my hand until I go to sleep?" Belinda asked, not wanting to be alone. Hester and Diana exchanged glances, understanding exactly how their youngest sister was feeling. Thomas too wanted to make the same demand but was afraid of seeming a baby.

"I will let you sleep in my bed with me tonight," Diana offered quickly. The fact that they had shared a room the previous evening had made them all feel more secure.

"No. I want cousin Luc," Belinda demanded, tightening her grip about his neck.

"Then you shall have me," he promised. "You can sleep in my room." He took another look at Thomas's face, noting the disappointment there. "And Thomas can sleep in my dressing room so that he will be close if you need him." Diana's and Hester's faces fell. "And I will tell Mrs. Greene to prepare my mother's room for you girls. That way you will all be close together tonight." The children sighed with relief and nodded. Wentworth looked on in amazement. Nothing he knew of his friend's experiences away from the Priory had prepared him for the family man he was now seeing. No wonder the old man liked him so much.

By the time Luc had finished talking to the children, he was exhausted. But his work was only beginning. His housekeeper asked to see him. "Tell her I will talk to her tomorrow, Dudley," he said tiredly.

"She says it is urgent, my lord," his butler said. "Something about the fete."

"The fete?" Since the disaster, Luc had given no

thought to the party or to the mission he was supposedly on. He straightened his shoulders and looked at his friend. Wentworth merely shrugged. "Send her in."

In a few minutes, Mrs. Greene bustled in, her keys swinging on her belt. "And what may I do for you, Mrs. Greene?" her employer asked.

"Answer a few questions, my lord." She paused. "Do you plan to cancel the fete?"

"You cannot, Luc," his friend reminded him. "People are already on their way here. And it is not as though your governess will be missed." Except by the children and me, Luc answered silently.

Both of the other occupants in the room glared at him. Wentworth quickly rethought what he had planned to say next and was silent. Luc thought for a moment, his eyes closed. When he opened them, he said, "He is right. No one would understand our canceling the affair. We will have to go on if you think you can, Mrs. Greene. I know Miss Montgomery was helping with the arrangements. Do you think you can manage without both Miss Witherspoon and her?"

"I am not saying it will be easy, but we can. Miss Diana and Miss Hester both know as many of the plans as Miss Montgomery did. If they are willing to help, and if I can hire some extra help to replace Miss Witherspoon and Rose, we will be ready."

"I have probably made things more difficult for you, Mrs. Greene," Luc said as he explained the arrangements he had made for the children. "Will this upset your arrangements for rooms?"

"Hmmm. We had not planned to use that room anyway. And if the children are willing, we can put unexpected guests in their rooms or perhaps Miss Montgomery's room."

"No!" Both the housekeeper and Wentworth stared at him. "Use the children's rooms if you must, but leave Miss Montgomery's alone. And hire anyone who is willing to work, men as well as women. I do not want the children out of the sight of an adult at any time."

"Yes, my lord," the housekeeper said, making her curtsy and her escape. As she walked down the stairs to her office, she wondered about his refusal to allow her to use Miss Montgomery's room. But he was going on with the fete, she reminded herself.

As soon as supper was over and the children settled in their new rooms, Luc and Wentworth walked into the study. His eyes heavy from the hours without sleep, Luc tried to keep a conversation going. Finally his friend took pity on him. "Go to bed, Forestal," he said, using his friend's title mockingly. "I will not think you a bad host if you leave me to entertain myself. In fact, I am thinking of retiring early myself."

"You? You are used to staying up until dawn," his friend reminded him.

"But then I sleep until noon. Which I was not able to do today," Wentworth reminded him, laughing. Then his face sobered. "You have my respect. Do not know if I could have done what you did." He smiled to himself when he saw his friend's reaction.

"What are you talking about?"

"Those children. Never knew there was so much to do in taking care of them. How do those fellows with large families manage?" He thought of trying to keep up with Belinda for more than a few hours at a time and felt exhausted.

"I imagine they leave them for their wives to manage."

"Poor ladies. But I suppose they are used to it."

"Or depend on their governesses," Luc said reflectively. He yawned widely and offered his apologies.

"No need. Governess. Yes, I met the older one today. Is the younger one truly recovering?" Wentworth asked, covering a yawn himself.

"We do not know for certain. The doctor seems cautiously optimistic," his friend said, glad he could be completely honest for once. "I will ride over in the morning to check once more."

"You cannot leave. You have guests arriving. Know my parents always stayed at home when expecting someone."

"I will leave before dawn and be back by noon. I do not really expect anyone before tea," Luc told him. "Do you want to go with me?"

"Before dawn? Not for me. Take a groom instead."

Slowly both gentlemen made their way up the stairs to their rooms. When Luc walked into his chambers, his valet was waiting. "The children are already asleep, my lord. I thought it best to stay close at hand. As soon as you are ready for bed, I will open the door between this room and that of the young ladies."

"Very good. I knew I could depend on you," his master said. The valet had just dropped his nightshirt over his head when Luc spoke again. "Call me at four. I am sorry to wake you up so early, but I must be on my way. And could you stay within earshot when I leave? The doctor said the children could have nightmares." Quickly the valet agreed.

Asleep earlier than he had been in years, dreaming of holding Frederica in his arms, Luc was grateful for the few hours of restful sleep he had early in the evening. Before the night was over, he was wakened by Thomas's cries. Hurrying into his dressing room, he stumbled over a stool, stubbing his toe. Cursing fluently, he finally sat down on the edge of the cot where his valet usually slept.

"I am sorry for waking you, sir," Thomas mumbled, entranced in spite of himself by the words pouring out of his cousin's mouth.

"No trouble. Just hit my demmed toe. Now, what woke you? A bad dream?"

"The same one. I see him falling backward, his hand over his shoulder, and a big burst of red under it. And I know I killed him," Thomas said in a rush. He pulled the covers up under his chin and tried to hide his shivering.

"Thomas, nothing I can say will change what happened," his guardian reminded him. "You must remember that what you did saved the girls and your governesses. If I had been there, I would have done exactly the same thing."

"You would have?"

"Yes. And I would also have had trouble sleeping. Would you feel any better if you slept with me?" he asked hesitantly, remembering how safe he had felt as a child when his mother would stay with him while he was ill. "The bed is big enough for six or so."

"You wouldn't mind?" the boy asked cautiously.

"Not at all. I will be getting up quite early to go to check on Miss Montgomery, though. Do not expect me to be still in bed when you get up. Come on now." He walked the boy back across the dark room and helped him find the stool to step up onto the bed. He slid in beside him, closing his eyes wearily.

A short time later, a loud wail woke both Luc and Thomas. They sat up straight in bed. "That's Belinda," Thomas said.

Luc slid from the bed and hurried to the chaise where Belinda had been put to sleep. "Were you frightened, little one?" he asked when he picked her up.

"I want Miss Witherspoon," she sobbed.

"What's wrong?" Diana and Hester asked, standing in the doorway rather self-consciously. They had hastily pulled on their robes, but their nightcaps were askew.

"Belinda was frightened by the strange room. Go on back to bed. I will take care of her," Luc said quietly, smiling at them. The flickering light of the candle that Diana carried made them both seem so very young. "I'm sorry she disturbed you." The girls lingered. Luc glanced at them, smothering his own weariness. "Were you sleeping?"

"Mostly," Hester said hesitantly.

"Bad dreams?" She nodded. "What about you, Diana?"

"Restless. It does not seem right for us to be here

safe when Miss Montgomery is lying hurt in that small inn," she said in a depressed voice.

"She would not want you to worry about her," her cousin reminded her. "Now, run back to bed."

"Do we have to?" Hester asked. "Thomas gets to sleep with you."

"Do the two of you want to join us?" he asked, hoping his friends would never find out what he was suggesting. Even though the girls were his wards, he could hear the gossip already.

"Yes," Hester said and jumped into the bed next to Thomas.

"Don't push," her brother said grumpily.

Diana looked at the bed and then at the chaise. "I will sleep over here if it is all right with you, cousin Luc," she said softly, thankful that he could not see the blush in her cheeks. Although he was her guardian, she felt strange about appearing in her nightrail in his bedroom when he was wearing only his nightshirt.

Luc nodded and carried Belinda, who had snuggled into his arms and gone to sleep, back to his bed. He put her down and climbed into bed beside her. When his valet woke him at four the next morning, he was lying on the edge of the bed half covered.

"Do not light a light. I will dress in the dressing room since Thomas is in here," he told his valet. Quickly throwing on riding clothes, he stepped into boots and was ready to leave. "You might as well get some rest yourself. Let the children sleep as late as they can," he said as he got ready to walk out of the room. "Thank you." The older man smiled, picked up the discarded clothing, folded it, and then lay down on the cot.

Before the sun was very high, Luc entered the inn. The first person he saw was the doctor. "How is she this morning?"

"You are up early, my lord," the small, round man said in surprise. He reached for the tankard of ale the innkeeper had poured him.

"How is she?" Luc asked again, his voice cold and dangerous. His dark blue eyes stared at the doctor.

"Not as well as I had hoped," the doctor admitted. "Miss Witherspoon called me when she realized something was wrong. I had to open her shoulder again to release the infection. Fortunately, it had not spread."

"Will she be all right?" Luc demanded, his heart racing wildly with fear.

"She is a brave little lady," the doctor said encouragingly. As much as he loved the ladies, he hated giving families news they did not want to hear. "I will look in later today to check on her again," he said in a soothing voice. "Now there is someone who needs me to help bring a new life into the world."

Luc did not wait to see him leave. He rushed up the stairs and threw open the door. "Lord Forestal," Violet said reproachfully. "You should have knocked." She finished smoothing Frederica's nightrail and covered her again. Luc noticed that the pillows he had had put in place were still there, but the sheets were stained.

"I saw the doctor below, but he did not say much. How did she sleep last night?" he asked, his eyes never leaving the pale face of the lady on the bed.

"Not well. She was restless," Violet said, exhaustion clear in her face and her voice. Her age showed more than it had ever done before. She got up slowly.

"Have you given her willow bark tea?" he asked sharply.

"As much as it is safe to give her. I also had to give her some laudanum for the pain. That is why she is sleeping now. There was no need for you to come, my lord. Rose and I can manage," she said tonelessly.

"I know you can, but I could not stay away," he admitted. Almost without willing it to happen, his hand went out to touch Frederica's forehead gently. It was warmer than it had been the day before. As tired as she was, Violet watched him and let her hopes revive. "You take yourself off to bed. I will stay with her for a time," he said firmly. When she started to protest, he hushed her. "Nothing you can say will change my mind. Go and get some sleep. I will watch over her until Rose awakens. But I must be home before luncheon." He saw her eyes widen as she remembered.

"How will you manage, my lord?"

"Mrs. Greene has assured me that she has everything in hand," Luc told her with a smile.

Violet nodded and left. Frederica needn't have worried about the house party, after all, she thought wearily. What a waste. She fell into bed, fully clothed, too tired to do more than pull the covers over her.

As Luc sat by Frederica's bedside, he wished there was something more that he could do for her. He accepted a tankard of ale the landlord offered but waved away the food. When Rose entered, he left, wishing that he could stay, not happy with the look on Frederica's face or her rising temperature. "Tell Miss Witherspoon I will return later this evening," he said firmly, ignoring the disapproval he read on the maid's face. She nodded.

As Luc greeted his guests and consulted with Hester, Diana, and Mrs. Greene about the party, Violet watched Frederica with dismay. Her shoulder especially seemed hot. Her temperature grew higher. Not even the laudanum gave her peaceful sleep. The maid began to wring her hands. Violet thrust her from the room, telling her to get some rest, and called for Mrs. Sneed.

"We need to cool her off," she said confidentially. "Do you have a slipper tub?"

"Nothing so fancy. Just one that we use when someone wants a bath," the innkeeper's wife said defensively. "But it'll take hours to heat the water."

"I do not want hot water. I want the coldest we can find. Does anyone keep an icehouse nearby?"

"An icehouse? What is that?"

"Never mind. If you wanted the coldest drink of water you could find, where would you go?" Violet asked.

"You want a drink of cold water?" Mrs. Sneed asked, puzzled.

"No."

"Then why would you ask where I would go to get a drink of cold water . . . ? " she began. Then her face lost the confused look. "Oh, you want cold water for her ladyship. Well, that would be from our well. Always clear and cold, it is. Never runs dry."

"Go and have someone bring the tub in here. Then have them bring buckets of that cold water up here too. And brew up some more of that willow bark tea," Violet said as though she were commanding troops. "Do you have anything to make a poultice with?"

"My ma always swore by a mixture of yeast and charcoal," the innkeeper's wife explained. "The yeast works as a drawing agent. Is that what you mean? Or do you want a mustard plaster?"

"I was thinking of a bread and laudanum poultice, but if you have the ingredients for the other, make that. We will try it after we have reduced the fever."

Working together, the two women undressed the restless patient and put her into the tub, holding her there as they poured buckets of cool water over her hot body. Like Frederica, Violet was in tears. Frederica, her shoulder aching with pain, shuddered with cold although her forehead still felt warm. When her lips began to turn blue with cold, Violet told the other woman to stop. Calling Rose to help them, they got their arms around her, lifted the helpless woman from the tub, and rubbed her dry.

Then they loosened the bandage over her wound. Its edges were oozing pus. In spite of Rose's protests, Violet and Mrs. Sneed agreed that it would be best to leave her unclothed so that it would be easier to change the poultices. They put her back into a fresh bed on her stomach, her injured side propped up once again by pillows, her arm draped over them, her skin almost as white as the sheets that covered her modestly. Working quickly, they fed her some broth and willow bark tea laced with laudanum.

Sending Rose off to a meal and for some more rest, the other two applied the first poultice, wincing when Frederica moaned when the mixture hit the open wound. As soon as one poultice cooled, they added another. Some time late in the evening, the doctor returned, looked at his patient, and told them to continue their efforts. Mrs. Sneed was replaced by Rose. Then the other two sent Violet for a rest. But as the evening progressed, Violet returned and sent the other two away.

At the Priory, after hours of being the gracious host, seeing his guests had everything they wanted, answering questions about his journeys—questions that he did not pay much attention to but Wentworth and Lord Moulton did, Luc was finally free. Once again the children were to sleep in his suite. Visiting each of them before they closed their eyes, Luc had explained that he would not be there that night but that his valet would be sleeping nearby. He left Thomas in his bed while Diana and Hester took Belinda into theirs. With the fete the next day, the children were almost too excited to sleep, but he reminded them that they needed to be at their best the next day. Belinda and Thomas went to sleep easily, but Diana and Hester stayed awake talking for a while.

Both Wentworth and his mentor knew where he was going. Because of their fears, he rode with a groom, mounted on fast horses. When he reached the inn, he threw the reins of his horse to his groom and told him, "Be ready to leave by seven."

"Yes, sir." Not by tone or lifted eyebrow did the groom reveal the curiosity he felt. He watched Luc enter the inn and then turned to find stables for the horses.

Luc was up the stairs and in Frederica's room almost before anyone noticed him. When he entered, he stopped, shocked at the disarray. Rags littered the floor by the bed. Violet was asleep in the chair, her hair straggling about her face. Her skin had the pale gray color of someone suffering from exhaustion.

"Violet," Luc said softly. "Miss Witherspoon?" He shook her gently, reluctant to rouse her but knowing she would sleep better in a bed.

"Oh, it is you, my lord," she said tiredly, making an attempt to straighten her hair.

"Never mind that. How is she?"

"Better. Her fever broke a short time ago. And her wound is beginning to close." In spite of her exhaustion, her triumph was evident. "She should be better soon, my lord."

To her surprise, he picked her up and hugged her. "And I know who to thank for that, Miss Witherspoon. When this is over, ask me anything and I will try to grant your request," he promised. "And I know Frederica will thank you too."

"Lord Forestal," Violet said, her shock evident in both her tone and her stiff body. She wondered if he meant what he seemed to promise.

"You have done enough for today. I will sit with her until seven. Then I must go. The fete is today, you know."

"The fete," Violet sighed, thinking of all the plans they had made and all the worrying they had done. Too tired to think clearly and without considering Frederica's state of undress, she allowed Luc to bustle her out of the room.

"I will watch over her carefully, I promise," he said as he closed the door. Then he walked back to the bed. Unable to resist the impulse any longer, he ran his hand over her forehead, delighted by the coolness he felt there. She breathed deeply. He pulled the covers up over her bare shoulders. Then he sat down beside her, her hand in his.

The long hours of riding and watching finally took their toll on him. He yawned, stretched, and walked around the room for a minute. Then once again he took his seat, holding her hand firmly in his. He lifted it to his lips, being careful not to jar her. Then he yawned again.

When he awoke the next time, he was half lying,

half sitting on the bed, his hand on Frederica's bare shoulder, her covers having slipped. It was not a position that he kept for long. A man who looked enough like Frederica that Luc knew he must be related to her grabbed him and pulled him from the bed, throwing him to the floor.

"It is not what you think, Lord Bassett," Violet said breathlessly, her eyes wide with horror.

10

DAZED AND SURPRISED, Luc looked up and found himself staring into Frederica's wide-open blue eyes, clear of fever for the first time in two days. He started to speak, but she shook her head slightly, wincing as the slight movement reminded her that she had been wounded. "Stay still," he whispered.

Unfortunately for Luc, George Montgomery's hearing was very acute. "What's that?" he demanded, turning to face Luc again. His face, naturally ruddy, was almost purple with rage. His hands clenched and unclenched as he thought of the scene he had disrupted. "Whoever you are, sir, you will be my sister's husband by tonight!" he thundered. His anger was not appeased when Luc smiled.

"And good morning to you too, George," Frederica said weakly, deciding that she was too weary to wonder why her brother and her employer were in her room. "Now, come over to the side of the bed so that I do not have to look up." The brief speech had taken more effort than she had dreamed possible. Her brother's words had given her the rush she needed to respond.

"Miss Frederica, you are awake," Violet said happily.

Watching her closely, Luc was well aware of the effort it had taken for Frederica to speak. He picked himself up and walked to the door.

"Where do you think you are going, sir?" Frederica's brother asked belligerently, not at all intimidated by the fact that Luc towered over him by at least six inches.

"To order some fresh broth for your sister," Luc said calmly. "I will be back. I promise you that."

"And how do I know you will keep your promise?" Bassett asked, his voice growing even louder.

"George, you are making my head ache," Frederica said weakly. She thrilled at the look Luc gave her.

"Master George, you should know better than to think such terrible things about Lord Forestal," Violet said sternly, forgetting as she always did under stress to give him his proper title. "He is a man of his word. He will return. Now, you sit down here by your sister and listen to me."

Luc slipped out of the room before he could burst out laughing. Then his face changed as he realized that he would have probably reacted in just the same way had he been faced by his own nurse again. Quickly he made his way into the common room. "Mrs. Sneed?" he called.

"Yes, my lord?" she asked, rubbing sleep from her eyes.

"My wife is awake and hungry. Do you have any more of your broth warmed?" He smiled to think the word *wife* would soon be true.

"Yes, my lord." After her struggles the previous day, the innkeeper's wife took Frederica's recovery as a personal victory. "I could shir her an egg and make some toasted bread," she suggested.

"Maybe later. For now the broth will do." He turned to go, and then he turned to face her again. "My wife's brother has just arrived. Naturally he is upset by what has happened. Do not be upset by anything strange he says. Do you understand?"

"Yes, my lord. Will you be wanting breakfast for yourself and the other gentleman, then?" He nodded and took the stairs two at a time. She watched him go. "Strange. Very strange. Always said quality was different," she said as she walked back into her kitchen.

Luc paused for a moment before going back into Frederica's room, wondering if he had only been dreaming, but why would he have dreamed George? As he waited, he realized that during the past two days, he had begun thinking of Frederica as his, and he was already beginning to think of her brother as his own. Therefore, it was a shock when he walked in the door and saw the man glaring at him.

"So you are the one who put my sister into danger and then compromised her?" the viscount asked, his voice lower than earlier but no less forceful.

"I told you it was my idea to say I was Lady Forestal, George. Lord Forestal was not even present when I told the children what to do," Frederica said weakly. Violet had washed her face and given her a drink of water before she had pulled the covers back up to her charge's chin again.

"Well, I do not understand what you were doing with his children anyway. You a governess?" her brother asked in astonishment. "What if the *ton* had discovered what you were doing? Had you no thought for the family name?"

Both Frederica and Violet were used to the viscount's constant questions, but Luc was not. "Bassett, apparently you and I have need to talk. Come down to the common room. There's no one there this early in the morning. We can talk privately." He held the door open for the other gentleman. As soon as George had left, still protesting, he turned toward Frederica and Violet. "I ordered some breakfast for you, Frederica. Drink it like a good girl. I will be up to say good-bye before I leave." He shut the door behind him.

"Leave?" Frederica asked, feeling an emptiness that was not physical.

"He must, my dear," Violet said. "It would be improper to hold the fete if he were not there as host. You said so yourself."

"The fete? The children? Who is taking care of the children?" Frederica began to cry in earnest now, her weakness overcoming her usually steady nerves.

"Do not worry, sweet. Mrs. Greene has them in

hand. And his lordship spends part of the day at the Priory with them," she said soothingly.

"They are safe? Truly safe?" Frederica asked, letting her friend wipe her face dry.

"Yes. You should have seen Diana. She took charge of the other children while I was watching you. You would have been proud of her."

"She did?" Frederica laid her head on the pillow again. She had just gotten comfortable when the door opened.

"Here's the broth his lordship requested. Must have been quite a relief to her ladyship's brother to see her so much better. When you wrote that letter to him, you must have been very worried. He certainly arrived quickly enough. 'Course, I would have too if I had received a special express that my sister had been shot—if I had a sister, of course," Mrs. Sneed said as she set the tray on a table next to the window. "Do you want me to help you get her dressed, Miss Witherspoon? Won't do to have those gentlemen in and out of her room—at least won't do to have her brother—in the state she's in. I suppose his lordship's seen her that way plenty of times," she added with a chuckle. "He seems quite a devoted husband, if you know what I mean."

In a tone meant to quell any more remarks of a similar nature, Violet said, "Your help would be most appreciated, Mrs. Sneed." Frederica's cheeks were flaming as she realized just how little clothing she was wearing and that Luc had seen her that way. In spite of the fact that the women jarred her wound as they lifted her and dressed her in a fresh nightrail, she gritted her teeth and did not utter a sound. Violet talked quietly while they worked. "Mrs. Sneed—she is the wife of the innkeeper of this inn—helped me make poultices for your wound yesterday. You owe her your life."

"Nonsense, Miss Witherspoon. Even without my help, you and Rose would have managed," the innkeeper's wife said, beaming from ear to ear at the praise she had been given. "Quality, real quality know how to treat people," she told her husband later. She fingered the purse of coins her ladyship's brother had given her, determined to put them by in some place where her husband could not find them.

Frederica drank her broth, making faces as she did so, and then drank the even worse-tasting willow bark tea. When she complained, Violet said soothingly, "We do not want you to grow worse again, do we?"

Violet thought Frederica was asleep when she asked, "He has not left yet, has he?"

Her friend had no doubt to whom she referred. "He is downstairs still with your brother. He promised to say good-bye," she said.

"Make him wake me up if I am asleep," Frederica whispered. "Promise?"

"I promise."

In the common room below, Viscount Bassett glared at the gentleman across the table. As usual, his first, white-hot heat of anger had disappeared. "And how did this whole sorry mess happen?" he demanded, ready to continue questioning, but the innkeeper placed a plate of rare beef in front of him and a tankard by his elbow. He allowed the man to serve them. As soon as they were alone again, he asked, "Well?"

"Your sister answered my advertisement for a governess."

"A governess? Freddie? You said that before, but I still cannot believe it."

"And a very good one," Luc assured him. "She had the right touch for my four."

"She is the governess for four children? You have four children? You have ruined my sister, and you are married?" George's voice got louder and louder with each question.

"Be quiet. You do not want the entire neighborhood to hear what you are saying," Luc said sternly. "They are not *my* children; they are my *wards*. And

I haven't ruined anyone. Everyone here believes that Frederica and I are married."

"Everyone but Violet and your servants," George reminded him, cutting a thick piece of beef and shoving it into his mouth. "Violet won't say anything, but you can believe those servants will."

"They will have nothing to say because I am going to marry her," Luc said firmly, his face set in rigid lines and his voice rich with conviction.

"We will have to see about that, won't we, Lord Forestal? As her brother I have the right to make that decision."

"She's of age. She can make it herself."

"Not if you hope for a dowry."

"What do I have need of a dowry for? I would rather have Frederica," Luc said, hitting the haft of his knife against the table to make his point.

"And who gave you permission to call her Frederica?" her brother demanded. "Just what kind of man are you anyway to take advantage of your governess?" Then he thought of another thing and added, "And how did you get Violet on your side? She was supposed to convince Frederica to come home."

"I did not take advantage of your sister," Luc said angrily. "And if Violet was supposed to get her to return home, she did a very poor job of it. When I offered the pair of them jobs, Frederica was at her wit's end."

"Frederica? Ha! She has never been at her wit's end," her brother retorted. "If she doesn't like the rules, she makes new ones."

Thinking about his first interview with Frederica, Luc had to agree. Then he had another thought. "How was it that you allowed her to become a governess in the first place? I had my man of business check out her references, and they were genuine."

"Me allow her? Ha! The chit ran away from home," George said.

"And you did not bring her back? And you talk about my ruining your sister," Luc said indignantly.

"I tried." George began to explain. "This is the first time I have known where she was in over eighteen months. The only word I have had from her has been through her solicitor and Violet."

"You allowed a solicitor to get away with not telling you? I would have fired him," Luc said.

"So would I if he were my employee. But he isn't. He works for her," George explained wearily. After thirty hours on the road, he was exhausted. He had stopped to change horses and eat, but that was all. And his curricule, as well sprung as it was, had grown increasingly hard.

"For her? What do you mean?"

"A great aunt died and left her a fortune. Didn't believe in puffing up the importance of the men. She controlled the money and thought it should go to one of the girls. Frederica was the oldest."

"Then why was she working as a governess?"

"Solicitor did not approve of her leaving home. He has some kind of control until she is thirty."

"Good God," Luc said reverently. "Didn't he realize what she was doing?"

"Apparently felt she would come to no harm. Said he had investigated the situation fully and was satisfied. Talked to him only a month ago. He must have investigated you too," George said in satisfaction, taking the last bite of beef from his plate and washing it down with ale. "Not bad for an inn as small as this, Forestal. Lucky to find the place."

"Well, I will not have it. She is going to marry me so that I do not have to worry about her getting into scrapes again," Luc said.

"I doubt then you will be able to keep her out of trouble," her brother said. He was willing to agree now that he was full.

"But you did not tell me why she ran away in the first place," Luc reminded him.

George cleared his throat nervously. "Disappointed in love," he said so low that Luc almost did not hear him.

"Who was he?" It was all Luc could do to get the question out without revealing his pain.

"Neighbor. He married our younger sister, Tina. According to Violet, Frederica had had me turn down all the offers she got because she was waiting for Henry to ask. Asked for our sister instead. She ran away right after the wedding." George ran his hand over his face, embarrassed.

"She is in love with someone else?" Luc asked, stunned. He had been so certain that the attraction between them was mutual. It was that thought that had kept him from exploding in despair the past few days.

"Violet thought it was infatuation only," George said quietly, wishing he had said nothing. The look on Luc's face told him the news had been a shock.

Just then the door to the inn yard opened. "The horses are ready, my lord," Luc's groom said. "If we are to reach the Priory in time for you to change—"

"Yes. I will be there in just a moment."

"Where are you going?"

"Home. No, no need to look like that. You can follow me. My home will be more comfortable than this inn. And we should be able to take Frederica home before long. I will leave my groom with you to show you the way," Luc explained quickly. "I am having a fete to introduce my oldest ward to my neighbors. Come as soon as you can. I will be expecting you." He hurried out of the room, leaving George staring after him.

After George had taken a walk to calm his stomach and his mind, he went back up to his sister's room. "You look more the thing," he said bracingly as he walked in, looking at her freshly washed face and neatly combed hair.

"Oh, it is you," she said listlessly. Then casually, as though the answer were of no importance at all, she asked, "Is Lord Forestal going to be here soon?"

"Already off to his home. Some kind of party today," George explained. He broke off in dismay as tears began to spill down her face. "He's invited me to stay with him. Talked about taking you back there as soon as you are well enough."

"He did?" Frederica raised her head, trying to read his face. What she saw there did not reassure her. "What did you talk about?" she asked, not certain she wanted to know the answer.

"You. He took me to task for allowing you to run away. Hmph. He let you be shot!"

"George, he had nothing to do with that," she said, refusing to admit to her brother that Luc had any weaknesses.

"Well, I told him I had nothing to do with your running away. It was all Henry's fault."

"You told him about Henry?" Frederica asked, feeling her world rock.

"I was not about to let him go on thinking it was my fault, now, was I?" her brother explained reasonably. He stared in horror as she burst into sobs, sobs that seemed to wrench her very being.

Entering the room, Violet hurried to the bedside. "There, there, sweet. Everything is going to be all right," she said soothingly.

"No, it won't," Frederica cried. "It will never be right. George told Luc about Henry!" She sobbed so hard she shook.

Violet put her arms around her friend as though she were still a child. "Well, you can tell him the truth as soon as you see him again. Has he already come to say good-bye?"

The tears that had been subsiding began in earnest again. "He has already gone. He will never want to see me again. I just know it."

"Now, you just listen to me, Miss Frederica. You stop those tears and stop talking nonsense. The gentleman who has ridden hours every day to see you is not going to give up so easily. But if you continue this way, you will be ill once again and never able to return home." She smoothed Frederica's forehead and helped her get comfortable again. George began to move toward the door. "And where are you going?" Violet asked, much as she had asked when he was a child.

"To the Priory. Forestal suggested that I make his home my headquarters. Now that I know that Frederica is improving, I might as well be on my way," he said defensively. He glanced from Violet to his sister, wondering how he found himself on the defensive again.

Frederica turned her head toward him, although he could tell that doing so hurt her. "Will you tell him that I realized that Henry meant nothing to me?" she asked. "It was merely my pride." She was willing to sacrifice anything, even her pride, to get Luc to return to her.

"I will tell him, word of a Montgomery," he promised. A few minutes later, his gifts given to the couple who had sheltered his sister, he was on his way once more.

Upset by Basset's revelations, Luc was careless of his own safety and had forgotten the promise he had made Wentworth and his mentor, riding alone across the open fields. The pounding hoofbeats seem to hammer the idea that Frederica was in love with someone else into his heart. Despite his preoccupation, he was still aware of danger. He had just jumped the fence into the large meadow near the Priory when he saw a flash of metal in front of him. Acting more from instinct than conscious thought, he dropped low on his horse's neck. The buzz of a shot cut the air only inches from his body. Keeping his head low and his body hidden by his horse, Luc sent the horse forward at a full run. Before the marksman could load again, he wanted to be in the trees at the edge of the park.

His horse winded and sweating, Luc rode into the stable yard minutes later. Masters looked at the horse and then up at his master, a question on his face that did not leave his lips. "Give him an extra ration of oats. He may have saved my life today," Luc said, making certain no one else could overhear the conversation. His head groom nodded, his eyes narrowed ominously. Too many strange things had happened recently.

As soon as Luc slipped into the house and up the recently reopened staircase, he breathed a sigh of relief. "Your bath may be cold, my lord," his valet said primly, "but it will be only a matter of moments to order some hot water."

"Never mind that. It will not be the first time I have taken a cold bath. I need to see Mr. Wentworth and Lord Moulton as soon as possible, certainly before I go down to receive my guests." Ignoring the services of his valet except for help to remove his top boots, Luc stripped off his clothes and walked toward his dressing room. He stepped into the tub, finding it not cold but merely lukewarm. Washing quickly, he was toweling off by the time his valet returned, his mind completely blocking out his despair over Frederica.

By the time his friends arrived, he had just finished tying his cravat, and his valet was helping him into a deep blue coat that fit him so tightly that when he moved his shoulders, the play of muscles was evident. "What is wrong?" Wentworth demanded. "Are you all right?"

"Who was missing this morning?"

"Other than you?" Wentworth asked acidly.

"Stop playing games. He is serious," Lord Moulton said. "What happened?"

"Someone shot at me as I was crossing the Wide Meadow. Had I not seen a glint of metal, you would be explaining my absence to my guests," Luc said as calmly as he could.

"I told you it was dangerous to ride alone. And you promised to take a groom with you. Where was he?" Wentworth demanded. "Did he search the spot from where you think the shot was fired?"

"I left him with Frederica's brother, to show him the way." Lord Moulton simply stared at him, dismayed at his careless attitude toward his own life. "He would not have been any help anyway. Had he been with me I might not have seen that warning. Who knew I was gone?"

"Anyone who came down for breakfast," his friend explained. "I said you had gone for an early ride. You promised you would be home before anyone was up."

"You knew he was leaving?" Lord Moulton asked, his eyes narrowed dangerously. "And you did not tell me?"

Wentworth squirmed for a moment and then nodded. Then he turned to his friend. "What kept you?"

"Frederica's brother, the Viscount Bassett, turned up."

"Bassett, from Yorkshire," Lord Mouton said thoughtfully. "Some controversy about his younger sister last year, but it was hushed up quickly."

"She became a governess, my governess," Luc explained, pain once more wracking his heart.

"So that is who she is," Wentworth exclaimed. "Thought I recognized her when I came down the first time after she arrived, but I never got a good look at her face."

"A governess? With her money and background. I wonder at that. Perhaps reversal of family fortunes," Lord Moulton said thoughtfully.

"Not according to her brother. He said she is impulsive"—and brave, Luc added to himself, thinking of the way she had protected the children with her own body. He was not going to give up his dreams, not yet.

"Every time we try to talk about who is trying to kill you, you change the subject," Wentworth complained.

"Have you had all of them watched?" Moulton asked, his face serious.

"Yes," Wentworth replied, assuming the role of a lieutenant to a general.

"Talk to your watchers. And let me know the results. And you, my Lord Forestal, are not to leave the Priory unless I agree," Lord Moulton said sternly.

"Watch yourself this afternoon. I doubt he would choose to act in such a crowd as this, but our man seems to be desperate. Now, I'd best be off before my wife thinks I have forgotten her. She said to compliment you on the arrangements. She is most impressed. Thinks that oldest ward of yours will do well next Season if you decide to present her."

"Not her too." Luc sighed like a father who had just seen his last hopes destroyed.

"What's wrong?" his mentor asked, smiling wryly.

"I do not think I am ready to supervise Diana's presentation," Luc grumbled. "I want her to put it off for a year."

"You will come around. Talk to my wife. She will steer you right. It will give her something worthwhile to do. Might be able to fire her off her first Season."

"Not that too," Luc said hastily. "Remember I am still having trouble with just the Season. Diana's too young."

"She does not appear that young to me," Wentworth said in his ear as they walked down the stairs to where Diana and Lady Moulton waited with the other children.

Dressed in a white muslin embroidered with white flowers with pale green leaves and stems, Diana glowed with happiness. Her hair, up for the first serious occasion in her life, gleamed golden under the small straw bonnet that merely shaded her eyes and highlighted her small chin with a large bow.

"Are you ready, my dear?" Luc asked, holding out his arm. He smiled at her and acknowledged that Wentworth had been right when he said she was no longer the child he remembered. He smiled at Thomas and Hester, who were ready to follow them from the house. "Where is Belinda?"

"We, that is, Miss Montgomery, thought it best that she stay inside until all the guests arrive. Then she will take luncheon with us," Diana explained hurriedly. "You do think that will be all right?"

"Certainly," he said as he led her from the house. "Let us greet our guests." He felt her hand tremble on his arm. "Just remember to smile," he reminded her as they walked toward the tent that had been set up on the front lawn.

11

THE AFTERNOON PASSED like a dream for Diana as she met all the young people of the area. For Luc, however, it was more of a nightmare as he watched his friends, wondering who was the traitor. Never before had he known such direct danger. He felt as though he were walking a fine line between discovery and death. As he moved from one group to another, introducing Diana to his neighbors, he also found himself distracted by thoughts of Frederica and her lost love.

Although Hester, Thomas, and Belinda soon grew tired of following their cousin and sister about, there were enough young people their own age to distract them. When Frederica had planned the invitations, she had made it clear that the activities were for the whole family. The oldest girls from the Priory farms had been hired to watch the little ones and to lead them away as soon as they became tired and cranky. Belinda was one of those who disappeared early that afternoon. For those somewhat older, grooms provided rides on small ponies or comfortable old nags. Thomas had protested that no one would bother with such tame sports, but he was soon proven wrong, although he refused to participate himself. Games such as hide-and-seek and blind man's bluff provided still other opportunities for the children to play with others their own age away from the eyes of their parents.

While Luc was performing his duties as a guardian, Viscount Bassett was taking advantage of his host's hospitality. Before he stepped into the hot bath that had been prepared for him, he penned a letter to his solicitor. Handing it to his valet to express, he said, "Ask a footman to find a groom. Explain that this must be hand-delivered in London as soon as possible. Have him wait for an answer." The valet nodded and hurried into the corridor, where a footman waited. Bassett slipped out of his robe and stepped into the hot water. "Ah," he sighed and closed his eyes.

The door to the room opened again. "It is on its way, my lord," his valet assured him. He handed his master a ball of soap and stood ready to help him out of the tub. A short time later, Bassett slipped into bed, choosing to take a short nap before he met the other guests. "Meet them later," he explained as he closed his eyes. "Too old to go chasing across the country. Just too old." His valet, who had accompanied him on the more than thirty-hour ride agreed, wishing that he too could steal a nap.

Exactly as Frederica and the children had planned, the afternoon was a complete success. Diana, remembering her governesses' lesson, slipped away before she went up to her room to change for her very first supper as an adult and found Mrs. Greene. "Everything was wonderful," she said excitedly. "Everyone had such a wonderful time. It was a beautiful day. Thank you for everything." The housekeeper smiled at the young girl, wishing that she had the energy of a sixteen-year-old once more. And Diana's compliments, repeated over the servants' supper table, did much to destroy the girl's previous reputation for haughtiness.

At supper that evening, in spite of the presence of the servants who worked for the visitors, Dudley stood up and cleared his throat importantly. Everyone fell quiet. "Lord Forestal also expressed his gratitude. I will be distributing his gifts after supper." At first everyone was silent. Then a buzz began.

"Gifts, is it?" asked Lady Moulton's dresser. "In our household we do not need to be bribed to do a good job." She turned up her nose, an action she was very good at.

Mrs. Greene merely smiled at her. "Lord Forestal's servants always do a good job. However, he feels that extra service should be rewarded. I am sorry your employer does not agree." The dresser flounced off, conscious of being bested.

With guests in the house, the servants had little time to enjoy their rewards. Fortunately, the meals had been planned in advance, and even the addition of Lord Bassett made little difference except to increase the covers.

That evening shortly before supper, Bassett walked into the drawing room, where all the guests were assembled. When his name was announced, more than one eyebrow went up, and more than one pair of eyes narrowed in thought. Two men on opposite sides of the room glanced at each other; one raised an eyebrow as if asking a question and then looked hastily away.

"Thought we might see you this afternoon, Bassett," Lord Moulton said as the younger man walked up to where he sat.

"I arrived too late. Did not want to disrupt my host's arrangements. Have you seen Forestal this evening?" he asked as casually as he could. As soon as he had awakened, he had remembered the promise he had made to his sister and had begun feeling guilty.

"He was talking to my wife a moment ago." Moulton swept the room with his eyes and then motioned for Wentworth to join them. "Have you seen Forestal recently?" he asked, not letting his irritation show.

"He went up to say good night to the children," his friend explained. Like their mentor, he was more comfortable when his friend was in his sight. "Never thought he would become so domesticated. After the last few days, I plan to avoid marriage for a long time."

Bassett shifted nervously, not really certain how to respond. One could never be certain if Wentworth was joking or serious. All he knew was that Wentworth liked to win, to win at any cost. "He is back," Wentworth said quietly to Lord Moulton. Bassett looked around the room, hoping for a few words with his host.

"Where?"

"He just has come into the room and is talking to Wilberforce. See, they are standing by the windows."

"Tell him I want to see him," Moulton said, his face set in serious lines. But before Wentworth could cross the room, the butler was opening the door to the dining room and announcing supper.

Neither Moulton nor Bassett could find a way to have a confidential talk with Luc. As the host, he escorted Lady Moulton, the highest-ranking lady there, to her seat at the foot of the table and took his seat at the head. Even though the evening was not formal, there was no way they could get him alone without causing comment.

Waiting for their chance, they ate the lobster patties, enjoyed the fresh peas and trout caught from his own streams, and allowed the footmen to serve them fresh strawberries and thick, clotted cream. When Lady Moulton rose and the few other ladies withdrew, the gentlemen knew that soon their time would come. As bottle after bottle of wine disappeared—but not down Moulton's throat or that of their host's—they watched the others of their party grow more and more drunk.

The party finally broke up when Luc had the footmen help the gentlemen up to bed. Wentworth and Moulton stayed behind, their disapproval hidden behind the masks of unconcern each had learned to wear. Just when they were about to broach the subject they had waited all evening to discuss, Bassett came stumbling back into the room. Totally oblivious to the others, he walked unsteadily across the room to stand before Luc.

"Meant to tell you I had changed my mind," Bassett said, "And something else." He stared owl-eyed down at Luc, who had sunk into a chair as soon as the footman escorted the last reveler from the room.

"Changed your mind about what?" Luc asked, reminding himself that it would not do to offend Frederica's brother any more than he already had.

"About marrying m'sister. Sent for a special license today. Be married when it arrives," Bassett said with a big smile. He turned and walked away, not even waiting for an answer. He had reached the door when he swung around and almost fell over. "Mustn't forget. Promised," he muttered as he pulled himself up by the door frame.

"Promised? Bassett, what are you talking about?" Luc demanded. Still torn by the thought of Frederica in love with someone else and exhausted from hours of stress, he did not want to hear any more about marriage then.

"Frederica. Made me promise I-I'd tell you," he said carefully. "Tell you that . . ." He paused, his head spinning. He held on to the door even more tightly and took a deep breath. "That she does not love Henry. Told me so this very morning. We can talk about settlements tomorrow. Good night." Catching sight of the other two gentlemen, he smiled at them and made a very credible bow—credible, that is, until he tried to stand up straight again. He slid to the floor.

"Call another footman, Forestal," Lord Moulton said crisply. "It will not do to have your future brother-in-law asleep on the dining room floor." He took a quick look at his protégé, noting that the hard line about Luc's mouth had disappeared with Bassett's last speech.

Luc crossed to the bell pull, feeling as though tons of worry had just been lifted from his shoulders. Frederica did not love Henry. But that did not mean she loved him, he reminded himself. Then he chuckled bitterly to himself. How many of his friends' marriages were built on love?

A short time later, the three remaining members of

the party were in the library, the door closed tightly behind them. "Well, what did you discover from your watchers?" Moulton asked, settling back into a comfortable chair, a glass of brandy in his hand.

Wentworth shifted restlessly. Although he had had the opportunity to divulge the information earlier in the evening, he had kept postponing the moment. He tapped his fingers together nervously, a tactic that Lord Moulton used himself in moments of great stress. "We cannot account for three of them," he admitted. "That is the problem with using servants," he said hastily. "Too often they must obey the head groom or butler or be dismissed."

"From seven to three," Luc said slowly. "At least we have made some progress. Who are they?"

"Gregory, Wilberforce, and Lindsey," Wentworth said, all his usual humor and sardonic tones absent. For a moment Moulton closed his eyes—the three youngest members of their group, the three most eager to serve.

"Not one of them is old enough to know what he is doing," Luc said harshly, thinking what the news would do to the family of the man who was betraying his country.

"Men younger than they are dying in the Peninsula every day," Moulton reminded him, "men that could still be living had not one of them been false to his country."

"Can we be certain that the traitor is one of them?" Wentworth asked. "If he has a confederate, he would have no need to carry out the task himself. He might be a dupe for someone more clever."

"No. Too much evidence points to someone in the group," Moulton reminded them. "What do you know about the three?"

For the next hour or so, the men pooled their information but could find no definite clue. Finally, deciding that fresher heads would lead to more definite answers, they climbed the staircase to their rooms.

Stripping off his clothing, Luc fell into bed. He was

asleep before his head hit his pillows, not even hearing Thomas's question before he went to sleep. Although normally an early riser, it was almost noon before Luc stumbled out of bed the next morning. "Are the others up yet?" he asked sleepily.

"The children and one or two of the others. Most are still resting," his valet said. "Shall I lay out your riding clothes for this afternoon?" Because the footman who had helped Lord Bassett to bed the previous evening had been standing close enough to the door to hear the viscount welcome their master into his family, the news that their master was to be married had quickly spread until all the other servants at the Priory had heard. Most of them declared that the news was not unexpected. That morning the Priory was buzzing with the news. "May I offer my congratulations, my lord?" the valet asked.

"Congratulations?" For a moment Luc looked confused. Then a wide smile spread across his face. "I think you should wish me luck. She has not yet agreed," he explained, wondering if he could spare a moment to visit Frederica. "And I doubt I will be free today to ask her," he added ruefully, thinking about the guests who remained.

As he took his guests fishing, played billiards with them, and took a fourth at cards, he wished he had not promised to be the decoy. But it was too late now to change the plan. That meant he had to play the gracious host.

While Luc was entertaining his guests and keeping watch on the three suspects, Frederica was fretting. Once Violet and Mrs. Sneed had destroyed the small pocket of infection, she had begun to grow stronger immediately. Always healthy, she did not enjoy staying in bed, but her nurses would not hear of her getting up. Indeed, the only time she had tried, she had discovered that she was weaker than she thought. Only by holding onto the bed was she able to stand for a moment before her knees and legs began shaking.

When she told the doctor she wanted to get up, he

laughed at her. Twinkling his eyes at Violet, he teased, "You do not like me. I am wounded."

"And I thought it was I," Frederica said crisply.

"Give yourself some time to heal," the doctor said brightly. "I do not want you to strain your shoulder. You would not want to have a relapse." Violet blanched, her face as washed-out as her simple lavender gown.

"Listen to him, Frederica," she begged. Her eyes were deep-set from the stress and lack of sleep she had suffered. Even though the fever had broken, Violet had stayed with Frederica the previous night, bringing her cups of broth or glasses of water. And after only a few hours of sleep she had returned to her bedside, afraid that when she left Frederica somehow would grow worse.

"I will if you will do the same," Frederica said, worried by the exhaustion she read on her friend's face. Suddenly, Violet seemed old, much older than she had when they left London.

"Nonsense. You are the one who was injured," Violet argued, trying to convince her to change her mind, but Frederica would not budge.

"You go to bed and do not get up until I say you can," the patient said strongly. "Tell her she must, Doctor."

Like Frederica, the doctor had been growing concerned about the older lady's health. "Have a cup or two of chamomile tea and try to get some sleep," he advised her. "I will have Mrs. Sneed prepare it. Come along, now." He swept Violet out of the room and down the stairs before she knew what was happening.

As Frederica had done the previous day, she settled in bed and thought about her employer—if he could still be called that, she reminded herself. Her despair early on had given way to anger and then to resignation. After trying to get out of bed and discovering how weak she was, she had realized that there was no way she could go to him. She had to wait for him to return to her. The day before she had been so weak that all she had wanted to do was sleep, but today she was stronger. Inventing reunion scenes in which Luc swept her up in his arms and pressed burning kisses across her face helped her doze away the day.

Sending Rose to check on Violet, she would lie there, her cheek pressed against her pillows, her hands pretending they were running over Luc's strong shoulders. She had just drifted into one of these sequences when her brother entered the room. "Are you all right?" he asked anxiously as he saw her arms move restlessly. "Is there something you want? Are you in pain? I will call Rose."

"George?" Frederica asked sharply. She turned over carefully so that she could look up at him.

He shifted restlessly, noting the way she winced. "Should you be doing that?"

"What?"

"Turning over. Is it good for your wound to lie on it?" He sat down in the chair beside her, worried.

"I am fine, George. The doctor says I am healing nicely." She smiled at him, and he realized how much he had missed her over the past eighteen months.

"Why did you do it, Frederica?" he asked, his hurt evident in his voice. "Why did you run away instead of talking to me about the situation?"

"Would you have forbidden the marriage?"

"No." He sat there and stared at his sister. Then he cleared his throat nervously. "But I would have arranged something. You could have visited relatives."

"And have everyone know that I was in love with my younger sister's husband? It was better my way."

"Dash it, Frederica. It was not. You left chaos behind you. I was frantic until I received that first letter. How could you do that to me? To all of us?" he asked. After his first panic at her disappearance, he had grown angry. As the months flowed past, he had believed that his anger was gone. Now it was back full force. "No matter how carefully we tried to hide your disappearance, word leaked out. Can you imagine how I looked when the *ton* discovered that you had disappeared? Before you decided to leave, did you ever sit down and think what it would be like for us?"

No matter how impulsively she behaved, Frederica was not afraid to admit her guilt. And the knowledge of what she had done to her family had haunted her as soon as she realized the position she had put them in. She blushed. "No," she whispered.

"That is what I thought. If you ever in your life think something through before you do it, I will be amazed," her brother said bitterly. He let his breath out sharply and reached out to take her hand. "We love you, Frederica. Do not frighten us again." He closed his eyes. "When I received the letter from Violet about your having been injured, I could not get here fast enough. Tina wanted to come too, but Henry refused. He said they had interrupted their honeymoon for you, but they were not going to take a chance on their heir."

Frederica leaned up on her elbow in spite of the pain it caused. "They interrupted their honeymoon?"

"As soon as Tina heard you were missing," he said sadly. "I kept it from them as long as I could, but I thought you might have said something to her."

"To Tina?"

"Well, I did not know that you thought she had stolen Henry from you," he said defensively. "You and Henry? Freddie, what were you thinking of?"

"Do not call me Freddie," she said firmly. Then she sighed. "It seems so far away now, almost in another life," she admitted.

"Where did you go at first?" he asked. For the next few hours they discussed her first post as a governess, working for the family of a colonel. "No wonder Violet went about looking guilty," he said as he heard of her governess's part in Frederica's escape. "I wonder if she thought you would not find a post."

"Probably. But I surprised her—and myself," she added. Her brother looked at her, astonished. "The first week I wanted to come home so badly," she admitted. "More than once I started a letter to you. Then, somehow, I was part of the family's life."

"Why did you seek another post instead of coming home when you left them?"

"I did not know that I was no longer in love with Henry, if I ever had been. I was afraid to come home, afraid I would do something to interfere with Tina's happiness. After the colonel was invalided home, I again got in touch with Violet's friend who ran the employment agency," Frederica said. That time seemed so far away. How strange to think that less than six months ago she had not known Luc. If it had not been for Violet. "And Violet," she added. "Did you think I would come running to you, begging you to take me back, just because you had discovered she was the one who had helped me and had thrown her out? It did not sound like you, George. But you do have a temper."

"And you do not?"

"I did not say that," she said virtuously. "I have simply learned to control it better since I have been on my own."

"Well, you had a great deal to learn," he said with the tactlessness older brothers sometime display.

"George!"

"Hope Forestal knows what a virago you can be," he said with the air of someone bestowing a great gift.

"Forestal?" Frederica's voice was sharp. "What are you prattling about now?"

"Told him I withdrew my objections to his suit. Even sent for a special license," he said proudly, puffing out his chest as though he were a peacock displaying his feathers. His words sent a thrill of hope through his sister. For a few moments she was speechless.

Then a horrible thought struck her. "George, you are not forcing him to do this, are you?" she asked, her voice shaking almost as much as her hands. "He was helping take care of me. Nothing happened."

"Nothing? Humph! I do not call finding him sprawled all over your naked back nothing," he said teasingly.

As he watched the light drain from her face, he relented. "How could I be forcing this marriage on him when I told him no when he first asked?" He paused. "No, I suppose he did not ask. He simply told me. That is right. When he told me you were going to marry him."

Frederica smiled broadly. Then as suddenly as it appeared, once again the joy disappeared from her face. "Was this before or after he learned about Henry?"

"Before." Frederica pulled her covers up over her head. "But last evening he did not say he had changed his mind when I told him I was willing to agree," he explained. "No settlements, yet. Maybe something tentative until our solicitors have time to talk. But I do not think the wedding should be postponed."

"Wedding?" Frederica had pulled the covers back down around her neck. "He has not yet made me an offer."

"He will. You will see," her brother said proudly, certain that without his help the marriage would never occur. He beamed at her. "I will ask him to ride over with me tomorrow."

"You are not to force him to do anything, George," Frederica said. The door to the room opened, and Rose walked in.

"It is time for more tea, miss," the maid said firmly. She avoided looking at the gentleman who had spent most of the afternoon visiting. Even if he was Miss Montgomery's brother, he had no business being in the bedchamber of anyone who was not his wife, she told herself piously. The past few days had made Rose seriously consider finding a new position, no matter how reckless that sounded. Her mother, who lived in a small town not far away, had been asking her to return home for some time. And the squire always had a place for a hardworking maid. Her family would never believe the tale she had to tell. Of course, she would not leave until Miss Montgomery was out of danger, but she made up her mind at that moment that she would return to her family. She poured the medicine for Frederica and then hurried from the room.

Frederica likewise was ready to return home. "No one here knows my real name," she reminded him. "I could simply return home with you. You could say I had been visiting in—in . . ."

"Jamaica perhaps?" he asked sarcastically. "No one looking at your pale skin would believe me. Besides, too much of your story is known by too many people. Wentworth knows who you are."

Once again she buried her head under the covers, muffling her words. George peeled them back. "I hope those were not the words I think they were," he said with a smile. "Violet will wash your mouth out with soap."

"And who will tell her?" she asked, fire in her eyes.

"Children, stop arguing," Violet said fiercely. She had entered the room so quietly that neither of them had noticed her. She wanted to smile: their actions reminded her so much of the way they had behaved when they were children. "Your brother's visit seems to have done you some good, Miss Frederica." She glanced at the color in her charge's cheeks and smiled. "Tell me about the Priory," she said, taking the chair George had vacated. After her rest she was very much improved.

"The little one . . ."

"Belinda?" Violet asked in alarm, her hand over her heart.

"I think. She is really very sad. Forestal said she looked for you in every room. Wouldn't go to sleep until her sisters took her to bed with them." Violet's face filled with alarm. She glanced at Frederica, noting the returning glow of her cheeks, wondering if it was good health or a fever. Quickly she put her hand to Frederica's head. It was cool. She breathed a sigh of relief. She cleared her throat several times but was too choked up to get any words out.

Frederica was not as reticent. "Violet, you must go

to her. Indeed, I would feel much better if you were at the Priory overseeing all of them. I know you said Diana showed remarkable presence when I was injured, but success has been known to cause a lady's head to be turned." She glanced at her brother, who was shifting from foot to foot as he stood at the end of the bed. "You did say Diana was a success, George?" He nodded.

"But I could not leave you here alone, Miss Frederica," Violet protested, torn between her love for Frederica and her knowledge that Belinda needed her.

"I will not be alone. I have Rose. Now that I am better, I do not need someone to sit up with me all night," Frederica reminded her. "And if you stay, you will have to share a room with Rose. While you two were usually not in the room at the same time, sharing was no problem. With two of you sharing the bed it may be."

"I do not like the idea of leaving you here with only a maid for protection. What if those horrible men appeared?" Violet asked.

"I will stay with you," her brother said heroically.

"And where would you sleep? There is only one other chamber, and that is where Violet and Rose sleep."

"Rose could sleep with you," her brother said so firmly that both ladies knew he expected their arguments to cease.

Violet, however, felt compelled to say, "That would not be wise." She shifted nervously.

"Why ever not?" George asked in surprise.

"She snores," Violet explained. "That is one reason Mrs. Greene sent her here, I am certain. No one else wishes to sleep in the same room with her. With so many extra servants to provide room for, Mrs. Greene solved a difficult situation by sending Rose to us. It is what I would have done."

"Violet is right. But I know I would feel more comfortable if there were someone other than Rose nearby," Frederica admitted.

"Perhaps Forestal could spare a groom. He could be close at hand to run any errands or take messages for you. He should not enter your room, however. Frederica, you must promise that he will not come in here," her brother said anxiously.

"Master George, now you are being foolish. Miss Frederica would not entertain a strange man in her bedchamber," Violet said in a scolding tone.

"That is what I would have said too, until I walked in on Lord Forestal and her," he said with a frown.

"I was delirious," Frederica reminded him. "How was I supposed to stop him? Even Violet could not." Her friend nodded her head and blushed, remembering all too well that she had made little protest that evening.

"Do you plan to return with me this evening, Violet?" George asked, wisely refusing to answer the last comment.

"How did you come?"

"In my curricle."

"Of course, I think you should leave immediately. I do not want to think of those children alone with strangers for another minute," Frederica said firmly.

"I will have to talk to Mrs. Sneed," her friend began hesitantly, "and pack and make certain you have enough willow bark for more tea."

"Nonsense. Talk to Mrs. Sneed if you must, but leave packing for Rose. It will give her something to do. Nothing you have with you here is irreplaceable," George reminded her. "Hurry on, now. I wish to leave within the hour."

A short time later, Violet bade Frederica a quick farewell. "If you need me for anything, my dear, send the groom and I will be here as quickly as possible," she said, tears in her eyes.

Frederica too felt teary but was afraid to show it for fear Violet would refuse to go. "Tell the children hello for me. See that they practice their math."

"No need to go into all that. I am certain the doctor will soon declare you ready to return to the Priory.

You can teach them math yourself," her brother said bracingly. "Now, if we are to return before it grows too late, we must be on our way." Taking Violet's arm, he led her from the room. Frederica, determined to be strong until they had left, felt tears start down her face.

As Violet made her way out the door, Mrs. Sneed called after her, "I will give Lady Forestal my personal attention, Miss Witherspoon. You need not worry about a thing."

The two men who had spent that afternoon in a corner by themselves, drinking and gambling, stopped for a moment. Then calling for their bill, they sauntered out into the sunshine only moments behind Lord Bassett and Miss Witherspoon.

"Strange men," the old gray-haired man who had talked to the children said. "Didn't talk to nobody but Sneed all afternoon." He called the innkeeper over. "Wot's those two want?" he asked, leaning close enough that the innkeeper smelled the gin on his breath.

"A place to drink and gamble, I suppose. Never said more than two words to me all afternoon. 'Wine.' Pay their shot, though, which is more than I can say for some of you." Sneed turned his back on the men and ambled back to the kitchen. The old man glared at him.

12

BASSETT'S ARRIVAL with Violet released Luc from his nighttime responsibilities. With Belinda once more established in the nursery and Diana and Hester in their own rooms, only Thomas continued to share Luc's apartment. And the boy moved into the chambers next door.

Although Luc had slept well the night before, that night he was restless, awake as soon as Thomas's nightmare began. Waking the boy, he sat with him and talked calmly until Thomas once again dropped off to sleep. Still wide awake himself, Luc stayed beside Thomas's bedside until he was certain the boy would not awake again. Then he began to prowl about the room, wondering if Frederica would like it.

The thought of her made him even more restless. Had he not promised Moulton and Wentworth that he would not leave his estate without notifying them, he would have ordered his horse saddled immediately. As eager as he was, he was also conscious of how abruptly he had left her the previous day. As a result, he was not sure how she would receive him. It was one thing to allow him to care for her when she was ill and yet another to agree to marry him. But he saw no other choice, no matter how she felt. He had compromised her. There was no other way. I should have listened to Violet, he told himself bitterly.

As the dawn began to break, he slipped back into bed, still thinking of Frederica. She was also the first thing on his mind when he awoke the next morning. As he sat up and stretched, he noticed a tray that contained two notes. As he opened the first, written by Wentworth, his eyes narrowed. Two grooms who had arrived with Lindsey and Gregory had been gone for hours the day before, although their masters had stayed at the estate. They had not returned until shortly after Bassett brought Miss Witherspoon home. If they disappeared again today, Wentworth had arranged for someone to follow them. "Lindsey and Gregory," Luc muttered to himself. His face was set in somber lines.

The second note was from Bassett. The groom he had sent to London had returned with the special license, and Frederica's brother had gone to find a vicar who would perform the ceremony. The instructions he left for Forestal included arriving at the inn for the ceremony early that afternoon. Frederica would be his before nightfall, Luc thought. He smiled. Calling for his valet, he slid from bed, eager to be on his way. Only occasionally did he worry about what their marriage would be like.

Carefully groomed and looking as though he were going on a visit to one of his London clubs, he walked down the stairs, whistling happily. "I am pleased you are in such a good humor, Lord Forestal," said Moulton, who had just left the library. His face was a mask that hid his thoughts. "Did you receive a note from Wentworth?"

"Yes." Luc paused, remembering at last his promise to stay under their watchful eyes. "Wentworth seems to have the situation in control," he said as if asking a question.

"Perhaps," his mentor agreed. "And what are your plans this day?"

His good humor overcoming his good sense, Luc said jokingly, "To marry."

Lord Moulton stopped, his face a mixture of pleasure and dismay. "From the Priory, I would hope," he suggested.

"From the inn where my bride lies waiting," Luc explained. "I am marrying Frederica Montgomery."

He held his breath, waiting for his mentor's disapproval. When the man said nothing disparaging, he let his breath out slowly.

"Congratulations, my boy," the older man said. "I trust you do not plan to travel alone. You will take Wentworth with you." Luc nodded reluctantly. "You will need a witness and someone to guard your back."

"Since the traitor has not done anything since the day of the fete, do you think he has given up the chase?" Luc asked, hoping the answer would be yes. His mentor simply looked at him, disapproval in his eyes. "I did not really think so," Luc sighed. "I do not think I will hunt this year," he said seemingly in a random fashion.

"Why not?" Moulton asked, recognizing the gambit for what it was.

"I know what the fox feels like when the hounds are on its trail."

The older man laughed and slapped him on the back. "Take Wentworth and be careful," he said with a laugh. "I do not expect trouble. In fact, I believe they will wait until the exchange is made tomorrow before striking again. But do not take chances. Your wife would not appreciate wearing widow weeds as soon as she was wed." Then he grew more serious. "This wedding of yours may cause some talk. My wife and I will remain after the others leave. When you announce your marriage, the *ton* needs to know that the marriage has our support." He paused, his hand on Luc's shoulder. "And we do approve," he added heartily. "Now find Wentworth and be off."

"Would you like to come with me?" Luc asked hesitantly. He pulled the sleeves of his dark blue morning coat down once again, taking his hat from his butler.

"You would never escape unseen with me along. Know that my thoughts will be with you," his friend said, wishing that he could stand in the father's place for his friend.

Taking the longer route by the roads instead of riding across the fields, Luc and Wentworth discussed the situation with the traitor. But Luc could not keep his thoughts on that issue. They kept returning to Frederica, the way she had nestled against him, had turned to him in her pain and sickness. If she would only turn to him now, let him protect her from the rumors of the world. She had to marry him, but he wanted her love too.

From the moment that Bassett walked into his sister's bedchamber with the news that she would be married that day, Frederica had done little but think of marriage to Luc. She closed her eyes and saw his deep blue ones fixed on her, blaming her for the need for their marriage. Her ears echoed with his deep, rich voice telling her everything was her fault. Her arms ached to wrap around his neck and pull him close to her, to feel his heart pounding, his arms holding her tight, but he rejected her. Finally, plunging down the waterfall of despair of whether he would ever forgive her into the placid pool of acceptance, she ranted and raved at her brother until she realized that there was no way to change his mind. She would marry Luc. Her brother would accept no other solution.

Already dressed in a fresh nightrail, Frederica let Rose help her into the dressing gown that Mrs. Greene had sent. A soft, pretty blue, it boasted flounces of blond lace and ribbons that fluttered whenever Frederica moved. Though dulled by the fever that she had recently suffered, her hair had been brushed into a fashionable style. When Rose held up the glass for her to look into, Frederica did not know whether to be pleased or to cry.

"I look like someone laid out for burial," she muttered. How were they ever to make this marriage work? He would resent her and would run back to his mistress. That thought made Frederica worry. She knew men in her class usually were not faithful to their wives, but she wanted a husband who loved only her. The thought of Luc returning to his mistress erased what little color she had in her cheeks.

Refusing the meal Mrs. Sneed served for luncheon,

Frederica lay in bed and worried. What would he say? Why had George ever told him about Henry? As her thoughts grew more frenzied, her shoulder began to ache.

When Luc walked in a short time later, she lay still, her eyes never leaving his face. Although Luc greeted George, his attention was on his future wife, noting the white line about her mouth, the dull look in her eyes. She is being forced into marriage, he thought helplessly.

Wentworth cleared his throat. Then Bassett made the introductions, ending casually, "Wentworth was the one who ran after Tina for a week or two."

"I recognized you on my first visit, Miss Montgomery," Wentworth explained. "But you were in a setting that was unexpected. My apologies." His eyes narrowed thoughtfully as he thought about what he had just said. There was something they were missing about the traitor, something unexpected. Everyone thought they had the traitors in their pockets, but he wondered.

Frederica said quietly, "I deliberately hid from you."

"As she did from all her family," her brother added. Now that the situation was in his control, he could joke about her absence.

Luc, his stomach twisting and turning, tried to enter into the conversation, but his words stuck in his throat. He looked at Frederica, enjoying the way the blue of her dressing gown made the blue of her eyes richer. She licked her lips, and it was all he could do to keep from crossing to the bed to take her in his arms and kiss her.

"The vicar is waiting," Bassett reminded them, shifting back and forth on his heels as he sometimes did when he was nervous.

Frederica glanced at Luc in panic. Recognizing the desperation in her look, he turned to his friends. "May we have a few minutes alone before the vicar comes up?"

Rose, totally forgotten by the others, sniffed. She did not care what the Viscount Bassett said; she knew what was proper. Frederica, no matter who she was, was no better than she should be. Bassett looked from his sister to Luc. "Please, George," Frederica begged.

"Who am I to quibble about a few minutes after what has already gone on?" he said, shrugging his shoulders. Rose's eyebrows went up in disapproval. But in a few moments, Luc and Frederica were alone.

At first only silence filled the room. Luc shifted restlessly. Frederica looked at anything but him. Finally, Luc crossed to stand beside the bed. Sitting on the edge, he took her hand in his. Her fingers naturally curled up around his, clinging to them. She licked her lips again nervously. Slowly he bent down and kissed her, gently at first and then hungrily. Frederica returned the kiss, parting her lips, inviting him to enter. He wrapped his arms around her, lifting her up so that she was pressed against him, her heart echoing the beats of his.

His arms tightened. When he put his hand over her wound, involuntarily she cried out in pain. He let her go, and she fell back onto the bed. This time, in spite of the ache, she bit her lip so she did not cry out. Noting the dismay on his face, the way he withdrew, she reached out to him, pulling his face down to her. "I am not hurt," she lied.

Luc pulled away, feeling guilty for hurting her. "No, we cannot. Your brother might come in at any time." But he took her hands and held them in his. His midnight blue eyes bored into her, demanding that she tell the truth. "Dare I?" he began, stammering like a schoolboy. Then resolutely gathering his courage, he asked, "Have I the right to hope that your kiss meant something, that you care for me as I care for you?"

As impulsive as always, Frederica said, "I care for the children. Is that the way you care for me?"

"No." The one word emptied his vocabulary. He simply stared at her. She played with the ribbons on her dressing gown, not certain what his answer meant. "Is that the way you care for me?" he asked finally.

She shook her head, her lips slightly parted, her breath coming fast. Taking courage from her question, he leaned closer and brushed her lips with his. "Is that more the way you feel?" She shook her head again. This time the kiss was longer. "What about that?" he asked, the faintest smile on his face. Once again she shook her head. This time when Luc kissed her, he nudged her lips apart and let his tongue introduce hers to new sensations. "Now?"

Her voice husky from the desire that was now burning in her, Frederica whispered, "Yes." The sound disappeared into the kiss. Her arms wrapped around his neck, and she refused to let go even though her shoulder was hurting.

Luc had just raised his head to ask her something new when George walked in. "If you did not need a vicar before, you would now," her brother said severely. "You had better smooth your hair, Frederica, or the vicar will have the wrong impression. And I had to travel quite a way to find one who did not know you personally, Forestal. He is eager to be on his way."

"Why did you want one who did not know Luc?" his sister asked, her voice beginning to return to normal. She looked up at her husband-to-be and could not get her breath, the flame in his eyes sending thrills up and down her spine.

". . . without scandal." Only the last two words made any sense to her.

"Oh!" She pulled her eyes away from Luc's and felt her cheeks flame. "Yes." Instead of an answer to her brother's question, the word was a promise gleaming in her eyes, which did not waver from Luc's.

"Call in your vicar, Bassett," Luc said, his eyes on Frederica. He took a deep breath.

Before many more minutes were past, Luc and Frederica were married. Only when the ceremony was over and the vicar had left did Frederica remember

Violet. "She will be so hurt that I did not arrange for her to be here," Frederica said, worry filling her eyes. "George, what are we to do?"

"Blame it on me," her brother proposed. "She will anyway. You did not know I planned for the ceremony to be today."

"Write her a letter and explain it to her," her husband suggested, wishing that he could somehow empty the room of all save Frederica and him. "Wentworth or Bassett can take it with them when they return to the Priory." He smiled at her. She smiled back, and he felt as though he were burning with fever. In just a few moments they would be alone.

His fever was quickly quenched. "What do you mean, 'When Wentworth and Bassett return to the Priory'?" Wentworth asked, his tone as carefully neutral as he could make it. To him the marriage had been a necessity that had been accomplished easily. Now that it had taken place, they could return to weightier issues.

"I will be staying with my wife." Luc smiled at her. Her heart began to beat faster.

"You cannot." Frederica, Luc, and Bassett stared at him in astonishment. Wentworth hesitated. Then he said, "How will it look to your guests? You marry but instead of announcing at the fete, you hide your wife away in a small inn. And you do not bring your wife home to the Priory. I think I hear tongues beginning to clatter. Far better to have Lady Forestal"—he made a slight bow to Frederica, who smiled at his use of her new title—"remain here in safety"—he emphasized the words and was pleased when Luc grew serious—"until your guests leave. In a few weeks, you can announce your marriage, and no one will be any wiser." By this time he had crossed to stand near Luc, his arm hung across his shoulder. He gave his friend a pinch to remind him of the other game in which they were involved. When Luc turned to complain, he gave him a look that sent disappointment raging through the new bridegroom.

His ruddy face flushed, her brother nodded. "Cannot be helped. Not what I would have wished, but I think it is the best plan."

"Well, I do not like it," Frederica said, looking up into her husband's face, hoping she would see agreement there. All she saw was his nod. He glanced at her regretfully, his lips longing for hers, his arms hungry for her. But that regret was quickly masked by concern.

"Everyone but Lord and Lady Moulton are scheduled to leave tomorrow," he told her. "As soon as the last one drives away, I will return. Then when the doctor says I may, I will take you home," Luc promised, his hand reaching for hers and his thumb caressing her palm. "I cannot remain here without some explanation, and to tell my guests the truth would expose you to needless gossip."

She wanted to kick and scream the way her sister had whenever her will was crossed when she was a child, but her good sense forbade it. She tightened her fingers around Luc's. "You will return as soon as they leave?" she asked as wistfully as Belinda had ever done. He nodded, his eyes almost as sad as hers. "When must you leave?" she asked.

Luc looked at Wentworth, who was looking anywhere but at his friend. When he had agreed to accompany Luc that morning, he had had no idea that he would be forced to separate a newly married couple. But he had promised Lord Moulton that Luc and he would return in time for dinner.

"You keep country hours, Luc," Wentworth reminded him. "Your guests have a right to expect to see you at dinner."

"I will stay with my sister for a while," Bassett said firmly. "We want no one to suspect what happened today. I paid the vicar enough to keep him from talking." He stood up and crossed to the window.

"That is one expense that is mine and no one else's," Luc said firmly. "I will repay you when we return to the Priory." He stood beside the bed, his hand reaching for his wife's hand. Their fingers intertwined. He stared down at her hungrily.

Wentworth looked at his friend and his new wife, embarrassed by the emotion he read on their faces. He cleared his throat. They jumped. "Perhaps you could join me in the common room to toast this marriage, Lord Bassett," he suggested. "We have time before Luc and I must leave."

Bassett looked at the two so recently married. They did not respond. "After you," he said, opening the door.

As soon as they realized they were alone, Frederica asked, "Do you really have to go?" She raised her eyes to his, pleading faintly.

"Wentworth is right," he said, more to convince himself than her. "Dash it, I wish I had never thought of that dratted party." He sat on the bed beside her.

"You did not, my lord. Need I remind you that I was the one who made the suggestion?" his wife reminded him. "And it is my fault that we are now married. If I had not been so clever, George would not have been able to force you to marry me." She pulled her hand from his and tucked them under the covers.

His dark blue eyes blazing, Luc bent down to where she lay, his eyes boring into hers. He put his hands on either side of her face and forced her to look at him. "He did not force me to do anything, Frederica. That I promise you. And it is not your fault you were injured; it is mine."

She had put her hands over his, stroking them lightly. At his words the motion stopped. "You said that before, I think. When I was very ill." She looked up at him with a question in her eyes. "What did you mean?"

He bent and kissed her, hoping to erase the question from her mind. Although a fire raged in her veins, the question remained. "Luc?"

He glanced at the door, knowing very well what his friend and mentor would say if they knew what he planned to tell his wife. "Frederica, I cannot say much." When he saw her frown, he brushed her lips with his again. It did not erase her look. He sighed, knowing he had already said too much. Then he said, "I am involved in work for the War Office."

She sat up in bed, both anxious and proud. "Then those men did not really want the children," she said slowly, thoughtfully. Her eyes searched his face.

"They wanted someone to force me to bargain with them," he explained. "Do not ask me more, Frederica." He closed his eyes. Then he opened them, staring at her as though she were a ripe peach and he a hungry man.

Frederica took a deep breath. "Are the children safe?" she asked, fearing his answer.

"As long as they are at the Priory. With Violet there and the footmen I have assigned to guard them, I doubt anyone will try to harm them again," he reassured her.

"What about you? Are you in danger?"

He did not try to lie to her. "Yes." She straightened her back even more and tried to smile bravely at him. The deep breath she took did nothing to hide her shiver of fear.

She glanced at the window at the afternoon sun and shivered again. She took his hand in both of hers, holding on tightly. She tried to speak but could produce no sound. She cleared her throat and tried again. Her voice was shaky. "Then go. Leave now so that you too will be safe," she said with tears in her eyes.

He leaned forward, a smile on his face. "No one knows I am here," he told her. "I am probably safer here than I am at the Priory." He bent and kissed her, holding her gently so that he did not reinjure her shoulder. "And I do not want to leave," he whispered in her ear, sending shivers of delight through her. Never once when she thought she was in love with Henry had she thought of his sitting on a bed with her, sending shivers of delight up and down her body.

But with Luc all it took was a look. The kisses and his touch were added delights.

"Luc." She murmured his name against his lips. His hand untied the first bow on the dressing gown. His hand slipped inside to caress her. "Oh, Luc." She threw her arms around him, bringing him closer.

A knock at the door tore them apart. His face flushed, Luc got up hastily, moving toward the window, trying to get himself under control. "I say, Forestal," Frederica's brother said gruffly, "Wentworth is waiting for you below." He looked at his sister, noticing a flush fast fading from her cheeks, and then directed his attention to the straight back that was all he could see of his new brother-in-law. "Is everything all right?"

"Fine," Luc said curtly. "I will see you tomorrow, madam wife," he said as he walked to the door. His voice did not give away his unhappiness. Before Frederica could master her emotions and answer him, he was gone.

As soon as the door closed behind him, Frederica moved to the edge of the bed. "Come here, George," she said firmly. "I am going to get up. Either you help me or watch while I try this myself." Her tone of voice told him not to argue with her. Frowning, he crossed to the side of the bed where she waited impatiently. Slowly he helped her stand up. "Now help me walk around the room," she demanded.

"Forestal would not approve," he reminded her. She stared at him as if to remind him that she was the mistress of her fate and no one else. "All right," he said weakly, giving in. "But you sit on the side of the bed until I can find that maid to help us." With her brother on one side and the maid on the other, each step that she took made her feel stronger. Each step she took made her more determined to be ready to return to the Priory with Luc the next day.

During his ride home, Luc was silent remembering the way Frederica had reacted to him and dreading the interview that he knew was just ahead. As soon as he had changed clothes, he walked up the stairs to the schoolroom. In his haste to leave that morning, he had not seen the children. When he walked into the room, they had just begun their meal.

After talking to them briefly, he left them in the care of the nursery maid and the footman, calling Violet into the next room. "Is she worse?" the older lady asked, concern in every line on her face. "I knew I should not have left her."

"No. Nothing like that," he said hastily. He tried to think of a way to tell her, wished that Frederica had written the letter, prayed that Bassett would appear miraculously and take care of the problem for him. "It is just that . . ." He paused and ran his handkerchief over his forehead. Then he rushed on like one of the new locomotives gathering steam. "Frederica and I were married this afternoon."

"Oh." The one word told him that she was deeply wounded, although her face was carefully blank.

"Her brother wanted us married before anyone learned about his sister's presence in the neighborhood. He wanted as little scandal as possible. In fact, he visited with vicars until he found one who did not know me," he explained. "Neither Frederica nor I had a choice of the time. Bassett arranged it all, but we do not plan to announce the marriage for a few weeks." She looked down at her hands, a tear slowly running down her cheek. Luc felt as though he were hitting a helpless puppy. "You were the first person she thought of. She wanted you there, but there was no time," he tried to explain.

"Do you plan to tell the children?" she asked, her voice only the tiniest bit shaky. She was proud of her reaction.

"Not until the other guests leave. You know Hester." He smiled at her, willing her to smile back. She did not. "Please forgive us," he said, a hint of pleading in his voice.

"I must see to the children," she said, longing for her own room and a good cry. She had always dreamed of preparing Frederica for her wedding. Now it had occurred, and she had not even been there. Her disappointment showed plainly on her face. Then another thought struck her, "Will you want me to leave when Lord Bassett does?" she asked, fearing the answer.

"Leave? Nonsense. I know Frederica depends on you. And so do I," Luc said forcefully. Then he began to wonder if her question had been merely a way to tell him that she wanted to return to retirement. "Of course, we want you to be happy. If you would be happier with Lord Bassett . . ."

"No, I prefer to remain here," she said firmly, her spirits beginning to rise as she realized that he had no intention of separating her from her favorite charge. "Give your wife my best wishes, my lord." She made her curtsy and swept from the room.

"Blast," Luc said, running his finger around the cravat that now seemed too tight.

13

THE NEXT MORNING before his guests were up, Luc joined the children for breakfast. He smiled at Violet and was pleased when she returned the smile. "What have you planned today?" he asked the older lady.

"Thomas is returning to his lessons with your vicar," she said. "Diana has promised to make calls with Lady Moulton, and Hester, Belinda, and I plan to walk in the gardens." She held up the teapot. "Would you like a cup?"

He refused, pleading the necessity of waiting upon his guests. Before he left, he pulled Diana and Thomas to one side. "While you are away from the Priory today, be careful," he said in a voice too low to be heard by the others.

"What do you expect to happen?" Diana asked, her voice not exactly steady. Thomas took a step or two closer to his cousin's side.

"Nothing," he assured her. "Just do not put yourself in needless danger. Make sure the groom is with you when you leave." They nodded, their eyes big. Luc hugged Belinda and Hester and left, disturbed by the fact that he had had to ruin the excitement the children felt.

If he had been able to see the conference that occurred shortly after he left the schoolroom, he would have been even more distressed. "Something is wrong," Diana said, her lovely face worried. "Those men the other day must have wanted more than one of us."

"Of course they did," Thomas said, his tone suggesting that Diana had an empty cockloft if she thought otherwise. "I have been thinking about one of the men's voices, the one who entered the coach."

"What about him?"

"His voice was too refined."

Diana looked over at the table, where Hester was finishing the last muffin. "And what does that mean?" she asked sarcastically. "Perhaps he has fallen on hard times."

"No. Had he been after our money or your jewels, I would have agreed," Thomas said seriously. "They did not ask for money. Did you notice that?"

"How do you know they did not plan to ask cousin Luc for money to get us back?" Diana said in her best manner, achieving the same disdain if not the same style as Lady Moulton.

"I don't," her brother admitted. "But there seems to be something missing." He stood up, a tall boy dressed in neat riding clothes that fit well today but by tomorrow would be too small. "I need to talk to Miss Montgomery in order to figure something out."

"Well, go and talk to her. If you take your groom, I am certain cousin Luc will not mind. You can go after you finish your lesson," his oldest sister said quite crisply.

Her brother simply stared at her. Sometimes she had the ability to get to the heart of the situation while he was still fumbling around the edges. "Violet will worry," he said hesitantly, still playing with the idea in his mind.

"I can tell her you plan to eat your luncheon with the vicar. But you must be home by dinner," she suggested.

Never had a morning crept by so slowly. Thomas read the translations his tutor suggested; Diana tried on clothes, trying to find something she liked but that Lady Moulton would not condemn as hopelessly out of style.

With each passing hour and each departing guest, Luc grew more and more restless. Most of his friends had come down early for breakfast, choosing to make an early start for their homes or Brighton. But the three that they had been watching were late risers. Finally, Wilberforce appeared, as jovial and pleasant as usual. "The fishing you promised lived up to your praises," he said. "I pulled in a large one yesterday afternoon late and sent it to the cook to prepare for breakfast." He searched the sideboard until he found the dish he wanted. Filling his plate, he sat down.

After his friend had finished eating, Luc accompanied him out to where his curricle waited. Wilberforce had just said his good-bye and was swinging up into the curricle when he got back down suddenly. "Forgot to tell you. Late last evening while we were playing cards, Lindsey and Gregory decided to leave at first light. I said I would give you their thanks. Rather shabby, really," he apologized. "I told them they should speak to you first." He climbed back into his curricle and took the reins from the waiting groom. Luc simply stood there for a moment stunned. Then he turned and hurried back into the house.

"Where are Lord Moulton and Mr. Wentworth, Dudley?" he asked as soon as he had walked through the door.

"In the library, my lord."

Walking quickly down the hall, Luc threw open the door. "They have made their escape," he announced. Moulton and Wentworth looked up, puzzled. "Lindsey and Gregory left at first light," he explained. Then he asked, his voice determinedly neutral, "Maybe they were not involved after all?"

Lord Moulton put his fingers together and tapped them. His face was carefully impassive. "Did they say anything to you last evening?" he asked Luc.

"Nothing. They left Wilberforce to extend their thanks," he said. He walked over to a chair and pulled it closer to where the other two were sitting.

"What about you, Wentworth? Did you take any precautions against this?"

"I assigned a watcher to each of the three with instructions to watch the stable carefully. I thought they might make another attempt on your life, Luc," his friend explained. "I am glad I am wrong."

"We did not give them a chance," Moulton reminded him. "But something about this does not feel right. They should have tried something."

"Remember the day of your wedding, Luc? I said I had not seen Miss Montgomery—Lady Forestal—the first time I came down because I had not expected to see her," Wentworth said. "That idea has been running through my head ever since. Maybe we should be looking at the unexpected.

"Maybe it is because we have been suspecting the wrong people," his friend once more suggested. He had known the three they were watching since they all had first come to town to gain a little town bronze.

Lord Moulton cleared his throat. He said sadly, "Wilberforce is in the clear. The other two," he sighed heavily, regretting the loss of two young men and his own error in judgment, "have not been as clever as they hoped they were. When I sent someone to London to see if there were any indications of impropriety, there were more than a few. In the last few months, both men have been spending large sums of money, but neither has any debts." At that his companions raised their eyebrows. "Although there is some family support for both, neither has the income to spend as freely as they have been. And they both have been gambling heavily."

"They could have been winning," Luc suggested, still hoping that their suspicions were not true. Their families would be the center of gossip once the scandal broke.

Wentworth laughed. "The way they play?" he asked. "They are as reckless as if they did not care whether they won or lost. Wilberforce was winning from them all last evening. I stood and watched for a time."

"I wish you had watched more closely," Moulton said with a sigh. Wentworth looked up, his cheeks reddening with anger at the unexpected rebuke.

"Is it time to make the switch?" Luc asked, wondering if he would ever be able to return to Frederica.

"Not yet. Last evening I dropped a few hints that the next courier had not yet arrived but that we expected him today."

"I thought I was to be the next courier," Wentworth said, his body suddenly stiff. Moulton and Luc looked at him, puzzled.

"You are too visible, my boy," Moulton told him. "You are the one everyone would suspect. No, the courier will arrive sometime this afternoon."

For a few more minutes they talked. Then Wentworth stood up. "I think I will wander down to the stables to see what I can discover. Perhaps their grooms will have said something to one of your men." He sauntered out of the room as though he were going to amuse himself instead of search for spies.

Luc and his mentor looked after him with impassive faces. Then Moulton asked, "Have the children recovered from their experience?"

"All but Thomas. He is still having nightmares," the younger man said. "If I am there quickly and we talk, he can usually return to sleep and not have another."

"I am sorry that they were put in danger. When I suggested you take this part, I did not realize to what lengths the man would go."

"Men, you mean."

Moulton did not answer. Luc shifted in his chair restlessly, uncomfortable with the new thought that had just appeared there. "Do you mean that you think Lindsey and Gregory are not the ones?" he asked, his voice louder than he had intended because of his astonishment.

"Things are not always what they seem" was the only thing the older gentleman would say. Lord Moulton rose from his chair. "Watch your back today, Forestal," he said sternly. He walked to the door, his face impassive as usual.

While Luc said good-bye to his guests and the children went about their daily activities, Frederica was bullying her maid. As soon as she awakened that morning, she felt more herself. She ate every bite of the egg and beef that Mrs. Sneed sent her and let Rose comb her hair and replait it. Then she was ready to get up and walk some more. Rose, however, resisted. "It is not as though I will fall," her mistress scolded. "You saw how well I was walking yesterday."

"That was when there were two of us to hold you up," the maid reminded her. Rose was not about to be blamed when Lady Forestal took a fall, as she was sure she was going to do. She might have decided to leave the Priory, but she did need a recommendation.

"Half of the time I walked with only my brother's help. And I even took some steps alone," Frederica reminded her. She glared at the maid, wishing Mrs. Greene had sent someone else to stay with her. Then changing her tactics, she smiled at Rose. "I had so hoped to be able to walk to my husband when he comes today," she said plaintively. She looked up under her dark eyelashes to see if that would change Rose's mind.

"I am certain if Lord Forestal had wanted you to walk, he would have told me to help you," the maid said pompously.

"And I am going to walk even if I have to do it myself," Frederica said angrily, moving over to the side of the bed and swinging her legs over the edge. She slid down until her feet touched the floor. Holding onto the bedpost, she stood up, delighted to find her legs so firm under her.

Before Rose could utter more than a squeak or take a step, there was a knock at the door. Hastily the maid wrapped Frederica in a dressing gown. "Come in," her mistress called, still standing.

The doctor walked in. When he saw her by the bed, he broke into a smile. "That is what I call determination," he said in a pleased voice, forgetting his previous opposition. "Can you walk?"

"With some help," Frederica said, at last admitting

that she did not want to let go of her support. She smiled at him winsomely.

"A few days ago, I thought we might have to bury you. Now look at you." The doctor crossed to stand beside her. "Here, you," he called to Rose. "Help me with her other side." Together they walked Frederica about the small room. At first more shaky than she had been the evening before, she soon gathered strength, finally making one circuit of the room by herself. "Now back to bed with you," the doctor finally said sternly. "I need to look at your shoulder.

"Does it hurt very much?" he asked as he put a smaller bandage on the wound.

"Only when someone tightens his hand over it," his patient said with a blush. Fortunately, the doctor made no reply. As he began to put his equipment back into his bag, Frederica asked more hesitantly than was usual with her, "When may I return home?"

"Anxious to return to your husband and children, are you?" he asked gruffly. She nodded her head vigorously. "Well, is your coach well sprung?" She nodded again, her throat too full to speak. "Then, if you are careful, you may leave today." Frederica smiled so broadly that the doctor felt that the sunshine outside had invaded the room through more than just the window. "Remember, if you have any trouble, any trouble at all, call in your doctor immediately. The wound is healing nicely. Unfortunately, you will have a scar but only in back. You were lucky that the ball was almost spent," he said seriously. "Now, take care," he warned as Frederica swung her legs over the side of the bed again. "You need to rest if you plan to take a journey today. The trip will be harder than you imagine."

"Thank you, Doctor," Frederica said with another smile. As soon as he had left the room, she put her legs back on the bed and demanded, "Go and find our groom. I want him to take a message to Lord Forestal." Her face set in disapproving lines, Rose did what she was told.

When the groom appeared, Frederica gave him his orders. "But I am not to leave you alone," he protested. "Lord Forestal gave specific instructions."

"My husband," Frederica said, subtly reminding him of her new position in the household, "would not want me to remain here if I did not have to." She waited. The groom, acknowledging the accuracy of her words, nodded. "Then tell him to bring the coach and some pillows." Although she had not appeared to be seriously listening to the doctor, his words had made an impression. She did not want to return home too weak to stand or to . . . Even to herself, she was not willing to complete the thought. But her cheeks burned with her blush. She watched in satisfaction as the groom nodded. More exhausted by her exertions than she wanted anyone to know, she made no protest when Rose brought her a cup of tea and covered her with a blanket. Soon she was asleep.

Her brother, still recovering from the shock of his sister's accident and his long journey, slept late that morning, awakening only a short time before luncheon. Dressing leisurely, he finally strolled into the salon, where the few remaining guests had assembled for lunch. He greeted Lord and Lady Moulton and then looked over at his host, who was seated beside Diana with Hester leaning on the arm of the settee beside him.

"He is quite remarkable, I believe," Lady Moulton said in a warm voice that would have surprised those that did not know her well.

"Forestal?" Bassett asked.

"Yes. So many men would have sent those children off to school or married quickly and let their wives take care of the problem. The children have lovely manners. I believe your sister can take part of the credit."

He smiled and wished he could release some of the pressure around his neck. "She has a great deal of fondness for them," he said. Then as if just realizing that the guests who were still at the Priory were assembled, he turned to look at his host, a hint of disapproval in his eyes. "Where is Wentworth?" he asked. "He told me that he was not leaving with the others."

Luc looked up in curiosity. Lord Moulton explained. "He received a message and had to leave very suddenly," he said. The look he gave Luc told the younger man not to ask questions. Before Bassett could question him further, luncheon was announced.

As soon as the meal was over, he sought out his new brother-in-law. "Shouldn't you be with Frederica?" he asked, his voice slightly censorious.

"I plan to be. Do you want to ride with me?" Luc asked. Before Bassett could answer, the butler appeared. "Yes?" Luc asked.

"The groom you left with Miss Montgomery has returned," the butler said.

"Show him in." Luc's face wore a worried look.

"What is wrong?" Lord Moulton asked as he walked up to the pair of them.

Before Luc could answer, the groom was there. Clearly surprised to see the other two gentlemen, he waited until Luc asked impatiently, "Well, what is wrong?"

"Nothing, my lord. Lady Forestal sent me to tell you that the doctor has given her permission to return home."

Luc smiled broadly and threw the man a coin. "Go and get something to eat," he said. "But first tell Masters to get the traveling coach ready. It has better springs."

"Lady Forestal said to tell you to bring pillows with you," the groom said.

"She is coming home!" Luc's face showed his excitement. Then he realized that he had not told the servants or the children about the wedding. "I must talk to Mrs. Greene, tell her we are married and to get my mother's chambers ready for Frederica."

"I will definitely be going with you, Forestal," Bassett said. "After her last journey, I want her to have a safe trip. I will order the pillows. You see to extra grooms."

Before Luc could follow Bassett out of the room, Moulton said, "Be careful today."

Luc stopped. "Should I wait to bring her home?" he asked.

"No," his friend told him. "She should be safe. But until that message, decoy or not, is safely on its way, you must watch yourself." Luc nodded solemnly. "And do not trust anyone," Moulton said. His eyes had a curiously despairing look. Once again Luc nodded. When Moulton did not say another word, Luc took his leave, hurrying out to talk to his housekeeper. His friend sighed heavily and took up one of the letters his associates had sent on to him.

Thomas, like his guardian, was in a hurry. His tutor had insisted that the boy share his luncheon while they finished their discussion of a particular passage by Cicero. Then he had had to convince the groom who had been assigned to him that Luc had given him permission to visit Miss Montgomery. Not wanting to seem impatient, the boy had traveled at a moderate rate, seemingly enjoying the bright sunshine and blue skies.

When he arrived at the inn, he hurried inside, followed by the groom. "If it isn't the nipper that shot the highwayman," one of the men sitting in the common room exclaimed. Mr. Sneed, who had been pouring a fresh tankard for one of his guests, looked up, curious.

As soon as he had finished what he was doing, he hurried over to Thomas. "What can I do for you, sir?" he asked, bowing. The last time the lad had come in, he had made a goodly sum of money—two goodly sums, in fact.

His foot on the first stair, Thomas paused. "Nothing. I simply came to see how my mother does."

The innkeeper's face was puzzled. "Your mother?" he asked.

"Lady Forestal."

"Did you not pass the coach on the way, lad?"

"What coach?"

"The one that Lord Forestal sent to fetch her home."

Thomas stared at the innkeeper as though he had two heads. "What are you talking about?"

" 'Bout an hour ago a gentleman arrived to take Lady Forestal and that uppity maid Rose back to the Priory. He said Lord Forestal had sent him. He had the coach she had ordered and everything," Mr. Sneed said, wiping his forehead nervously with the rag he had in his hand.

"When did she order a coach?" Thomas asked, his words careful and slow.

"This morning. She sent that groom to tell his lordship to come and get her as soon as the doctor told her she could. Real sorry to see her go. But my wife won't miss that maid of hers. Never heard such complaining," the innkeeper said helpfully.

"And Lord Forestal came to get her?" Thomas asked, using the Socratic method he had been studying to get more information. Pleased at the minor success he had had, he kept asking questions.

"Not him. Heard Lady Forestal call the gentleman Mr. Wentworth. He was here the same day her brother brought the vicar to call."

"A vicar?" The idea confused him. Thomas tried again. "And how long ago did they leave?"

"Not more than ten minutes before you arrived." The innkeeper glanced toward the common room, where one of his patrons was waving an empty tankard. "Is there anything else I can do for you?"

"Nothing," Thomas said, not allowing his confusion to show. He walked back outside with the groom close at hand. "Did we pass a coach on the way here?" he asked, wondering if perhaps he could have missed such a large object during one of his daydreams.

"A coach, sir? Is this one of your riddles, Master Thomas?" the young man asked, his face showing his confusion. "It would be hard to miss one of those."

"Where could a coach go if it did not go down the

road that we traveled?" Thomas asked, his brow still creased.

"Down a road that we did not travel," said the groom, delighted because he had solved the problem.

"You're right!" Thomas exclaimed. "How many roads lead into this town?"

The groom looked around. "Two."

"Are you certain?" the boy asked impatiently.

"We came in here," the groom pointed. "The road goes out there." He turned and pointed to the opposite end of the small village. Thomas turned around and realized that the groom was right. The village was built on either side of the road.

The boy hurried back into the inn. "Is this the only road through the town?" he asked.

"Except for a footpath or two," the innkeeper said.

"Are they large enough for a coach to go down?"

"A coach? No way, young sir. They be so overgrown that takes an effort just to walk that way after dark. Some say the paths are haunted," an old man said with a cackle.

Thomas turned and raced out of the inn. "You return to the Priory. Follow the road. When you meet my cousin, tell him that Miss Montgomery has disappeared."

"Disappeared?" the groom asked, his voice strained. Thomas ignored him. "I am going to try to find her." He swung up into the saddle and rode off down the road in the opposite direction from his home.

"Disappeared?" the groom asked again. Then he shook his head and headed back in the direction from which he had come. Then he swung back around. He had ridden only a few yards when he turned around again. "Best follow Master Thomas's instructions," he said to himself.

The groom had been on the road for a while when he met the outriders and coach from the Priory. "My lord," the groom said when he caught sight of his master.

"What are you doing here, Turner?" a loud, gruff

voice shouted. "You are supposed to be with Master Thomas."

"Mr. Masters," the groom said, stumbling over his words in his eagerness to get them out. "Master Thomas sent me to find his lordship. Miss Montgomery has disappeared!"

"What!" Frederica's brother, who had chosen to ride rather than be jostled inside a coach, swung his horse around and pulled up in front of the coach. "Get out here, Forestal!"

"What is going on?" Luc asked, climbing down from the heavy traveling coach.

"Turner, who was supposed to be with Master Thomas, has some news," the head groom replied. He glared at the young groom, who by now was beginning to wish he had never left the boy's side.

"Well, speak out, lad," his master said firmly.

"Master Thomas said he had your permission to visit Miss Montgomery," the groom began.

"Lady Forestal now," her brother added.

"Lady Forestal." The young groom looked around to see how the others were taking the news of their master's marriage but was disappointed at the lack of astonishment on their faces. Had he been at the Priory a few hours earlier, he would have seen all the amazement he desired. "When we arrived, the innkeeper told Master Thomas that Miss—Lady Forestal had just left with the man you had sent to take her back to the Priory."

"What man?" Luc asked sharply, his anxiety giving his voice a cutting edge. He motioned the groom to get down. "What man?" he repeated when the groom was face to face with him. Bassett too had dismounted, holding his reins in his hand, his face concerned.

"Mr. Wentworth, or so the innkeeper said," the groom said, wondering what was wrong.

"And where is Master Thomas?" Like his employer, Masters too had dismounted. The three men and three horses surrounded the young groom. He took a step backward.

"He followed the coach. The innkeeper said it was only ten minutes down the road."

"Which road?"

"The one that leads through the village," Turner explained. He swallowed, wishing that anyone but he had been chosen to accompany Master Thomas that morning.

"You ride with the coach to the village, Turner. I will take your horse," Luc said, stretching out his hand.

"I will take that one, my lord. You take mine," Masters said firmly. He put his reins in Luc's hands and took those Turner held.

"Do you ride with me, Bassett?" Luc asked, his voice cold and hard.

"As far as we need to go," the other man said firmly.

"Take the coach to the village," Luc told the coachman. "The rest of you come with me."

As they covered the mile or so into the small town, Luc tried to reassure himself that Wentworth was only trying to protect Frederica. But Moulton's words, "Be careful," rang in his ears. His stomach rolled with the thought of what this might mean. Wentworth?

14

WHEN THE COACH had arrived so early that afternoon, Frederica had been overjoyed. Only the absence of her husband and the pillows she had requested cast a damper on her happiness. Willingly she allowed Wentworth to hand her and her maid into the carriage. "I will be your outrider this afternoon," Wentworth said with a smile as he closed the carriage door.

For the first few miles, Frederica relaxed and tried to sleep. However, each time the coach hit a bump, her mouth tightened in pain. "I should have had some of that wretched willow bark tea before we left," she said once when they hit a particularly deep rut.

"I put some in the basket Mrs. Sneed sent with us," Rose said, pulling the bottle out. "Shall I pour you some?" Just then the coach lurched again.

Frederica bit her lip, trying not to cry out. "Just give it to me. I will drink from it," she said when she could speak again.

"But you might drink too much," the maid protested. "Let me have the coachman stop," she added. Pulling aside the curtain that separated her seat from the underside of the coachman's seat, she called, "Stop!" Nothing happened. "Stop!" she called again. Still nothing happened. "I suppose Lord Forestal gave them orders not to stop for anything," she suggested, handing the bottle to her mistress.

Frederica took it, held it to her lips for a moment, and took a drink, trying not to swallow more than she usually did. "Put it away," she said with a gasp, handing the bottle back. She leaned back into the corner of the carriage, her face a careful mask. No matter how worried her husband was over her safety, she knew that had she asked to stop the carriage, he would have expected his servants to do so.

After a few more minutes had gone by, ones in which she seemed to be sleeping, she said as calmly as she possibly could, "Open the sashes, Rose. I would like more air."

Frowning, the older woman did as she was told. She tied back the first sash and glanced out the window. Although Frederica had been unconscious during her ride to the village, Rose had not. In fact, she had ridden on the top of the coach because it had been full of supplies that Mrs. Greene had sent. Because she had been filled with the excitement of the situation, she had asked the coachman many questions and observed the countryside closely. The landscape through which they were now passing was not the same as she had seen on that earlier trip. She opened her mouth to tell her mistress what she suspected.

"Shut the sash!" The order could not be mistaken. Mr. Wentworth had pulled alongside the coach and leaned down to glare at her. The maid nodded and drew back, pulling the cord loose.

"What is wrong?" her mistress asked, her face pale. The concoction she had drunk had dulled the pain she was feeling.

"We are not on the road to the Priory," Rose whispered, afraid of the men who surrounded them.

"I see." For a few moments Frederica was silent, any fear she felt carefully hidden. Then she asked, "Do you know where we are?"

"No, my lady." Big tears began to roll down the maid's face. "I want to go home," she sobbed. She covered her face with her hands.

"I am certain that we will be at the Priory before long," her mistress reassured her, not feeling at all certain herself. When her husband had said he was working for the War Office, she had feared the worst—but for him not for her. Then she reminded herself that Mr. Wentworth was her husband's friend and would not lead them into danger.

"Not the Priory," the maid cried, her tears falling faster. "I want my mother."

Feeling as though she were comforting one of the children she had been a governess to, Frederica tried to soothe her, to erase her fears. In spite of the seriousness of their situation, she chuckled to herself. Rose was at least ten years older than she and should have been comforting her.

"What are we to do?" the maid asked, finally gaining control of herself. She wiped her eyes and face on the hem of her gown.

"For now, nothing. When we stop, if we are not at the Priory, we will decide." As Frederica lay back into her corner, she tried to formulate a plan that would release them if they really were in danger. Then they hit another rut, deeper than before, and all she could do was keep from crying out in pain. Her shoulder that just that morning had seemed the merest scratch now burned like a curling stick accidentally allowed to touch her skin.

Had she realized that help was only a short way behind her, she would have been able to truly relax. It had not taken Thomas long to find the coach's trail. Following directions given to him by a farmer leading a cow to market, he soon had them in sight. When they turned into a smaller, less traveled road, he let them move almost out of sight before he followed them. And at each turn, he remembered to mark the way. If he turned right, he put a strip torn from his handkerchief on the right side. If they turned left, he put the strip there. His only worry was whether Luc would understand the markings. He followed closely, but when he saw the man on horseback pull up next to the coach and lean down, Thomas fell back, afraid he would be seen. When he recognized Wentworth, he started to call out. Then he stopped, remembering his cousin's words that morning.

Still farther behind were Luc, Bassett, and the servants. Hoping to discover that it had all been a mistake, they had stopped at the inn only to learn exactly what Turner had told them. Luc took a moment to gather his thoughts and then turned to the grooms. "I need a volunteer to ride back to the Priory," he said. "Lord Moulton must know what has happened." One of the older men stepped forward. "I will not be long," Luc promised. "Mr. Sneed, I need pen and paper." He turned back to the men who waited for him. "Get something to drink and eat. We do not know how long this will take."

Bassett followed him into the small chamber where only hours before Frederica had slept. Luc looked around, his eyes bleak. "What is happening, Forestal?" his brother-in-law asked as the silence began to close in around him.

Luc looked up from the letter he was writing almost as though he were surprised he was not alone. He looked down again and continued writing. "Do not ask," he said. He finished the letter and sealed it.

"Do not ask? My sister disappears with a friend of yours, and you tell me not to ask," Bassett yelled.

"Wentworth may not be a friend of mine."

"What? You go everywhere with him. He was your witness at your wedding."

"I know, Bassett," Luc said as calmly as he could. "But I am not certain that the man I thought I knew and the man he has become are the same person. This involves the war," he added quietly.

"The war! I knew I should have forbidden the match. Now you are planning to run off to play soldier." Bassett threw up his hands and let them drop.

"Not in the sense you mean. Come. We must be off." Luc strode out of the room, his brother-in-law at his heels.

"You do not mean to tell me anything else, do you?" Bassett cried.

"No."

In a few moments, the letter was on its way, and

the rest of the party were once again on horseback. "Which way did Turner say they went?" Luc asked.

Before long they were following the winding road that Thomas had so carefully marked for him. "Quite clever, that cousin of yours," Bassett said when Luc bent down and picked up another piece of handkerchief. "I would never have thought of this myself."

Before they could get any farther up the lane, they saw Thomas riding toward them. "Cousin Luc," the boy shouted excitedly. "I am so glad to see you."

"What has happened?" his cousin asked, his eyes like two blue stars blazing with fire.

"He has them in a cottage not far from here. It looks like it is deserted, maybe has been for a while," the boy told him. "Hurry up. Let me take you there."

"Not just yet. Bassett, Masters, we need to talk." Luc swung off his horse and threw his reins to a groom. He walked over to a large tree and leaned against its rough trunk. Thomas and the other two followed, looking puzzled.

"Well, talk," Bassett demanded when they were once more face to face.

Just then they heard approaching hoofbeats. Looking at one another in astonishment, they pulled their horses off the road and into the woods, hoping they would be undetected.

"That is Rose," Luc said as he watched the figure on horseback ride past them. She was holding on the horse as though she was afraid of falling off. "Quick, one of you, after her." The men were on their horses in a moment and gave chase.

When they returned several minutes later, one of them was holding a hysterical Rose in front of him, trying to keep her from falling off while warding off the blows she was swinging. "She said she had to go to the Priory, my lord," he said as he put the still crying woman on the ground and moved away as quickly as he could.

"Rose, Rose," Luc said as he moved closer to her and grabbed her hands in his.

"No. Do not hurt me," she cried, twisting and trying to get away.

"Rose, it is I, Lord Forestal," he said again. He tried to hold her still. She looked up, her eyes wide with fright. "It is all right," he promised. "What did they do to you?" he asked, fearing the worst.

"Oh, my lord, I was so frightened." She began to cry again, raising her hands to cover her face.

"Shh. You are fine now. They cannot get you again," he said soothingly, longing instead to shake her and get her to tell him what was happening to his wife. "Masters and the rest of us are here to protect you. And as soon as you are ready, someone will take you back to the Priory."

"The Priory! Oh, my lord, I was supposed to give you a message when I reached the Priory," she said in a voice that still shook from her sobs.

"What message?" Bassett and Thomas moved closer.

"You are to bring the document"—she stumbled over the unfamiliar word—"to the inn in the village at eight and wait in the common room for a signal."

"Or?" Luc said the word in a dangerous drawl, his tone low and cold.

"Or he will kill Lady Forestal," Rose said in a rush. "I knew something was wrong. I tried to tell her, but they would not stop. I could do nothing, nothing," she cried, covering her face once again with her hands.

Although Luc was raging inside, he tried to maintain control of his temper. Neither Bassett nor Thomas had any such restrictions. "When I get my hands on the man, I will kill him," Bassett promised. He kept hitting the gloves he carried against his leg. Thomas cursed fluently, his recent visits to the stable apparent in his vocabulary.

"No, you will not," Luc said, his eyes blazing with anger. "I believe that privilege belongs to me."

"Let's go get them, cousin Luc," Thomas pleaded. "I know where they are."

"Not yet. There are a few more questions I need have answered first," his cousin said. He turned back to the maid. "Why did he send you?" he asked. "Didn't he realize I would find out where he was?"

"He said you would ask that. He plans to move Lady Forestal again sometime this afternoon," Rose said, her voice still shaky. "And he said you would not have enough time to return to the Priory for the plans, make a search, and still meet him on time."

Like a general making plans for a battle, Luc began issuing orders. "Thomas, you and Masters go and watch the house. If they start to move my wife, let me know immediately," he said. "And stay well hidden." The two nodded and led their horses away.

"So he knew that you were expected at the inn today," Bassett said thoughtfully. "But he was not there when the messenger my sister sent arrived."

Rose blushed. "Lady Forestal told him," she said. "She thought you had sent him to bring her to you." She hung her head as if to deny her part in the proceedings. "She did not even want to wait for me to finish packing."

"Sounds just like her," her brother said, his voice dry with emotion. "Impulsive as always."

"He will not be expecting to see us, then," Luc said coldly. He smiled, and Rose shivered.

"He said to warn you that he would know if you made an attempt to rescue her," the maid said hesitantly. "Do you think he had someone following me?"

"If he did, the man would have found us by now," Bassett reminded her. "I imagine that he was certain that we would not do anything to injure Lady Forestal."

"Tell me about the cottage," her employer demanded. "Where are they keeping my wife?"

"In an upstairs room. The window is so small that hardly any light enters it. It has a bed and night table, but that is all. When they carried Lady Forestal in, they allowed me to look after her there for a short time."

The question he had been holding inside since they discovered her popped out. "How is she—Lady Forestal, I mean?" he asked, his voice revealing his worry.

"Jostled and in pain," the maid said. "She pretended to be unconscious while they carried her inside. She thought they might not be as cautious if she appeared weaker than she really is."

"How do you know this?" he asked impatiently.

"She told me. After they locked us in. When they came for me, she pretended to be unconscious again," Rose explained. "Apparently they believed her. No one tried to rouse her."

"Did they lock the door when you left?" Bassett asked eagerly.

"No. Yes. Well, now, I am not certain," Rose began. "There was a key. But whether they used it, I do not know. I was not allowed to dally, you see."

"What did you see? Can you draw a plan of the house here in the dirt?" Luc asked, handing her a stick.

Thinking for a moment, Rose took the stick and began drawing lines. At first there was only a hallway with closed doors beside it and an upstairs room. Soon, as she closed her eyes, she could see more and quickly drew it into place. "I can remember no more," she said after a pause, laying her stick on the ground.

"You have done well," Luc said, meaning every word that he said. "How many people were there?"

"Mr. Wentworth, the coachman, and the groom were all I saw," the maid said slowly. "But . . ."

"Go on," Bassett urged her.

"The fires were lit, there was water in the pitchers, and somewhere in the house someone was cooking apples," she explained, waiting for them to laugh at her.

"One at least, maybe more," Luc said thoughtfully.

"Better plan on more," Bassett said dryly. "Better to be overprepared." He drew Luc to one side away from the others. "Are you planning a rescue?" he asked, letting his worry show on his face.

"Do you doubt it? I cannot leave Frederica in

Wentworth's hands. Nor can I wait for him to release her. If things go wrong, he will kill her—you may be sure of that," Luc said bitterly, thinking about the determination of the man he had only yesterday considered his best friend.

At that moment Thomas dashed up the road, his horse lathered. "Get farther into the woods," the boy called. "He has sent someone up this road. One of his servants is coming."

Luc smiled, the kind of smile a wolf has just before he takes an antelope down. Thomas felt a shiver run down his spine as he looked at it. Slowly, carefully, the men moved back into the woods. "As soon as he passes, you follow him," said Luc, pointing to the man known to be the best stalker. "As soon as you can, bring him to me," he said with a firm voice. "Now we shall have more information." He watched with satisfaction as his groom noiselessly moved into position to shadow the rider.

They watched as the man rode by, never once looking in their direction. "Lazy, probably hired just for today," Bassett said, his face set in hard lines.

Thomas looked at him, curious. "How can you tell?" he asked.

"The way he rode. He is in no hurry, and when Forestal's man catches him, he will be willing to talk," Bassett said as though he could read the man's mind.

Luc, still talking to Rose, wore a serious look on his face. "Take her to the inn as soon as we have that man a prisoner," he said, calling to one of the grooms. "You can ride pillon, Rose." He turned to the groom. "As soon as you get to the inn, bring back Turner and the coachman." He paused for a moment, his forehead creased in thought. "In fact, bring the coach. Riding on horseback may injure Lady Forestal more."

"No, your lordship," Rose said firmly, surprising herself and the others by disagreeing with her employer. "No coach will be comfortable on this road. You'd do better to take her on horseback." She remembered all too well the way her mistress had bitten her lip to keep from showing how weak she was.

"Then bring only the men," Forestal said. His voice had grown even colder. A few minutes later, the stalker returned, leading a horse with a man draped over the saddle. "Now, be on your way, and hurry back. Remember, be careful. And be quiet."

"He is unconscious, my lord," the stalker said with regret. "But he should be coming around soon."

His master simply nodded. "Thomas, come here," he called.

While her rescuers made their plans, Frederica too was thinking rapidly. As soon as she acknowledged that Wentworth was not taking her to her husband, she had decided that being a helpless invalid would be her best course. Let him think that she could do nothing to help herself. Following this course, she pretended to faint, determined to maintain the pretense at any cost. When they lifted her roughly out of the coach, the pretense almost became a reality. She moaned and left her good arm flop as though she had no control over it.

The few minutes she and Rose were alone in the upstairs room she used to discover what Rose had learned about the house. When the maid was dragged from the room, Frederica had to remind herself not to react, not to lose her protective coloring. But it was hard.

The quiet of that room was almost overpowering. Although she rose and crept unsteadily to the door, putting her ear to the thick plank, she could hear nothing. Then she heard footsteps. She moved quickly back to the bed, trying to recreate the exact position she had been in.

"Such a long fainting spell," her captor said mockingly. "This should bring her around." He held a bottle of sal volatile under her nose. The strong odor made Frederica twitch and try to get away.

Realizing that this spell at least must come to an

end, she opened her eyes. "Luc?" she said softly. "Luc?"

Her performance was good enough to fool the man who held her captive. "He has been delayed," he said soothingly. "He said for you to rest until he comes." Wentworth smiled wolfishly to himself. When Luc came, the game would be over. Of course, it also meant his having to leave England. The thought of having to leave his home did not please Wentworth completely, but with his prospects and money he could live a life of ease anywhere. Maybe he would go to the Indies and change his name. He had always enjoyed hearing about the tropics. He glanced down at the woman, who had obediently closed her eyes and seemed to drop off into sleep, and laughed to himself. When he decided to marry, he would choose a woman for her beauty, not a drab little thing like Forestal had chosen. He walked out of the room pleased with himself.

When the door closed behind him, Frederica sat up, muttering a few curse words she had learned from her brother. She walked to the door, steadier this time, and tried the handle. It was locked. She sagged against it for a moment, all her hopes destroyed. Then she pulled herself together. She moved across the room to the window, a small thing that let in only a small amount of light and offered no possibility of escape. Even had she been well, which she admitted she was not, she would not have been able to slip through it.

Having inspected her room, she crossed to the bed again and lay down. For some time she was quiet, simply thinking. Then she smiled. "Rose," she called weakly. "Rose." For a few minutes there was nothing. She called again, this time letting her voice seem more agitated. "Rose," she cried hysterically.

Finally Wentworth appeared. "Your maid is running an errand for me," he said calmly. "May I help you?"

"My medicine," Frederica said weakly. "I must have my medicine."

"Where is it?"

"The basket. Rose will know where it is." She lay back and moaned artistically. Wentworth grimaced and hurried from the room, leaving the door open just a little.

"Find the thing and bring it here," she heard him shout to someone below. Before she could think about getting off the bed, he was back. She moaned again. "How are you feeling?" he asked in a concerned voice. He needed her to trade for the letter; if she were too ill to speak, he would have more problems than he had planned.

"I hurt," Frederica moaned. "I am thirsty. Where is Rose? When will she return?" She tossed restlessly on the bed as though her fever were rising. She hoped the red in her cheeks where she had pinched them would convince him that she was indeed ill.

"Soon," Wentworth said curtly, wondering how to cope with the situation. "Would you like a cool rag for your head?" he asked, remembering the way Violet and the others had worked to get her fever down before. She nodded and moaned as if that slight motion had caused her head to ache even more.

"Water," she begged. He crossed to the pitcher, ready to pour her some, but discovered it empty. He cursed quietly. Then taking the pitcher, he hurried down the stairs, yelling at one of his men to fetch more water.

"Have you found that damned basket yet?" she heard him ask. A door slammed, cutting off the answer.

Realizing that this might be her only chance, Frederica slid off the bed. Although she was slightly unsteady, she made her way quickly to the door. Opening it slowly, cautiously, she peered out into the hall. She could hear noises from the floor below, but nothing was very clear. She glanced up and down the narrow hallway. There was only the one staircase. Taking a deep breath, she quickly made her way down it, hoping that it did not have any distinctive creaks.

Her foot was on the last step when she heard Wentworth's voice. She staggered down the hallway, knowing that the chances of her escaping were certainly slim but determined to try anyway.

"Give them to me," Wentworth said angrily. "If you were to walk into her room, she would know something was wrong. We want her calm, at least until Forestal is in our hands."

"Are you so certain he will come?" a gruff voice asked.

"Wot if he don't?" another asked.

"He will," Wentworth promised. "Everything else has worked out as I planned, hasn't it?"

"Cept stoppin' the coach. Never said Bert'd be shot," the second man complained. The sound of a fist hitting a face echoed down the hallway, where Frederica was struggling with the front door. She stopped for a moment and then worked harder.

"Give me that damned basket," Wentworth snarled. "And, you two, get back out there. I do not trust Forestal."

Finally, Frederica managed to lift the heavy bar that kept the door closed, feeling her wound tear open as she lifted it. Dampness began to trickle down her back. Refusing to give up, she slipped out, closing the door carefully behind her. She looked around wildly. The cottage was set in a small stand of trees, but none was large enough for her to hide behind. Determined that she would make her escape, she stumbled toward the trees that lined the path.

Behind her she heard Wentworth roar. "She's gone," he yelled. "Find her, you idiots. Search the house and the grounds."

The man he had just hit turned around in the kitchen. "She's not here," he said with a laugh. "Thunk he was so smart. Not his fault, that's wot he'll say," he told his mate.

"Well, I do not want to be around when he comes back. Let's go and look for her," his friend said, pulling the other man out the door.

Frederica reached the first of the trees. Suddenly a large hand covered her mouth. She screamed but not a sound could be heard. "Hush, my lady. It is me, Masters," a deep voice reassured her. She collapsed against him, completely exhausted by her exertions. "If you could walk just a little further," he said in her ear. "I have a horse nearby."

She nodded and stood up straighter, still holding on to him. Her heart was still pounding, and she was growing weaker by the moment. Behind them they could hear the sounds of the searchers. "They are getting closer," she whispered. "If they should catch us, you must leave me," she ordered. He simply helped her walk, knowing that what she suggested would never be his choice.

"Up you go," he said as he lifted her up onto his horse, wishing he had not traded with his master. He swung up in front of her and led the horse skillfully through the woods and to the road, knowing that surface would allow him to travel faster. With Lord Forestal only a short way down the road, he hoped they could elude her captors.

Just before they made the turn that would have hidden them from view, one of the searchers found them. "She's getting away," he called. "There she is on the road."

"Mount up," Wentworth yelled, his face distorted by anger. "Follow her." He swung up on his horse and bent low over its neck, determined not to lose his pawn.

Frederica clung to Masters, fearing at any moment the men behind them would catch up. The horse they were riding was carrying a double load and was already tired. The lather on its sides was hardly dry. A darkness seemed to be creeping over her, but she kept pushing it back, willing it to go away. She glanced back again. "They are gaining on us," she said, her voice weak.

"Just a few more minutes," Masters said. "Then they shall have a surprise." She could hear the satisfaction in his voice and wondered at it. The road to the cottage was not straight, and every time they turned and lost sight of the men following them, Frederica hoped they would give up. That hope was destroyed only seconds later when the men appeared again, whipping their horses to their top speeds. "Just a little farther," Masters said again, this time with an edge to his voice.

When Luc and the rest of his party had finished asking Wentworth's man questions, they tied him up. "Mount up," Luc called, his voice low but clear. Before he could give any more orders, they heard hoofbeats.

"Several horses," Bassett said, listening intently.

"Move back to the trees," Luc ordered. "Spread out on either side. Maybe we can hit them before they know we are here."

"Where is Masters?" Thomas asked, puzzled. Luc and Bassett exchanged looks but said nothing. If, as they suspected, Wentworth had captured Masters and knew where they were, their chances of succeeding were fast disappearing.

They watched the road anxiously. "That's Masters," Luc said, his eyes taking on a feral cast.

"And that's Frederica behind him," her brother said, his eyes hard and cold.

"Do not let the others by," Luc called out softly. The men waiting leaned forward, watching the road again. The sound of hoofbeats grew louder. The three men chasing Frederica and Masters came into sight. "Get them!" Luc called, sending his horse after Wentworth, whom he had recognized immediately.

The men who had been waiting all afternoon needed no more instructions. Easily they surrounded Wentworth's two men. Realizing they had no chance of escape, the two of them gave up quickly. "It were all him," the least educated said, pointing at Wentworth. "He made us do it."

Wentworth was not as easy to catch. As soon as he saw the men pouring onto the road, he knew his game was over. He turned his horse, hoping to make a dash for it, but Bassett was behind him, holding a pistol. He turned again and sent his horse into the woods. Thomas was in his way. He raised his own weapon, determined to get rid of the boy. A low voice behind him called, "Thomas, get out of the way." Not wanting to waste a shot, Wentworth turned slightly. He glanced back. Luc was only a short distance away. He glanced ahead again. The trees were beginning to thin out. He turned, taking careful aim at his chief pursuer. He pulled the trigger.

Using the trick that had saved his life once before, Luc bent low, sliding off the saddle to cling to the neck of his horse. The shot, which had been aimed for his heart, missed. Wentworth cursed. He turned and headed for the low wall that surrounded a nearby field. Before he could reach it, a shot rang out. Wentworth tumbled from his horse, a surprised looked on his face. Bassett lowered his gun.

As soon as they had passed the spot where Masters knew Forestal was hiding, he slowed his horse and then walked him slowly back. Frederica, her heart racing more than ever, searched the area frantically. Finally, Thomas appeared. Then she heard one shot followed almost instantly by another. Her face grew white. She lost control of her arms and felt herself begin to slide.

"Watch the lady," she heard Thomas call as she slipped into unconsciousness.

15

"I WILL NOT spend another night here," Frederica said as the doctor applied another bandage. "I want to go home." She glared at her husband and brother and at the doctor who was working on her. She had been complaining since she roused from fainting, but no one was listening to her.

Her husband looked at the doctor. "I tried to tell her that she needed rest before she traveled again," he said helplessly. If he had done as he wished, they would already be on the road to the Priory. He wanted her home with him so that he could keep her safe.

Her brother took one look at his sister's face and turned back to the doctor. "What is your opinion?" he asked. He sat on the edge of a table.

The doctor cleared his throat and looked from Frederica's determined face to the others. "Hmmm. Not exactly what I would prescribe for a wound, but perhaps Lady Forestal is right. She would undoubtedly rest easier in her own bed."

Luc smiled at his wife, his eyes glittering with excitement. And he would rest better when she was in bed with him, he told himself. "How soon may we leave?"

"I am finished here," the doctor said, washing his hands. "Travel slowly, and I do not think any further harm will happen. You can leave immediately."

Forestal was gone in an instant. Outside the door they could hear him shouting instructions. Then he was back.

"Thank you," he said, escorting the doctor from the room. Bassett heard rather than saw a clink of coins as Luc handed the doctor his payment.

The journey to the Priory was a quiet one. Rose, who had waited at the inn for word of her mistress, accompanied Frederica along with Thomas, who had been given strict orders not to answer any questions. To ensure the journey would not be difficult, the doctor had left an infusion of poppies to give her before they left. Thomas, who had been looking forward to avoiding her questions, watched in disgust as she dropped off to sleep. He and Rose soon followed, completely exhausted by the events of the day.

The sound of the coach coming up the drive alerted the household. Violet and the girls, Lord and Lady Moulton, and the servants rushed outside. As soon as the coach stopped, they rushed to surround the door.

"Cousin Luc," Belinda called. "Is our Miss Montgomery inside?" She tried to see, but Hester was in her way.

"She's not Miss Montgomery anymore, Belinda," Hester told her in tones that suggested that Belinda had forgotten her manners. "She is Lady Forestal."

"And our cousin," Diana said with a smile. "Wait here with me for a moment." The little girl, excited about the news and about staying up past her bedtime, jumped up and down.

Violet, her heart pounding, waited nervously for the young woman she had guarded so anxiously. Luc opened the door. Before he could climb into the coach, Thomas had jumped down. "She is still asleep, cousin Luc," he said.

"Did she have any pain on the trip?"

"She slept the whole way," the boy said, revealing the dismay he had felt over the situation.

"Thomas, where is cousin Frederica?" asked Hester, enjoying her first chance to use the name. She frowned. "You did not leave her behind again, did you?"

"Of course not," her brother reassured her. He

watched Luc climb into the coach. "Cousin Luc will have to carry her into the house, that's all."

"Carry her?" Violet asked, her hand going to her throat. Her face paled. "Has she had a relapse?"

"Do not worry, Violet," Bassett said as he walked up, his reins in his hand. "As soon as she has had a good night's rest she will be as right as rain." He handed his horse over to one of the waiting grooms. "It looks as though everyone in the house is waiting for us."

"We are," Lady Moulton assured him. She took his arm and led him into the house. "You look as though you have had a terrible day, Lord Bassett. What may I have the servants get you?" At the door she paused and motioned the rest of them to follow her.

As though she were on a string and in Lady Moulton's control, Diana turned. Belinda and Hester, however, clung to Violet's skirts and refused. "I want cousin Fredica," Belinda wailed.

"Frederica, you silly girl. Hush now, or you will wake her up," Thomas said as he picked his little sister up. After the excitement of the day, the action gave him a sense of returning to ordinary life.

"I doubt that anything could do that," Luc said as he stepped from the coach, Frederica in his arms. She was deeply asleep. "How much of that infusion did you give her?" he asked the maid.

"Just what the doctor told me," the older woman said defensively. She climbed from the carriage in his wake, relieved to be at the Priory once more. She stretched.

"What kind of infusion?" Violet asked, her eyes wide.

"Of poppies," Luc explained.

Violet ran her hand over her friend's forehead, pleased to find it cool. "Then you might as well put her to bed now, Lord Forestal. She will not awaken for some time. It takes very little to put her to sleep." The older governess gathered the little girls near her and watched with satisfaction as Lord Forestal, moving as though he were holding Venetian glass, carried his wife inside. The servants, ready for presentation to their new mistress, watched him, their faces confused.

"Is her chamber ready, Mrs. Greene?" Luc asked his housekeeper.

"Yes, your lordship." She led the way up the stairs. "I took the liberty of assigning a maid to wait on her ladyship. If she is unhappy with my selection, she can arrange something else tomorrow."

"I am certain your choice will please my wife." Once more Luc thrilled at those words. As he turned to go up the stairs, he saw Violet. "Miss Witherspoon, can you entrust the children to someone else for a moment and help my wife?" he called. The bleak look on the older lady's face disappeared.

"I will be there momentarily, my lord. Nancy, take Belinda up to bed. Diana and Hester, do not badger Lady Moulton." She gave each of the girls a stern look. "I will return shortly."

Muttering under her breath, Hester followed her sister and Lady Moulton into the drawing room. Lord Moulton took Thomas by the arm and followed. "You have had quite an adventure today, young man. Your sisters have been worried about you," he said. "And we worried about you too, Lord Bassett," he assured the older man.

"Need not have worried about me. This young man had everything under control," Bassett said heartily. The long ride home had given him time to think, time to accept what he had done that afternoon.

"I thought you were going to your tutor today," Hester asked her brother, the knowledge that she had once again missed out on being part of the excitement making her disgruntled.

"He did," Diana said. Then she noticed all the adult eyes watching her. "Or he said he was going to," she added hastily, trying to cover her mistake.

Thomas yawned and covered his mouth with his hand. "I did," he said indistinctly.

"Then what were you doing at the inn?" Lord

Moulton asked, wanting each piece of the puzzle in place.

"I had to ask Miss Montgomery—"

"Cousin Frederica now," Hester reminded him importantly. The three adults around her frowned, and she stopped talking.

Just then the door opened. "Mrs. Greene thought you might want a tea tray, Lady Moulton," Dudley said, directing the footmen to place the heavy silver service on the table in front of her.

"Are there any tea cakes?" Thomas asked. Although Mrs. Sneed had given him some bread and cheese, the long ride had made him hungry again.

"Yes," Lady Moulton said calmly. She handed him a plate filled with them and watched as he stuffed one into his mouth. "Continue."

As soon as he had finished chewing, he told them what he knew. He had just reached the end of his tale when his cousin walked in.

"How is Lady Forestal?" Lady Moulton asked. She put her needlework in her lap and folded her hands, waiting for his reply.

"Still sleeping. Violet is staying with her until I return," Luc explained. Leaving his wife in someone else's hands had been very difficult for him. The memory of her life in danger once more because of him was very real to him. "And Violet sent word to the three of you." He looked around at the children. They stared back at him. "You are to go to bed instantly." The girls moaned, but for once Thomas made no protest.

"Do you want to sleep in my dressing room tonight, Thomas?" Bassett asked, wanting to give his sister and her new husband some privacy.

"No, thank you, Lord Bassett. I will return to my own room," the boy said, his face impassive.

"You do not have to, Thomas. You can share my room," his cousin said.

"I know, cousin Luc. But I think I am ready now,"

he said, yawning widely. Bassett yawned also but managed to cover it more quickly.

"Then I shall see you in the morning. Say good night now," Luc said, proud of the young man.

"I will bid you good night also, gentlemen. Do not stay up too late." Lady Moulton swept from the room.

Taking their seats once more, Lord Moulton, Bassett, and Luc let their polite masks slip. Bassett yawned again. "Think I will go to bed also, gentlemen," he said. He yawned again. "I do not plan to rise until late. Keep your stories until then."

When they were alone, Luc glanced at his mentor. The older man's face was sad. Luc got up and crossed to the desk. Then he turned around. His face blazed with anger. "You knew," he said.

Lord Moulton nodded. "I suspected."

Luc turned his back on him and said, "I cannot deal with this tonight. We will talk tomorrow." He walked from the room. When the door shut behind him, Lord Moulton sighed heavily. His face for once looked his age. After a few minutes, he too left the room.

Upstairs, Luc entered his wife's bedchamber. "She is still asleep, Lord Forestal," Violet explained, getting up from her chair. "She may sleep all night."

"After what she has been through today, it might be best," Luc said, wishing he too could forget as easily. "You go to bed yourself. Tomorrow sometime we will explain everything." Everything we can explain, he thought to himself with a sigh. She nodded and walked from the room.

After he closed the door behind her, he walked back to the bed and looked down at his sleeping wife. Then he walked into his own room, where his valet waited. After a quick bath, he pulled on a fresh nightshirt and walked back into Frederica's bedroom. Now lit only by a single branch of candles, it was as shadowy as a cavern. "She will not know where she is when she awakes," he muttered to himself as he threw back the covers and crawled in beside her. "She will be afraid," he whispered, as if giving himself courage. Then he was asleep.

Hours later he awoke, his eyes wide, his heart beating wildly. A finger touched his lips lightly. He turned his head slowly. Frederica was awake, her eyes unclouded by fever or pain. He smiled and kissed her finger. She smiled back and put her palm over his mouth. He kissed that too. Turning on his side, he moved closer to her, his eyes never leaving hers. Frederica began to breathe more heavily, but she did not pull away when he kissed her. The first kiss was like the touch of a baby's eyelash against her face. Then he sighed and wrapped his arms around her. Frederica went into his arms as though they had been made to hold only her, a smile tilting her lips.

This time the kiss was deeper. As her finger had circled his lips earlier, now his tongue circled hers, slipping between them now and then, searching for an entrance. She parted her lips slightly, and he entered, drinking in her sweetness. His hand crept slowly up her left side, stroking her. Her hands reached out to pull him closer.

"How is your shoulder?" he whispered, wanting to turn her on her back but afraid in case he should hurt her.

"What shoulder?" she asked, pulling him down to kiss her once more. She turned so that he was above her. Luc untied the bow that kept the neckline of her nightrail in place. Carefully he pushed the gown off her shoulders, taking pains not to disturb her bandage. He leaned down and lightly kissed her breast.

"Did that hurt?" he asked as he pulled away.

"No." She pulled him closer to her. "Do it again," she begged. With a laugh her husband kissed his way across her shoulders. "Hmmm." She smiled up at him, her eyes lazy with newly learned passion. "Feels good."

"You like that?" Luc asked, leaning farther down to brush her bare breasts with his lips. She gasped. He freed the rest of her body from the nightrail, his hands stroking her as they uncovered each new part. His lips returned to caress hers, to dampen her breasts.

When Luc had kissed her in her bedroom at the inn, he knew that passion would flare between them. He did not know how hotly it would burn. Without shyness, she welcomed his embraces and returned them. Her body blossomed under his. Slowly, carefully, he prepared her for him, letting his leg slide between hers, letting her feel his desire.

As she writhed beneath him, he poised above her. In an instant they were one. The sharp pain of his entrance made her stiffen. Feeling her resistance, Luc stayed still until her body began to relax around him. He bent his head to her breasts, running his tongue around her nipples as he had run it around her lips only a short time before. "Luc," she moaned.

"Yes, say my name, sweet," he whispered in her ear. Then he kissed her again, giving his tongue full play in her mouth, teaching her what their bodies would do.

"Luc." His name, like a sigh, escaped from between her lips, and she arched upward. He kissed her again and began to move, slowly at first. He controlled himself and moved his hand under her to lift her to meet his thrusts. He placed her leg over his and reached between their bodies to caress her. His name became a litany on her lips until she moaned, shuddered, and then collapsed. He thrust again, feeling her leading him on to his own ecstasy.

They were still together some time later when he rolled over, taking her with him. "It is not fair," she complained, looking down at him.

"What?" Luc looked at her nestled against him as naturally as if she had been sleeping with him all her life. He smiled.

"You are still clothed," Frederica protested.

"That is something we can take care of very quickly," he said, sitting up and pulling his nightshirt over his head. He lay back down and pulled her close again. "Is that better?"

"Much." She ran her hand over his chest, playing with his hair. "Luc?" Her voice was wistful.

"Hmmm," he answered, already almost asleep.

"Would you have married me if my brother had not insisted?" she asked, needing an answer but afraid of what it might be.

"What?" He sat up straight. "After what happened tonight, you need to ask?" He felt rather than saw her nod. He slid back down beside her, his arm pulling her close. "I might ask the same of you," he replied.

"I would have," she said, covering his chest with soft kisses. He smiled and pulled her closer.

"When I was in London, I could not stop thinking about you," he told her. "I planned to ask you to marry me when I returned home." He kissed her, and their passion began to build again. Just before they dropped off to sleep some time later, Luc said quietly, "I love you, Frederica."

Her lips covered his. "And I love you," she said against them. He tightened his arm around her and went to sleep.

The next morning as they lay nestled together, they whispered the same words to each other again, never tiring of hearing them. Finally, Luc slid from her bed. Frederica hid her face shyly, peeping out as he walked into his bedchamber next door. She turned over, thinking about the previous night, and smiled. Then she stretched. The soreness in her shoulder reminded her of what had happened the day before.

"Do you want breakfast up here or to go down?" her husband asked, walking back into her bedroom while he fastened his shirt.

"Here," she said.

"Was I too rough with you last night?" Luc asked, bending over to kiss away the shadows in her eyes.

"Never." She wrapped her arms around his neck and kissed him, wincing only slightly.

"Do you want Violet to have a look at that shoulder?" he asked. "Or we could send for the doctor."

"Violet," she said flatly. She looked up at him and marveled that he loved her. "Are you having breakfast downstairs?" she asked.

"No, love. I will eat with you," he said as he sat down and drew on his stockings. The idea that she could watch her husband dress made her heart race. "Then I must talk to your brother and Lord Moulton."

"About yesterday?"

"About yesterday." He stood up and approached the bed again. "Do you think you will be strong enough to tell about what happened sometime today?"

"To you?"

"To Lord Moulton."

"He is the one who put you in danger, isn't he?" she asked, her anger evident in her voice.

"No, love. I am the one who did that," her husband assured her. He put his shoes on.

"Are you going to do it again?" she asked, her voice very hesitant. She looked up at him and shuddered when she thought of the fact that she could lose him.

"No." The word was stated so firmly that she did not ask him any more questions. Soon he lifted her out of bed and put her on the chaise in his bedroom, in front of which a tray had been placed. "Can you pour or should I?" he asked.

"You." She smiled up at him as he waited on her, fixing her tea to her specifications. He cut her food into small pieces and fed them to her, stopping often for kisses. When they had finished, she was flushed, and his cravat had to be discarded. She watched him take another one from his valet and wrap it around his neck, carefully creasing it. When he was finished, she said, "Call Violet to change my bandage. Then I will dress and go downstairs with you."

Remaining by her side, watching Violet pull the bandage away from her shoulder, made Luc grow pale. Only the fact that Frederica was counting on him to give her strength helped him get through. He stared at the red, puckered hole that was beginning to close and gulped. His fingers tightened around her. She did not make a sound but only held on tighter.

"It is healing nicely, Lord Forestal," Violet said. His presence in Frederica's bedroom reminded her of the inn. She looked from one to the other, noting the way their eyes met, their hands clung to each other. The hurt over not being present at their wedding began to drain away. "Do you want me to help you dress?" her friend asked.

"No, Violet, you have done enough." Frederica smiled at her. "And until I am once again strong enough to take charge of the children, you will be busy enough."

"Take charge of the children again?" Violet asked.

"I thought we'd hire another governess," Luc said. "I want you with me."

"Hire another governess? Luc, you already have two."

"One is my wife, or have you forgotten?" He bent over her menacingly. She smiled up at him.

"Let me teach them just for the summer?" she begged, her eyes on his.

Violet watched as he smiled down at her friend. "The summer," he promised. Then his face grew serious. "Get dressed, and I will carry you downstairs."

"I can walk."

"And I prefer to carry you," he said sternly, spoiling the image by bending over and kissing her. Realizing that they had forgotten she was in the room, Violet blushed and slipped out.

A short time later, Luc, Frederica, Lord and Lady Moulton, Bassett, and Violet assembled in the drawing room. When everyone was there, Luc looked around the room. "Whatever we say today must go no further than this room," he said. Lord Moulton nodded. Luc looked around, waiting until each person nodded his or her agreement. "It began some time ago in London," he said, staring at Lord Moulton.

The anger he had felt the evening before had disappeared. Only a dull ache remained. Without giving away any of the network's secrets, Luc laid out the foundation of the problem.

"After I became aware of what was happening, I became suspicious," Lord Moulton said, breaking into his story. "Every time Luc was in danger, Wentworth was around." Luc looked at him, his mouth set in a hard line. "I know you think I should have told you, Forestal," the older man said, "but you cannot dissemble. You would have given everything away before we had any proof."

"At least then Frederica would not have been hurt or the children placed in danger," his protégé said bitterly.

His mentor ignored him. "When I realized what was happening, I appointed him your bodyguard."

"What?" Bassett exclaimed. "You put Wentworth in charge of Forestal's safety?"

"Who better? As long as they were alone together, I was certain nothing would happen. Wentworth did not want any suspicion to fall on him," he explained.

"What about Lindsey and Gregory?" Luc asked. He held his wife's hand as if afraid he would lose her.

"Wentworth's pawns. He supplied the money, and they played decoy. Of course, they did not know what they were doing, but they were only too happy to have their life-styles subsidized," Moulton said dryly. "I understand that both have been called home by their fathers. Urgent family business, I believe. I do not think we will see them in London very soon."

The older gentleman smiled. Then his smile faded. "What I have never been able to figure out, however, is why he did it," he said sadly.

"He told us that," Bassett said, remembering those few minutes the day before.

"Why?"

"It was a game to him. That's what he said," Luc explained, his face carefully expressionless.

"A game with men's lives at stake?" Lady Moulton asked, horrified at the man's callous nature.

"A game? He dared to threaten your life for a game?" Frederica asked. Violet simply stared at him.

"That is what he said. Apparently, he grew tired of carrying messages. He decided to see what would happen if they did not arrive," Luc said.

"Then he was not selling them to the French?" Moulton asked, seeing the first ray of sunshine in the entire affair.

"Yes, he was. Apparently, part of the game involved performing more dangerous tasks each time without getting caught. I was the ultimate challenge, he said." Luc remembered how his former friend had lain there laughing, the blood pouring from the corner of his mouth.

"Why you?" Frederica asked. "He was your friend."

"Lord Moulton began showing me too much favor," Luc said wryly. "I should have told Wentworth I was trying to get out."

"He was always asking me to send him to some place new," Moulton said. "But he was so careless. I finally stopped giving him assignments. But I did not know that he realized what I was doing. I must be growing old."

"Why was he so determined to get you out of the way?" Bassett asked. "He could have stolen the letter at any time. Why did he need to kill you?"

"With Philpot and me out the way, he was certain Lord Moulton would entrust him with the memorandum. He had already sold the merchandise and had merely to deliver it," Luc explained. "He said the excitement made the money worthwhile."

The ladies shook their heads, wondering at the mind of a man who became a traitor because he wanted more excitement. "How will you explain his death to the world?" Frederica wanted to know. In spite of his efforts to keep it from her, Frederica had known what had happened to Wentworth since she had come to the previous afternoon.

"At the hands of highwaymen, I think," Lord Moulton said quietly and firmly. He tapped his fingers together. "I think it is a fitting end for him." The others could only nod. He stood up, crossed to where his wife was sitting, and pulled her to her feet. "I think we shall leave today, my dear. Thank you for your hospitality, Forestal."

"I thought you were going to stay so the *ton* would not gossip about my sister's marriage," Bassett complained.

"I think Forestal and your sister can take care of any gossip without my help. Do you plan to be in London any time soon, Bassett?" Moulton asked.

"That is the way it begins, Bassett. Watch yourself," Luc called. He shook his mentor's hand, his look telling him as words could not that he understood. They watched him leave the room, Violet slipping out behind them.

The room fell silent about them. "When do you return to London with the memorandum, love?" his wife asked, dreading the answer.

"I do not have to return," he declared. "That dratted letter was sent on yesterday. Wentworth had no idea that the next courier was the tinker. He probably passed him on the road." He took a deep breath. "You missed much of the excitement last evening."

She looked at him and raised her eyebrow eloquently. Luc smiled. "I was not talking about that," he said, his ears turning pink around the edges. "The children and servants turned out to meet you, and you did not even wake up to say hello."

"That was not my fault, but perhaps I should visit them," his wife suggested.

"I will take you up to the schoolroom soon."

"Or you could send for them to share our tea," she said, smiling up at him.

"Perhaps. First there are some points we must clear up." Frederica knew from the look on his face that he was serious.

"What?"

"Rose, for one thing. She may be a snorer—your

brother said Violet had declared it was true—but she was loyal yesterday. How should I reward her?"

Frederica thought for a moment. "She wants to go home to her mother. Give her enough money so that she can."

He nodded. "We also need to discuss Thomas. If it had not been for him, Wentworth might have succeeded," he reminded her.

"I did get away on my own," she said severely.

"And if Masters had not been there, you would have been recaptured," he reminded her.

"Thomas wants to go to school," Frederica said, the last word almost choking her. "But do not send him this summer. Wait until fall. Give us a chance to become better acquainted," she begged. "I want him to think of us, of me, as his family." Her eyes were wet with tears. Blinking rapidly, she lowered her head.

"We are," Luc said forcefully. "And Thomas knows it. He would not have chased after that coach if he did not care for you, Frederica." He tilted her head upward so that he could look into her eyes. "All four of them know that you love them. A summer will make no difference."

"It will to me," she pleaded. "Wait until fall and then ask him." Her eyes begged him to agree with her.

"All right. Must I also start planning for Diana's presentation?" The tone of his voice told Frederica that he did not really want to consider it.

"We shall see," she said, knowing that next February would probably find them on their way to town, unless she could convince Diana that she needed another year to polish her social skills.

Luc heard a noise in the hallway. "Are you certain you are strong enough to handle this?" he asked, walking to the door.

"I have missed them," she said with a smile. "Besides, if I know Violet, she will allow them to stay for only a little while. What shall we do then?"

"I think you will need to go back upstairs to bed,"

her new husband said, smiling suggestively. She smiled back, delighted. He threw open the door, and the four children came in, some hesitantly and others dashing to her side.

"Cousin Fredica, I can count," Belinda said in her high, childish voice. "One, two, three . . ."

"Lady Moulton said she would present me, but I would rather have you," Diana said.

Hester smiled at her former teacher, silent for once in her life. She sat down beside her and held her hand. Thomas took his place behind her, one hand on her shoulder as if reassuring himself that she was still there.

As soon as Frederica and Luc answered the children's questions they felt were appropriate, Violet, who had followed her charges into the room, said sternly, "We must return to the schoolroom before your cousin Frederica is thoroughly exhausted." A chorus of groans accompanied her statement. She frowned. "You would not want her to have a relapse, would you?" Hester turned to stare at her cousin, an anxious look on her face.

"I will be fine," Frederica said, smiling at her.

"But Violet is right. She does need to rest," Luc said firmly. He smiled at the children. "I think she has been up long enough for today. You will see her again tomorrow."

When the door swung shut behind them, Frederica turned to her husband. "Tomorrow? What happened to the rest of today?"

"Today? Today is mine," he said. He picked her up as though she were weightless. A short time later, he carefully deposited her on his bed. He eyed his wife of two days. "This is not how I pictured beginning married life," he said. Her face lost its animation. He hurried on. "With four children, I mean." Casually, as if her reaction did not mean anything to him, he took off his jacket and threw it over a chair.

"Oh." She lay there looking up at him, willing him

to continue, to look at her. Her heartbeat was speeding up again.

"Are you certain this is the life you want?" he asked, his voice revealing his doubts. He stepped out of his shoes. He walked back over to the bed. She began to breathe more rapidly.

"As long as you are part of it, I will be happy," she said with a smile. She lifted her hand to his shoulder and then caressed his cheek as he bent over the bed. Her good arm crept around his neck, and she pulled him closer so that she could kiss him.

He kissed her lightly, teasingly. Then he stretched out beside her on the bed and whispered in her ear. She blushed and pulled away from him slightly. He reached up and stripped his neckcloth off and then pulled the top bow on her gown loose. She wet her lips. He kissed her again, this time more thoroughly. "I love you," he whispered, looking deeply into her eyes. Frederica answered him with a kiss.

Sometime later she put her cheek against his bare shoulder and listened to Luc's heart slowing to his natural rhythm. She yawned. Luc smiled at her. As she drifted off to sleep, she nestled closer to him, acknowledging rather soberly for her that she was irrevocably bound to him as he was bound to her. She smiled, listening to the soothing beat of his heart. "Mine," she whispered.